Caribbean Adventure Series

Book 3

RAGING WATERS

A Rick Waters Novel

ERIC CHANCE STONE

LOST AND FOUND
PUBLISHING

2021 by Eric Chance Stone

Published by Lost and Found Publishing

Printed in the United States of America

ISBN: 978-1-7341626-5-3 (paperback)
ISBN: 978-1-7341626-4-6 (ebook)

First Edition
10 9 8 7 6 5 4 3 2 1

ACKNOWLEDGMENTS

'd like to thank my beta readers Ron Dalton, Bavette & Dennis Battern, Sherry Whitten Petrivelli, Mike Keevil, Ross Ruschman, Michell & Gib Moore, David Dyer, Chuck Springs, Chuck and Linda Reed.

I'd like to thank my amazing editor, Stephanie Diaz Slagle.
I'd like to thank my proofreader, Gretchen Douglas.
Thanks to my graphic artist Les.
Special thanks to Nick Sullivan, Wayne Stinnett, Cap Daniels for all their input and advise.
I like to especially thank all the readers of my novels. It's all about the readers. I appreciate your continued support on this journey.

Find The Official Synopsis Music at:

GUM.CO/RAGINGWATERSMUSICFREE

RAGING WATERS

CHAPTER ONE

A sliver of light peeked over the horizon, and the night sky began to shift from black to a light gray as the stars retreated back into the galaxy. When Johnie turned the key and fired up *Nine-Tenths*, the sound of the mighty Mann twin diesels startled a great white heron that was hunting for pinfish in the shallows of the marina. Rick was on the stern of the boat, restringing the Penn reels. His cockatoo, Chief, delicately nibbled on a red grape while sitting on the mobile tree perch up on the flybridge. The fourth member of Rick's crew, Possum, filled the water tanks and sipped on a stainless-steel coffee mug with *The Crow's Nest* logo on the side.

"Rick, you want a mug?" asked Possum.

"Yeah, man, I need some brain fuel. See if Johnie wants one too."

Possum made Rick a coffee the way he liked it, climbed up to the flybridge, and gave Johnie one as well.

"How are the engines?" asked Possum.

"As smooth as a Velvet Elvis hanging in a bachelor pad with three-inch white shag carpet," replied Johnie.

Possum chuckled. "You have a way with words."

"What's our ETA?" yelled Rick from down below.

Johnie glanced at the chart plotter, then looked at his watch and said, "Happy hour!"

As the first mate aboard Rick's vessel, Johnie had plotted the course to the Hemingway International Yacht Club, a mere eighteen-kilometer cab ride to the famous La Bodeguita del Medio salsa bar, where a small autographed sign hung behind the bar that read: *My mojito in La Bodeguita. My daiquiri in El Floridita—Ernest Hemingway.* Many people believed it was his real signature. In reality, it had been proven to be a forgery by none other than the owner, who'd hired a graphic artist to create the sign based on several Hemingway signed pieces, in order to drum up business. What had started as a small joke among friends turned into a big lie once the place started hopping. There was no empirical evidence that Hemingway enjoyed mojitos or had even set foot in the place, but that didn't matter to Rick and the gang. They were determined to drink a mojito there and see the infamous sign. They also planned to visit the Floridita, where photographs of Hemingway bellied up to the bar sipping on his actual favorite drink—a daiquiri—hung on the wall.

Rick and Possum untied the lines from the dock as Johnie slowly maneuvered *Nine-Tenths* toward the end of the channel and open water. The route would take them back to the inside of the Florida Keys via the Channel Five bridge, around the end of Key West into the Florida Straits, and then to a small deep-water channel just to the east of Punta

Cabeza de Vaca, which translated to Cow Head Tip. They would side tie the fifty-five-foot Viking sportfisher as close to the yacht club as possible in the narrow inlet.

The seas were smooth today. Rick climbed up to the flybridge and took over for Johnie at the helm as they rounded Key West. Chief sat on his shoulder, mocking the gulls following the boat. Near him, Possum rigged up four rods with pre-rigged ballyhoo and bright, multicolored trolling skirts. Rick would slow the boat only for a short while once they hit the 6,000-foot drop-off in the center of the Florida Straits, giving a small opening for them to fish.

"Whatcha trying to catch?" asked Johnie, noticing Possum rigging up one of the rods with a high-speed trolling lure.

"A wahoo!" said Possum.

As Rick got into open water and Key West disappeared below the horizon, Possum loosened the drag on the gold Penn reel and fed line out a few hundred feet behind the boat. The normal cruising speed of a Viking 55 was thirty-two knots, but with Johnie's custom-built computer module plugins, they were easily doing over forty. The elusive wahoo could reach speeds of over sixty miles per hour.

Johnie kicked back in the fighting chair, studying Possum's fishing experiment with great skepticism, but anything was possible. Possum was one of the smartest people Johnie had ever met, and he always thought outside of the box.

After only twenty minutes, the reel sizzled.

"Fish on!" yelled Possum and Johnie simultaneously.

Rick slowed the boat down to four knots as Possum swapped places with Johnie and strapped himself into the fighting chair, already wearing the rod holder belt. The lightning-fast fish leaped into the air, shaking its head and desperately trying to dislodge the hook from its mouth. Possum reeled with all his might, and eventually, he brought the fish alongside the sportfisher. In one quick motion, Johnie gaffed the massive fish and pulled its flopping body onto the deck.

"Woohoo, wahoo!" shouted Possum.

Johnie grabbed the portable scale and pulled the fish up. After weighing it, he exclaimed, "Eighty-three pounds!"

"Great job, Possum!" yelled Rick from the flybridge.

Johnie quickly gutted the tasty fish and threw it on ice. He would fillet it once they docked the boat. It was too risky to do that with the boat cruising at high speeds.

Before Rick could get the boat up to a full plane, the reel sizzled again. A blue flash spun in the air. Possum secured the rod and sat back in the fighting chair as Rick once again slowed the boat to four knots.

"It's a sailfish!" shouted Johnie.

"Hell to the yeah!" said Possum.

Rick pulled up *The Best of George Jones* album on his iPhone and blasted it through the eighteen speakers of the boat. Possum looked up at Rick over his shoulder and shot him a big grin.

The sleek fish jumped repeatedly and eventually gave up. Johnie pulled it on board, measured it, and weighed it.

"Seventy-three pounds! You know, if you catch a bull dolphin, you get the Blue Water Grand Slam: wahoo, sailfish, and dolphin," said Johnie.

"Really? I've heard of that. Well, let's get a dolphin," replied Possum.

"Since you're so close to the Grand Slam, Possum, I'll go trolling speed for a while," said Rick from the flybridge. "Cuba isn't going anywhere."

Johnie released the sailfish and started letting out the three ballyhoo rigs as Possum changed his high-speed trolling rig to the same ballyhoo rig and let out the line. It wasn't long before two of the reels ticked, then started smoking. Johnie took the one on the starboard bow and strapped on a standing fighting belt. Grabbing the port rod, Possum sat in the fighting chair. Johnie's fish ran deep and never jumped. Luckily, Possum grabbed the right rod as a massive bull dolphin leaped into the air.

"Oh my God! If I get her on board, I'll have the Grand Slam," hollered Possum.

He fought the fish with finesse and skill, and Rick set the autopilot and came down to assist, as Johnie had his hands full. After a fifteen-minute fight, Rick gaffed the beautifully colored fish and swung it onto the deck.

"You did it, Possum! You got the Blue Water Grand Slam," said Rick, wearing a big smile.

He pulled out a gold medal on a red, white, and blue ribbon and hung it around Possum's neck. Possum rolled his eyes, and Johnie chuckled. Rick's sarcasm was obvious, because he had bought those for kids who caught their first fish ever on a charter. Still, Johnie could tell Possum was proud of himself. He was grinning like, well...a possum.

Johnie quickly documented the Grand Slam in the boat's logbook, and planned to later email the info to the FWC Saltwater Angler Recognition Program to make it official. He was sweating profusely, still dealing with whatever animal was caught on the other line, and Possum helped him into the fighting chair. Whatever he'd caught wasn't giving up much ground.

"What do you think it is, Johnie?" asked Rick.

"I don't know, but whatever it is, it's huge. Maybe a shark."

The mighty fish would give up a few feet then take more back. Johnie's arms were turning into noodles.

"Possum, give me a hand," said Rick.

Rick pulled out the big black case holding the underwater drone. Luckily, Johnie had just fully charged it and popped in an empty SD card. Rick and Possum launched it over the side and turned on the monitor as it dove down. Rick guided it, being careful not to get too close to Johnie's line. Suddenly, the colossal fish came into view.

"It's a bluefin tuna and it's massive!" yelled Rick. "We have to get that thing on board. One just recently sold in Japan for $1.8 million. They're super rare and sought after for sushi."

"You've got to be kidding me," replied a winded Johnie.

"I'm dead serious. That fish could make you a millionaire again," said Rick.

Johnie knew what he was referring to—his cut of Fletcher's gold was still hidden away under the settee on the boat.

"It'll be a team win if we can land it," said Johnie.

For over an hour, he fought the fish. The lactic acid in his arms burned and he was almost ready to give up when the tuna suddenly turned and gave up some ground. Johnie cranked as fast as he could, and with a last-minute burst of energy, he managed to pull the fish alongside the boat. Both Rick and Possum gaffed it together and tried to heave it on board. It was no use. The fish weighed well over 600 pounds. With the fish secure, Johnie rigged up a come-along and cranked the fish onto the boat. They all screamed in unison, including Chief.

"How are we gonna get it to the market in Japan? Plus, don't we need a commercial fish seller license to legally sell it?" asked Possum.

"Nope, you don't need a fish seller license, only a federal HMS permit—which I luckily applied for and have in my back pocket," replied Johnie, his eyes twinkling. "Best twenty-six dollars I ever spent."

"You are a genius," said Rick.

"Okay, but how do we get it to Japan from Cuba?" asked Possum again.

Rick pulled out his iPhone. "Easy, we fly it there. Air Canada has a one-stop flight from Havana to Japan. The US has a trade embargo against Cuba, but Canada doesn't, so we are solid. As soon as we get to Cuba, I'm gonna make some calls and see where we can sell this puppy."

"Okay, you make the calls, and I'll order the mojitos," replied Possum.

Johnie, Rick, and Possum worked together to get the fish on ice. It was no easy task and they had to move some beer from the giant in-deck fish box to dry storage. It was a tight squeeze, but they managed to get the fish down below.

"Well, that's it, boys," said Rick, wiping his hands clean. "No more fishing. We need to make up some time and we are out of fish storage space, not that I'm complaining. Besides, the big trench is on the south side of Cuba. Maybe we can fish that in a couple of days. I've read a lot about it. You could throw a tennis ball from shore and it would be floating over 7,200 feet of water."

"Sounds like a plan. You want me to steer for a while?" asked Johnie, holding his aching back.

"Naw, man, you rest your arms. I think there's some Tiger Balm in the first-aid kit. Rub down your arms and grab a beer; you earned it."

"You don't have to ask me twice," said Johnie.

While Johnie and Possum stayed below spraying the fish guts off of the boat and stowing the rods and tackle, Rick returned to the flybridge and brought the boat back up on plane. Chief sat on Rick's shoulder and munched on a red grape, dropping pieces of it on Rick's shirt. He was a content bird and seemed right at home on the water. Rick would have to stow him somewhere safe for their passage into Cuba. He didn't wanna take any chances of him being confiscated by customs and immigration.

Once Johnie came up from below, Rick instructed him to disassemble Chief's big cage and mobile tree perch and hide them in the engine room. "We'll put Chief in his travel cage and hide him in the anchor locker," said Rick, "in case the immigration officers want to inspect the boat."

"Got it, boss," said Johnie.

In a matter of a few hours, they would be entering the small channel along the edge of Punta Cabeza de Vaca and tying up at the yacht club.

As they entered Cuban waters, a boat with a high-powered gun on a tripod approached them.

"Rick, give me Chief," yelled Johnie.

Rick set the autopilot, climbed partially down from the flybridge, and handed Chief to Johnie. Johnie put several fresh grapes and water in the bird's travel cage, covered it, and stowed Chief down below in the anchor locker. He came back up after a minute and said, "He's well hidden, Rick. It should be fine as long as he doesn't squawk like crazy."

Rick nodded. It was dark in the locker and anytime it was dark, Chief generally fell fast asleep regardless of the time of day. Rick would keep the music loud in case of a random squawk, and also planned to grease the agent with a few Benjamins if needed.

The boat slowly approached alongside the sportfisher. Over a loudspeaker from the government, someone called out, "Hola. Bienvenidos a Cuba."

One of the men tossed Johnie a line and pointed at the cleat. "Planeas atracar en Cuba?" said the man.

Johnie looked up at Rick. "I have no idea what he just said."

Rick climbed down from the flybridge and said, "Give me your passports."

Possum and Johnie passed them to Rick.

"Nos alojaremos en el por solo unos días para visitar La Habana. Nosotros atracaremos en el Club Náutico Internacional Hemingway," said Rick to the man, and passed him all three passports.

The immigration officer took the passports and opened each of them. When he got to Rick's, he opened the page and saw five hundred-dollar bills folded inside. He looked over his shoulder at the captain and the other crewmember, who were talking, and quickly put the bills in his shirt pocket when they turned their heads. He put a stamped slip of paper in each passport and handed them back to Rick.

Rick smiled and said, "Gracias, que tenga un gran día."

"Disfruten de Cuba, mis amigos," the officer replied.

Rick handed him the stern line, and the man waved his hands in a circle to the captain. The boat backed away, heading east.

"What just happened?" asked Possum.

"He gave us stamped immigration papers and told us to enjoy Cuba," replied Rick.

"What did you give him and when did you learn to speak Spanish so well?"

"I gave him $500. When I started seeing Jules, I wanted to surprise her and polish up my Spanish, so I downloaded an app called Babbel, and I studied every night with my headphones on before I fell asleep."

Possum snorted. "Well, color me impressed, amigo."

"Muchas gracias, Zarigüeya," said Rick with a grin.

"Did you just say my name in Spanish?"

"Yeah, it was one of the first new words I learned. It has a certain ring to it. Don't you think, Zarigüeya?"

"Yeah, but I'll just stick to Possum, if that's okay."

"No problemo, Possum." Rick laughed.

Johnie climbed back up to the flybridge to check the chart plotter. "We're only about ten clicks from the channel entrance. You want me to steer now?"

"Sure, go ahead. I'll get Chief out of his dungeon."

Rick opened the anchor locker and slowly pulled Chief and his travel cage out. The cockatoo was fast asleep but startled awake. Chief hopped up and down with excitement. Once the cage was on deck, Rick pulled Chief out and gave him a kiss on the beak. Chief snuggled against Rick's neck and cooed like a dove.

"Possum, can you reassemble the big cage inside? I think we are solid now with the authorities."

"Sure, Rick. No worries."

Once the cage was reassembled, Rick put Chief inside with some of his favorite treats and climbed back up to the flybridge with Johnie. The lush green Sierra de los Órganos mountain range to the west and the whitewashed buildings of Havana, standing in stark contrast to the backdrop of green rainforests and blue skies, were breathtaking.

They slowly approached the entrance to the marina, and Rick took over the helm. Johnie and Possum went to their positions on the starboard bow and stern, ready to tie off the lines at the yacht club. A tall, thin, dark-skinned man wearing a canotier hat and chewing on a cigar approached the boat.

"Hola, amigos," he said.

Johnie and Possum tossed him the lines, and he secured them snugly to the oversized cleats on shore, just after Johnie lined the starboard side of the boat with huge fenders.

Rick climbed down and greeted the man. "Con quién hablo sobre las tarifas del muelle?" he asked.

The man pointed to the building at the end of the canal.

"You pay girl at yacht club," replied the man.

"Oh, you speak English," said Rick.

"Si. I watch your boat?" asked the man.

"How much?"

The man shrugged his shoulders and said, "No se."

"How about fifty dollars a day?"

The man's eyes grew wide. "Si, yes, yes, yes!"

"Where can we get some Cuban cigars?' asked Johnie.

The man looked perplexed. "Anywhere. This is Cuba."

"Duh," murmured Johnie, his cheeks flushing from embarrassment.

Rick looked at his watch. "It's 3:30 p.m. You know what that means?"

"My mojito at the Bodeguita del Medio and my daiquiri at the Floridita?" replied Possum.

"Exactamundo!" said Rick in Spanglish.

CHAPTER TWO

Rick, Johnie, and Possum stepped into the blue and white yacht building, and a voluptuous tanned girl walked over to greet them.

"Hola y bienvenidos al Hemingway International Yacht Club, permítame presentarle a nuestro comodoro," said the curvy woman.

Rick understood she was inviting them to meet her boss. He waved for Possum and Johnie to follow him.

"Comodoro Escrich, tenemos visitantes," chirped the beautiful woman to a man inside an office.

"Come in, come in," said the man.

They all stepped into his office, and the chubby, gray-haired man introduced himself with a smile.

"Hola. I am José Miguel Díaz Escrich, but you can just call me José."

"I'm Rick. This is Possum and Johnie. We are in the fifty-five-foot Viking on the east side of the canal. How much is it to stay here?"

"The fee to join the yacht club is $150. Dockage for a forty-five-foot or larger boat is one dollar per foot, so for your boat that would be fifty-five US dollars per day. That gives you access to all the amenities, including the pool and three restaurants," said the commodore.

"That's a deal! You speak perfect English, José," replied Rick.

"Thank you, Rick, I was an officer in the Cuban Navy until 1992, then I was out of a job. I decided to open a yacht club so I could make some money. We have assisted the Hemingway International Billfish Tournament, which is the second oldest tournament in the world, since we opened. I'm sure you know Hemingway was a huge sportsman and fished in the tournament many times."

"I think I read that somewhere," piped up Possum.

"Actually, that's why we're here," said Rick. "We want to get some great cigars and visit Hemingway's two favorite bars."

"Ah, El Floridita and Bodeguita del Medio. The second one is a rumor, but it's still a great place to check out."

The commodore walked over to a large bookshelf and opened a beautifully crafted humidor. He grabbed a large handful of cigars, put them in a Ziploc bag, and handed them to Rick.

"My cousin rolls these himself. The best in Cuba!"

"How much?"

"For you, my friends, a handshake is all I ask. And please help spread the word about our wonderful yacht club when you return to the States."

They all shook his hand and thanked him.

"We will definitely help you get the word out," said Rick. "Where can we get a cab into Havana?"

"Just see Floramaria. She will have your paperwork and you can pay her the fees. She will call you a cab. Have fun and don't worry about your boat; we have cameras everywhere," said the commodore.

"Ah, the flower of Mary."

"You speak Spanish, Rick?"

"Si, José. He estado estudiando para impresionar a una chica,"

José let out a hearty laugh and said, "It's always for a girl, isn't it?"

Rick paid Floramaria, signed a few papers, and within a few minutes, a 1957 Chevy pulled up in front of the yacht club.

"Tu taxi esta aqui," said Floramaria.

Johnie stepped outside to say something to the cab driver and returned with a bouquet of flowers. Both Rick and Possum looked at each other inquisitively, not knowing how Johnie got the flowers so fast, or why. The flush in his cheeks soon told them the answer, as he sauntered up to the receptionist. He had taken a liking to her.

Rick and Possum stepped outside to give him some space, sharing a soft chuckle.

"Flowers for the flower of Mary," said Johnie, repeating what he had learned earlier from Rick as he handed the flowers to the beautiful tanned woman.

"Oh, estan hermosas," said Floramaria.

"I'm sorry, I don't really speak Spanish," said Johnie.

"I said, 'They are beautiful.'"

Johnie's eyes lit up. "Oh, you speak English."

"Yes, I learned from the commodore."

"What time do you get off? Do you want to meet us in Havana?"

The woman blushed and covered her mouth. "I get off at five."

Johnie looked down at his watch. It was 4:22 p.m. "Would you like to ride with me? I can get us another cab."

She looked at Johnie, then looked back at her flowers and said, "Yes, but I don't even know your name."

"Sorry, I should've introduced myself. I'm Johnie. I'm the first mate and mechanic on Rick's boat." He gave her a big smile and said, "I'll be right back." He hurried outside.

Rick was sitting in the front seat of the cab, practicing his Spanish with the driver and trying to get some information about the area. Possum was leaning against the car with one of the unlit cigars hanging from his mouth.

"Rick, I'm gonna catch up with y'all in a little bit," said Johnie. "Where are you going first? She gets off in about a half an hour. I think I'm in love."

Rick smirked at him. "You sly dog! We're going for mojitos and a late lunch at Bodeguita del Medio, then we'll hit El Floridita for daiquiris. After that, who knows!"

"Okay, I'll see y'all at Bodeguita del Medio. I won't be far behind you."

Possum climbed in the back seat and they drove off. Johnie rushed back inside, humming to himself, to wait for his date.

"Rick, ask him where I can get one of those hats," said Possum. "It's good practice for you."

"Dónde puedo conseguir uno de esos sombreros?"

The taxi driver held up one finger, indicating for them to hold on a second. He took a sharp right down a back alley, then slammed on his brakes and pointed to a street vendor on the corner. A small cart stood there covered in hats and other types of Cuban clothing and some fresh coconuts and pineapple. Rick and Possum hopped out of the car and approached the vendor.

"Nos gustaría comprar uno de sus sombreros. Cuánto cuesta?" asked Rick.

"Cinco dólares por sombrero," said the vendor.

He then pointed at a pineapple and a coconut that had straws in them and made a gesture like he was taking a drink.

"Cuánto cuesta?" asked Rick.

"Dos dólares," said the man.

"Possum, do you want a pineapple and rum or coconut and rum?"

Possum started singing a song about putting lime in a coconut, and dancing like an idiot.

"Yo tomaré la piña y mi amigo estúpido tomará un coco con lima, hazlos dobles," said Rick.

Possum slung a slanted look at him. "Did you just call me stupid?"

"No se," replied Rick.

Possum just smirked as the man poured the Havana Club rum with a heavy hand into the cold fruit vessels he had plucked from the ice chest. He stuck a little Havana Club swizzle stick and a straw into each tropical concoction.

"Woohoo!" exclaimed Possum.

"He even put a lime in yours, Possum. Just like the song," said Rick.

They both got back in the cab bound for Bodeguita del Medio. Either the vendor knew how to make the perfect drink or Havana Club was an incredibly smooth rum. Both Rick and Possum were impressed. About halfway through each drink, they swapped the coconut for the pineapple. Their timing was impeccable. As soon the noisy air-sucking sounds came from the straws, the cabby pulled up to the front door of the famous bar. Rick paid the man and tipped him twenty dollars.

"Yo me quedo aqui para ustedes. Seré su conductor. Sí?"

Rick nodded and said, "Si."

"What did he say?" asked Possum.

He said he wants to be our driver from now on. I guess they aren't used to good tips around here."

"Oh cool, that will come in handy. I dig his car too," replied Possum.

A light brown 1962 Studebaker pulled up in front of the yacht club at five o'clock on the dot. Johnie told the cab driver to wait for a minute until Floramaria locked up the office. She stepped out looking even more stunning than she was while working. She had changed into her street clothes and ditched the Hemingway Yacht Club logo polo shirt. She wore a colorful flowered sundress, and red high heels that matched the silk scarf she had loosely tied around her delicate tanned neck. Johnie opened the door for her like a true gentleman and tapped the cab driver on the shoulder.

"Bodeguita del Medio, por favor," said Johnie, using the only Spanish he really knew besides baño and cerveza. "Do you like mojitos, Floramaria?"

"Yes, I do, very much, and they make the best at Bode-guita del Medio in Havana, with the exception of the ones I make at home."

"Oh, that's great. Where do you live? I mean, what part of the island?"

"I live in Vedado," she said.

"Vedado! Eres una chica rica?" interrupted the cab driver.

"No, no soy rica! Vivo en una casa de huéspedes. Yo les hago la contabilidad y en cambio ellos me dan un alberge," she blurted out.

"What did he say?" asked Johnie.

"Well, Vedado is one of the richest neighborhoods in Havana, and he said I must be a rich girl. I told him I live in a guest house and I trade accounting for my rent. It's my second job. Most people in Cuba have two, if not three, jobs. I am very lucky to work for a such a nice family. They own a coffee export business, and I have worked for them since I graduated from university."

"Wow, that's really cool," said Johnie.

"It's actually pretty close to Bodeguita del Medio— walking distance, in fact."

"That's great. You can stumble home if need be."

"Trust me, I have. I have a little moped and I have left it chained up in Havana and walked home few times, I must admit," she said with a light laugh.

When they pulled up to the famous tourist bar and stepped inside, Rick waved them over to a corner table.

"Hello again, Floramaria. I see you brought a stray dog with you," said Rick.

"He's a cute stray dog," she replied.

Johnie started to blush.

Rick waved his finger in a circle to the bartender for another round. The cute waitress brought over the drinks and sat next to Rick. She was definitely working him hard, but Rick was having none of it. She eventually got the hint and set her eyes on a couple of young German guys at the bar instead.

After taking photos of the famous faux Hemingway sign behind the bar and enjoying several more rounds, they all decided it was time to hit El Floridita. The cab driver was still sitting out front in his 1957 Chevy, and they all hopped in.

"El Floridita, amigo," said Rick.

"Señor rápido," replied the cabby.

He drove like a bat out of hell, and it reminded Rick of the scene from the movie *Captain Ron* where Kurt Russell stole a similar car and was chased by bloodthirsty, heavily armed pirates—pirates of the Caribbean.

When he arrived at El Floridita, the driver even slammed on the brakes and slid in sideways to the curb Captain Ron style.

"I like this guy," said Rick.

He looked in the back seat at his wide-eyed gang. They all had death grips on the back of the seat. Apparently, they didn't feel the same way. Rick chuckled as he opened the door for his compadres in crime.

El Floridita was hopping. Their timing was perfect though, as a group of four people at the bar were getting up to leave. Rick quickly secured their spots. He sat at the end seat next to a bronze statue of Hemingway leaning against the bar with his elbow resting on the edge. It almost felt like they were drinking with Hemingway. He made small talk with the statue, cracking everybody up. The bartender brought them all daiquiris, the drink that Hemingway always drank there. They were made the same way they were back in Hemingway's time: rum, simple syrup, lime juice, and a splash of maraschino liqueur, blended to perfection.

After several rounds, Rick noticed a sign on the wall for free Wi-Fi. He pulled out his phone and turned it on. His phone started whistling repeatedly. He was getting texts. They were from Jules.

> *Jules: I went hiking deep in the jungle with guides and found a crashed airplane. The pilot was dead and two people were inside. One was dead and one was holding on. The plane was full of stuff like you use to treasure hunt. The dying man gave me a backpack and said please find the Jewel of Orinoco. I'll send an email with more details.*

> *Jules: Rick, I am in trouble, please help.*

> *Jules: Someone is outside my door, I'm scared.*

Rick texted her back immediately.

Rick: Jules, are you ok?

Rick: Jules, please respond.

He waited a minute, then called her using Wi-Fi calling. It went straight to voicemail.

"Jules, it's Rick. I'm worried about you. Please call or text me as soon as you get this."

As he hung up, his heart was pounding. He quickly opened his email. He scrolled down a few and found the email from Jules and opened it.

Dear Rick,

I think I have gotten myself into some big trouble. As I said in my text, I found an airplane that had crashed with two dead guys in it and one who died not long after I found him. His dying words were for me to find the Sacred Jewel of Orinoco. He went on to say the Kayapó tribes' lives depend on it.

The name of the man who died and gave me the backpack was Kevin Clizby. He was an anthropologist. So was the other dead passenger. I went through all of his research papers in the backpack. They were searching for a giant sapphire that is the most sacred artifact of the Yanomami people. They worshipped this sapphire like a god, and it was stolen from the tribe's temple. The Yanomami believe the Kayapó stole it. From what I can understand from the documents in his backpack, Clizby met with Davi Kopenawa, the shaman and spokesperson for the Yanomami, and Kubei, the Kayapó leader. He talked them into a truce and promised to return the sacred sapphire to the Yanomami, who agreed to give it to the American Museum of Natural History in New York in exchange for one million dollars to aid them in their stand to stop a massive dam being built that will destroy their land.

If the Sacred Jewel of Orinoco is not returned to the Yanomami tribe soon, they will attack the Kayapós. The Yanomami are known as a fierce people and are 40,000 strong. There are only about 5,500 Kayapó left. They will be decimated. It will be genocide, Rick.

I made copies of all the documents and hid them in a drybag in a hole under the crawl space of my house in Fonte Boa in case anything happens to me. Clizby wrote that a group of men from England, one of whom was named Evan Taylor, were partners in an import/export business there called Armstrong Imports. They stole the sapphire and were arrested by the Brazil Federal Police and deported but managed to hide the jewel before they were captured. I have a map they made leading to its whereabouts in the backpack. Clizby got ahold of it somehow. I can't decipher it—that's more up your alley. The guys who stole it know I have the map and they want it back. The only person I told was my roommate, but I trusted her. She has been missing now for five days, and I got a call from her kidnappers demanding the map in exchange *for her release. I came home and my place was ran-sacked. I packed up my stuff and I'm staying at the Hotel Eliana in Fonte Boa under the name J.C. for Juliana Castro.*

 Rick, I'm terrified. Please help me. The address for the hotel is Avenida Gov Gilberto Mestrinho 220 Cidade Nova, Fonte Boa, State of Amazonas 69670-000 Brazil.

With love,
Jules

Rick pulled Possum aside and showed him the texts and email. Possum read them and looked up at Rick, his eyes full of concern.

"What are you gonna do, Rick?"

"I guess I'm going to Brazil," he said with a shaky laugh. "You and Johnie, get that tuna to air cargo in the morning. I've already arranged for it to be shipped to Japan. There's a bill of landing at the Air Canada freight office. Just use the company card Johnie has to pay for it. I need to book a flight to Brazil. After y'all ship the tuna, take the boat back to Destin. Johnie has some charters coming up in a few days. You can head back to Houston or stay with Johnie, just monitor your phone. I may need you."

Rick pulled up Google Maps and searched for the closest international airport to Fonte Boa. It appeared to be Manaus. He would have to fly back to Miami first, but there was a nonstop on Latam Airlines that he could make if he caught the first flight out in the morning to Miami, so he booked them both. His trip to Cuba would be cut short, but he didn't care. If anything happened to Jules, he wouldn't be able to live with himself.

Johnie was making googly eyes at Floramaria and having way too much fun, so Rick asked Possum to keep it on the lowdown until the next day. He didn't want to upset Johnie and interrupt his date.

They had a few more drinks and then sat down at a table and ordered some appetizers. The food and the service were surprisingly good, but Rick couldn't stop thinking about Jules.

Why won't she answer her phone?

After they all ate, Johnie said, "Hey guys, I'm gonna walk Floramaria back to her place. She lives close by and it's a beautiful night for a walk."

"Sounds good, Johnie," said Rick. "Be careful, and if you end up staying over, please be back at the boat by seven a.m. to help Possum get that fish to market. I have to make a run to Miami. Possum will fill you in on the details tomorrow."

A flicker of concern crossed Johnie's gaze. "All right, Rick. Everything okay?"

"Don't worry about it. Just take care of Floramaria."

"Okay, boss. Sounds good."

Outside, Possum and Rick climbed back into the cab and told their driver to head back to the yacht club.

Rick leaned over and got the driver's attention. "Conoce a alguien con un camión? Necesito llevar un atún al aeropuerto mañana por la mañana."

"Sí, mi hermano tiene un camión frigorífico. A qué hora lo necesitas?"

"Siete de la mañana, en el puerto deportivo," said Rick.

"No hay problema." The driver put the car into gear, bound for the marina.

"Okay, Possum, to our good luck, his brother has a refrigerated truck and he will be at the yacht club at seven a.m. to load the tuna for the airport. Once y'all get that tuna shipped to Japan, hightail it to Destin, and I'll keep you posted once I get to Brazil."

"Got it, boss," said Possum.

They arrived back at the yacht club, and Rick packed a suitcase. He had no idea what to bring but he knew he couldn't take a gun, so he packed his buck knife and hiking gear and put all of his surveillance gear in a carry-on. He threw in a birdwatching book to throw off customs. He would need to pose as a bird-loving tourist so as not to arouse any suspicion about all of his recording devices and his monocular and night-vision goggles. He remembered he had a book on bats that a friend from Indiana had given him. She was a chiropterologist, and had taken him on a couple of bat migration field assignments. Rick hated bats, but that book would help sell the night-vision goggles to authorities, so he was glad he had it.

Now all he had to do was sleep, which would be no easy task. He brought Chief into his cabin and let him sleep beside him. Chief was the only bird Rick had ever heard of that liked to sleep in a real bed. He didn't know how long he would be gone, so he tucked Chief under his chin on his chest, and eventually they both drifted off.

CHAPTER THREE

Rick rose before the morning sun peeked over the horizon. Chief hadn't moved all night. The cockatoo yawned when Rick picked him up and set him on top of his cage. It always amazed and impressed Rick that Chief could hold it all night and then as soon he put him on his cage, he would take care of his morning business.

For a change, Rick had awakened before Possum. He tried to say quiet as he made some coffee. He had arranged for his driver to be at the yacht club at 5:45 a.m. to get him to the airport in time. Coming in by boat and flying back to US soil worried him a little, as his passport hadn't been stamped; it only had a Cuban tourist card placed inside. There was nothing he could do about it now, though, so he would deal with it in Miami.

Possum stumbled out of his cabin looking rather disheveled. "Good morning, amigo." He rubbed his sleepy eyes. "You're up early."

"I guess I'm nervous about flying into Brazil and finding Jules."

"It'll all work out, man. Just have faith," said Possum as he patted Rick on the shoulder.

"You want some java?" asked Rick.

"Yeah, man. You want me to make some breakfast?"

"Naw, I'm too anxious to eat. I'll take a couple of breakfast bars with me for the flight. You go ahead, though."

Rick dragged his luggage up to the deck and sipped on a cup of coffee. He stared at the water as the sun began to appear. Bait fish broke the surface, fleeing from some jacks that were chasing them in the canal. It was a beautiful morning in Cuba, and he tried to soak it in as best he could.

Chief was bobbing and weaving on top of his cage, doing his morning dance they were all so used to. Rick stepped back down and gave Chief a kiss on the beak.

"You be a good boy. I have to head out, so you listen to your uncle Possum and Johnie," Rick told him.

The bird just cocked his head as if he understood Rick.

"All right, man," Rick said to Possum. "It's time for me to head out. I'll send you a text as soon as I find Wi-Fi in Brazil, hopefully at the airport."

"Let me help you with the bags and walk you to the cab," said Possum.

They strolled down the dock. An uneasy feeling sent a shiver down Rick's spine.

"You sure you don't want me to come?" asked Possum, who looked rather nervous about the trip too.

"Naw, man. I need you stateside in case I need something. If it goes sideways, I'll let you know."

Rick put his big duffel in the trunk and sat in the back seat with his carry-on next to him.

Possum leaned in and shook his hand firmly. "Good luck and Godspeed."

Rick just nodded.

"Vámonos!"

The cabby peeled out, and Rick waved goodbye to Possum out of the window.

The airport was surprisingly busy at such an early hour. Rick checked his bag through to Manaus and proceeded to security. The officers at the gate pulled him aside and went through the gear in his carry-on, asking what it was all for. Once he showed them the two books and explained about the birdwatching, they all nodded and sent him to the gate. He was sure he'd get the same treatment when he landed in Brazil. He knew one thing for sure: he would have to secure a gun once he arrived. He figured that wouldn't be too hard in a third-world country.

Upon landing in Miami, he sent a quick text to Possum to update him.

Rick: I'm in Miami, all good. Agent didn't seem to care.

Possum: Awesome, we got the tuna shipped and I emailed you a receipt. Getting boat fueled now.

Rick: Ok, be safe.

Possum: Ditto amigo.

Rick got a row to himself on the flight to Manaus. The plane had Wi-Fi, so he opened his laptop and studied the route to Fonte Boa. It was over four hundred miles to get there from Manaus. He did a search and found Azul Linhas Aeréas had a commuter flight into Tefé. The only way to get to Fonte Boa from Tefé was by ferry, and it was just shy of a five-hour ride on the Amazon. He sighed. This trip was beginning to sound like the movie *Planes, Trains, and Automobiles*, only with different modes of transportation.

The half-empty plane touched down softly in Manaus, and Rick made his way to the exit. It was a short stroll to customs and immigration. The agent spoke Portuguese and English, so Rick explained that he was heading upriver to study birds and the bidentate yellow-eared bat, something he'd memorized from his book. The immigration officer seemed uninterested and waved him through.

There was a huge message board in the center of the terminal. A ferry leaving for Fonte Boa was scheduled for 3:45 p.m. It was three o'clock, so Rick went to the main ticket counter to see if he could catch a flight to Tefé instead. That would put him much closer, and from there it would be a much shorter ferry ride. There was a flight at 4:20 on Azul Airways. It was only $120, so Rick opted for that.

The agent took so long to book the ticket that Rick had to sprint to security and then to the gate. It turned out to be unnecessary, though, as the flight crew seemed uninterested in being on time. The gate agent took his ticket and pointed to the door. The plane was only half full. Rick picked a seat close to the front and sat there fifteen minutes past the departure time. The gate agent eventually moseyed to the cockpit with the weight and balance papers. He nonchalantly gave his speech in Portuguese, English, then Spanish and closed the airplane door.

The captain fired up the twin props. It was very loud in the cabin, but the plane seemed safe and new enough, just extremely loud. Rick shoved a few pieces of cocktail napkins into his ears, wishing he had remembered to bring his noise-cancelling headphones.

It had been a long day, and Rick dozed off and slept though almost the entire flight. It was only a little over an hour long. Before he knew it, the little puddle jumper was touching down.

The Tefé airport was small but surprisingly clean and organized. Rick needed to find a ferry to Fonte Boa but didn't speak a lick of Portuguese. He wished he had bought a translation book back in Manaus, as there were no shops inside the tiny airport. He stopped several people who looked like sky caps and asked them if they spoke English. They all shook their heads, except the final person, who pointed to a lady putting brochures into a carousel rack.

"Excuse me, do you speak English?" Rick asked her.

"Yes, I do. How can I help you?" she responded.

"I'm trying to get to Fonte Boa. I read that there's a ferry I can catch."

"You will need to go to the Porto de Tefé, just on the edge of town. But the next ferry doesn't leave until nine tomorrow morning, so you will need a hotel," she said.

"Okay. Is there a cab nearby?"

"Yes, but I only live about a mile from the port and close to Stylos Hall Hotel. I run a taxi service, if you would like a ride."

"That would be great," replied Rick. "Do I need to make a reservation for the hotel?"

"As soon as I finish stacking the rest of these brochures, I will call for you and also arrange your ferry. Just have a seat and give me about fifteen minutes. They speak only Portuguese, so it will easier if I do it," she responded with a smile.

"Thanks so much. Oh, forgive me—my name is Rick Waters. Yours?"

"Nice to formally meet you, Rick. I am Regina. Just call me Gina."

Rick thanked her again and sat on a bench. As he waited, he watched people stroll in and collect their luggage and greet their loved ones. A vendor pushing a small cart labeled "água" sat near the exit. Rick recognized the word for water, as it was very close to Spanish. He then realized he had no Brazilian money. At the far corner of the building, he spotted a booth that read "Câmbio de Divisas" and had pictures of US dollars and lots of other Monopoly-looking money.

Rick got Gina's attention and pointed toward the money exchange while rubbing his fingers and thumb together. The universal sign for money. She just nodded and continued filling the rack.

Pulling out five one-hundred-dollar bills, he slid them through the glass hole toward the man behind the counter.

The attendant quickly started typing into a calculator and spun it around for Rick to see. It read 2,529.34. Rick just nodded, though he had no idea if he was being ripped off or not. After stuffing most of the cash inside his carry-on, he put a small mix of the colored bills in his front pocket, and made his way to the water vendor.

Rick held up two fingers and the man said, "Dez reais, por favor," and held up all ten fingers.

Rick handed him ten real and did the math in his head based on the currency exchange rate from the shop. The waters were basically a buck each.

Good price, he thought to himself.

He made his way back to the brochure stand as Gina was closing up the cardboard box and putting it on a small cart.

"Follow me," she said as she wheeled the small cart through the exit to the parking lot. She pushed a button on her key fob, and a small white van's horn beeped. The back side door slid open. She put the box inside, along with a few more, and instructed Rick to place his carry-on beside them and hop in the front seat.

Rick climbed in the passenger seat, relieved that this was a right-driving country in case he ever needed to rent a vehicle. One less thing to worry about.

Gina climbed in, started the Toyota van, and made her way out of the parking lot. As she drove, Rick took in the scenery, spotting a couple of tropical birds that made him think of Chief and miss him. He was sure Possum, Johnie, Chief, and the boat were making good progress toward Destin by now. He really needed to touch base with them, but his cell phone had no reception in Brazil.

"Is there anywhere I can get a Brazilian cell phone or SIM card?"

"Sure, but everyone here speaks Portuguese, even the operators. Do you need to call home or something?"

"Yeah, I wanna check on my crew back in Florida."

"Well, the hotel has good Wi-Fi, and if you have Skype that's your best bet," she said.

"Duh, why didn't I think of that?"

They both laughed.

"You sure speak good English, and I don't even detect an accent," said Rick.

"That's because I'm from So Cal, silly. I grew up near Newport in the OC."

"Ah, I see. You have such a dark complexion that I assumed you were from here. No offense."

"None taken. I fit in quite well here, actually. Even locals think I'm Brazilian."

"How did you end up here?"

"Well, that's a long story, but I can tell you the condensed version. Basically, I was studying botany at UC Irvine and I decided to go to Rio on my spring break ten years ago. I met a cabana boy at my resort and fell in love. He showed me all over Brazil, and I was smitten with the Amazon basin. I went back to school and we were married within two months. He ended up running off with a waitress shortly after he got his green card. I was just his way to get citizenship. Prick! Anyway, the joke's on him. After I got my degree, I came back on a grant I received to study the indigenous Cinchona tree. The bark is used for blood disorders. After the grant ran out, I was hooked and just couldn't leave. Now I run a huge plant nursery and just do the brochures as a favor for a friend. I realized I was happier here than anywhere else I've ever been, so I guess I owe that prick for showing it to me in the first place."

"Wow, that is a great story! Thanks for sharing," said Rick.

"My pleasure." She smiled. "We're not too far from the hotel. Is there anywhere you need to stop before we arrive?"

"Can you suggest a restaurant, not too far from the hotel?"

"I can do better than that. I have a local meal that's been cooking in my slow cooker all day. It's too much for me to eat and you're welcome to join me. To be honest, I don't get to speak English that much and it's been nice."

"Sure, sounds like a treat. How do you know I'm not a serial killer?" asked Rick.

"Ha-ha, how do you know *I'm* not?" she replied with a wink.

"Touché."

"I also make my own cachaça liquor out of fermented sugar cane. It's similar to rum but has a unique taste. I can whip us up some caipirinha cocktails, which kind of taste like mojitos, but I like them way better."

"Okay, I'm in. Sounds like a plan."

She continued to drive for a couple more miles, then pulled up to a huge gate with ten-foot-tall concrete walls surrounding the entire estate.

Rick's eyes widened. "Wow, this is quite the spread!"

"You'd be surprised what $100,000 can buy down here. My parents loaned me the money, and I've already paid them back with the profits from the nursery."

She put in a code, and the huge iron gates slowly opened. The driveway was curvy, and the grounds were immaculate. Off to the right were several huge greenhouses, nearly a football field long.

"What all do you grow in the greenhouses?" asked Rick.

"One thing, and one thing only. Well, I should say one species only. I grow orchids for export. Lots of different varieties. I'd love to show you," she said as she parked the car.

"That would be great. I've got a black thumb, but it won't hurt to look."

Rick stepped out of the van, only to quickly jump back in and slam the door. A ginormous dog was running full speed toward him.

"It's okay, Rick," said Gina, laughing. "It's just Mio. He's a Fila Brasileiro, aka a Brazilian Mastiff. They are bred to keep jaguars away. He's just a little snuggle bug."

The massive dog jumped up and put his paws on her shoulders. He was taller than she was. He licked her face as she nuzzled the side of his head. Rick slowly climbed out of the van, and the dog again bolted toward Rick.

"Down, Mio!" yelled Gina.

The dog stopped in his tracks a foot from Rick and bowed down in front of him with his paws crossed. Rick leaned down and rubbed him behind his ears.

"Well, that's it. You're friends for life now," said Gina. "Wanna see the greenhouse?"

"Sure!"

She motioned with her head for him to follow her, and Mio strolled beside him with his shoe-sized tongue hanging out. Gina opened the door of the first greenhouse, and the air was even more humid than outside. Once the mist from

Rick's eyes cleared, the color spectrum blew him away. The orchids were beautiful, some rows blooming and some not. Row after row of orchids stretched as far as he could see, with names and dates at the end of each one.

"Oh my God, I've never seen so many orchids in my life. How many are there?"

"Thousands."

"You export them all? To where, the US?"

"Not all of them. I'd say about 90 percent are exported. I also sell some to local shops and the occasional local if I like them."

"This is quite the business you have."

"It's a labor of love as well. I've always been fascinated by orchids. They're what drew me into botany to begin with. I got one on my sixteenth birthday and I was hooked ever since. How about a cocktail?"

"Sounds good. It's been a long day."

"Shall we retire to the dream porch?" she asked.

"Dream porch?"

"You'll understand when you see it."

"Do you have Wi-Fi?" asked Rick.

"I sure do. The password is Orchid16." She winked at him.

"Clever."

Rick jogged over to the van, snatched his carry-on, and caught up with Gina. They walked around toward the back of the house on the wraparound porch, with Mio close behind. When he turned the corner, he was stunned by the beauty in front of him. A huge, expansive backyard led to a lush row of trees with the Tefé River in the background. It was stunning.

"I see why you call it the dream porch. I could sit here and daydream all day," said Rick.

"Yeah, it's pretty special. Just beyond the trees to the right, beside the river, is the rainforest. That's why I adopted Mio. One afternoon near sunset, I was pruning some plants near the back of the property and I heard a growl. I looked up and high in the tree was a huge jaguar, and he looked like he was licking his lips and I was his next meal. Luckily, I had a pistol in my gardening bag, and when I fired it in the air, he bolted. If I hadn't had that, I might not be here today."

"Damn, I can't even imagine. I was kinda worried about leaving my guns behind, but I couldn't risk taking them on the plane," replied Rick.

"How about those drinks?" she asked.

He grinned. "You read my mind."

CHAPTER FOUR

They adjourned to the parlor after Gina gave Rick the grand tour. The house reminded him of the old antebellum homes he'd see so many times in Mississippi, with a touch of tiki style. Gina was an avid collector of wooden hand-carved tiki cups and anything tiki, for that matter. She handed him a glossy cup she'd named "Mug of the Monkey God." Hers was a zombie making a painful expression.

"So, Rick, tell me about yourself."

"Not a whole lot to tell. I'm just a good ol' boy from Texas."

"Texas? I know a guy from Texas. He won the lottery last year and bought the big place at the edge of town. We've gone out a few times. He likes to call himself my boy toy. He's too funny. His name is Gary."

"I know a Gary, went to school with him in Texas. Gary Haas, from LaBelle, Texas."

Her eyes grew wide and she almost dropped her drink. "You've got to be kidding me. My Gary's name is Gary

Haas, and he's from LaBelle, Texas, he told me. No way, it can't be the same guy. Wait, I have a picture of us on the river. A group of us, actually. Let me go grab it."

Rick sipped his drink, thinking it was impossible that the Gary Haas he knew was the same guy she was going out with. He frowned and stared at the floor as he waited for her to return.

"Here ya go! Is it him?"

He took the picture she handed him. His mouth fell open. "Oh my God, it is! I just saw him a while back and he was working at the refinery in Port Arthur. He won the lottery?"

"Yep, he's a multi-millionaire now. Let me call him and tell him you're here. He won't believe it."

She walked to another room and called him. She came sprinting back into the parlor, almost out of breath.

"He's freaking out and thinks I'm messing with him. He's on his way over."

"This is incredible. Talk about a small world," replied Rick, shaking his head in disbelief. "How did you meet Gary?"

"It's a funny story. Let's wait till he gets here or you'll be hearing it twice, ha-ha. He'll be here in like ten minutes."

They both sipped on their tiki mugs and made small talk as they waited for Gary. Soon, the doorbell rang and the door opened.

"Honey, I'm home!" bellowed Gary.

Gina jumped up, ran to the hallway, and wrapped her arms around him. She pulled away and pointed at Rick.

"See, I told you he was here."

"Son of a bitch, I can't believe it!" said Gary.

He reached to shake Rick's hand and then pulled him out of the chair for a big man-hug.

"What the hell are you doing here?" asked Gary.

"Me?" Rick laughed. "What are you doing in South America? Better yet, in Tefé of all places?"

"It's a bit of a crazy story. Babe, can you make me a drink?"

"Way ahead of you," Gina said as she handed Gary a tiki mug in the shape of a cactus. "That's his favorite. Reminds him of Texas," she explained to Rick.

They all pulled their chairs closer together, and the story of how Gary got there began to unfold.

"Remember that refinery job I got the last time you saw me, Rick? You gave me a ride home from the Boudin Hut."

"Oh yeah, how could I forget? That's when I beat the crap out of that tweaker who disrespected his girlfriend. You also met Chief that night."

"That's right! How's that little feller?"

"He's great. He's back on the boat with my crew. Speaking of which, I need to call them." Rick glanced at his watch and saw it was getting late. "Eh, I'll wait and call them in the morning."

"So, back to my story," said Gary. "I worked there for a few months and then got the notice that they were shutting down one of the lines. I was the lowest man on the totem pole, so they cut me loose. I was gonna collect unemployment because they said I'd only be laid off for six weeks. I had put away quite a bit of cash and decided to treat it like a mini vacation. I stopped off at Crawdad's convenience store to fill my truck and grab a six-pack. My change was three bucks, so I grabbed a Powerball ticket. I rarely play, but I just kinda felt like it that day. Plus, the jackpot was huge. It was over $730 million. I put the ticket in my pocket and forgot about it.

"A few days later, I saw on TV that there was a single winner who hadn't come forward yet, and the winning ticket came from Crawdad's. I found the ticket in my shirt in the laundry hamper. Thank God I hadn't done the laundry yet, 'cause I'd been planning on it until I remembered I needed to mow the grass first. I have a habit of leaving receipts and cash in my pockets. Anyway, I pulled out the ticket and got on my laptop, figuring I probably wouldn't get any of the numbers and some lucky son of a bitch had won from the same store I'd gotten my ticket from. When I opened the website and saw all my number matched, I fell back in my chair in total disbelief. I pretty much had a panic attack. It was about noon and I immediately jumped in my truck and drove straight to Dallas with the ticket sitting beside me in a Ziploc bag. It was a five-hour drive to the Dallas Lottery Claim Center, and I put the pedal to the metal. I was so afraid I'd lose the ticket or destroy it if I held on to it any longer. I pulled into the parking lot at 4:53 p.m. They closed at five. I flung open the doors and started yelling, 'I won, I won!' They took my ticket and verified it. I took the cash payment option of…are you ready for this, Rick? $546 million! I kinda went crazy for a few months and bought dumb shit and ran around town with thousands of dollars in my pockets."

"Holy crap, dude," said Rick. "I can't even imagine what went through your mind when you saw those numbers. But that still doesn't explain how you ended up here."

"Remember when we were kids and we used to ride all around the Green Acres subdivision on our bicycles, and Terry Dunaway would cruise by on his Honda CR125 dirt bike, standing up on the pedals the entire time? We were always jealous because he had a motor and we didn't, and we'd get bored after a while and say, 'I wonder what David Lee Roth is doing right now.' Later we found out that when he wasn't on tour with Van Halen, he was down here trekking through the Amazon like some crazy adventurer. We always said if we ever got rich, we would do the same thing."

"I totally remember that," replied Rick, smiling at the memory.

"It wasn't too long after I won the money that cousins I'd never heard of started popping out of the woodwork. I was giving away money and some were blowing it on drugs. I'm a very giving guy, and I had to get away from the area. That, along with the David Lee Roth story, sealed the deal for me. I did a little research and found this place, Tefé. About as far from LaBelle, Texas, as you can get. I planned to lie low here for a while, but now that I bought a place, I feel like this is home now. But what brings you here, Rick?"

Gina had stepped into the kitchen to make another batch of caipirinha cocktails. Rick gestured with his head toward her, looked into Gary's eyes, and asked, "Is she cool? Can she be trusted?"

"Dude, she is one hundred percent legit. I vouch for her. So, what's up?"

Rick pulled out a folded piece of paper and handed it to Gary. "This is an email from Jules, the girl I've been dating. She came down here to study the pink dolphins over near Fonte Boa."

"Jules. Do you mean Juliana? Juliana Castro?" asked Gary.

Rick's eyebrows lifted. "You know her?"

"Everyone knows her. She's very beautiful and popular with all the locals. She's a sweetheart. I never finished my entire story, but after I bought my place down here, which came with a dock, I needed a boat for that dock, so I had a three-story catamaran riverboat built. It has an upper deck complete with palm trees and a huge bar. I run trips up the river to Fonte Boa for tourists. I always wanted to trek down the Amazon like Roth, but I'm too old to do it in a dugout canoe, so I do it in style now."

Gary unfolded the copy of the email Jules had sent Rick. He read it silently and then lifted his head.

"Rick, tomorrow morning we are going to Fonte Boa on my boat."

"We're going where?" Gina injected.

Gary hesitated. "You have a nursery to run, and this is too dangerous for..."

Gina frowned, narrowing her eyes. "For what? A girl?"

Gary glanced at Rick. "Can I show her the letter?"

"Sure," replied Rick.

As Gina read it, her frown grew more intense and her dark face began to turn red. "I'm going! We all love Juliana and if she's in trouble, I wanna help. Besides, I have all the guns!"

"She has a point, Rick."

She waved Rick toward her, and they both followed her through the kitchen to a side library. She pulled out one of the books and the entire bookcase slid open, revealing over a dozen shotguns, more rifles and handguns than Rick could count, and an entire wall of ammo.

"You didn't think I only collected tiki mugs, did you?" she said, smirking. "Even though I was raised in the OC, my dad came from the hills of Northern California and taught me how to shoot almost before I could walk. So, what's the plan?"

"Do you have any duffel bags?" asked Rick.

"As a matter of fact, I have three tactical gear bags under that cabinet right there."

She pointed to a large cabinet under the long row of assault rifles. Rick opened the cabinet and set the bags on the ammo reload table in the center of the room.

"Are you sure you want to do this, Gina? These people are dangerous, and I have no idea what they're capable of. How much do you know about the Kayapó and Yanomami?"

"I know quite a bit. The Yanomami have been battling the building of a large dam that will destroy a giant swath of their land. The Yanomami are large in numbers compared to the Kayapó and they believe the Kayapó stole their sacred jewel. If the jewel isn't returned, they will most definitely eliminate the entire Kayapó tribe. So yes, I'm totally sure. Plus, I can come in handy. I'm pretty cute. I can be quite persuasive, and I speak English, Portuguese, and Spanish fluently."

Rick shot a glance over to Gary. "She's got my vote."

"Yeah, mine too!"

"Okay, let's load up." Rick took several shotguns from the rack and reached for an assault rifle. "Is this a fully auto M-16?"

"Well, it ain't no AR-15, I'll tell you that." Gina chuckled. "If you like that, you're gonna love this."

She opened a closed gun locker and pulled out two H&K MP7 mini submachine guns and two MAC-10s. She slid them across the table toward Rick, who was stunned.

"The MP7 shoots 4.7s, and the MAC-10 shoots standard 9 millimeters or .45 acps. Luckily, I have thousands of rounds for each," she said.

"I feel like a kid in a candy store." Rick grabbed a few more Springfield 45 handguns, which also shot the acp rounds, and one long-range Barrett M82 50-cal sniper rifle. "I can't believe you have a Barrett M82."

"Look closer," replied Gina.

Rick turned the rifle sideways and squinted for a better look. "Holy shit. This is a standard issue military M107. How'd you get this?"

Gina shrugged. "I have friends in low places. If I told you, I'd have to kill you." She flashed her teeth at him.

"Fair enough."

They took all the duffels into the parlor and sat around the table.

"This is a serious situation," he told them. "If either of you have any doubts, say your piece now and you can bow out."

"Besides the email, what else do you know, Rick?" asked Gary.

"Not much, to be honest. I really wish my crew were here. Possum, my best buddy, is a wealth of knowledge on precious jewels and one hell of a treasure finder. And Johnie is a jack-of-all-trades and has incredible intuition."

"Fly 'em here," said Gary.

Rick twisted his mouth. "There's no one to watch my bird, and we have charters all week."

"Dude, this is Juliana you're talking about. Cancel the damn charters and put your cockatoo in a boarding house. Better yet, fly him here too. Even better, I'll send my private jet down there and bring them all here. That way we can avoid immigration. My plane is in Birmingham right now and my pilot is on call. I can have him fly in to Destin and pick them all up and head here. We can meet them in Fonte Boa. I'll just have the pilot land in Tefé and then transfer them to a helicopter. If we plan it right, they won't be far behind us."

"Are you serious? Wait, you own a jet?"

"I'm leasing one right now. I've been taking flying lessons. So far, I'm only rated to fly a crop duster, but as soon as I get my multi-engine instrument rating, I'm upgrading to a Bombardier Global 7500, which can get here nonstop from Florida. The Gulfstream will have to refuel in Caracas, but they don't even come on the plane, so it won't be an issue for your cockatoo. I have a huge aviary on the boat, and he can hang there while we investigate Fonte Boa."

"Man, Gary, you've thought of everything. Being rich suits you well, bud!"

Gary polished his nails across his chest and gave Rick a huge grin. "I'm getting used to it. The funny thing is, even though I blew a lot in the beginning, I lucked out and found an amazing money manager. The investments he's made not only have protected my money, but I now have more than when I started. Like they always say, *it takes money to make money*."

Rick laughed. "So true, man. My charter boat is making bank. I could've never done that without a couple of windfalls I lucked into."

"Rick, I'll make up the bed for you in the guest room," said Gina. "It's late and there's no sense in you checking in to the hotel now, especially considering what we're doing tomorrow."

"Thanks for the hospitality, Gina. I've only known you a few hours, but it feels like I've known you my whole life."

"She's like that, Rick!" blurted Gary.

"Okay, one more drink and then bed. We need an early start," said Gina. Then she slapped her forehead. "Holy crap, in all the excitement, we forgot to eat. Let me get some bowls out. You're gonna love it, Rick. It's called Goat Water. Don't ask, just eat."

She ladled three large bowls of Goat Water and filled up everyone's mugs. Reaching out, she took each of their hands.

"In God's name, I pray. Thank you, Lord, for the bountiful feast we are about to enjoy. Thank you for bringing Rick and Gary back together in the way only you can do. Please protect Juliana and her roommate and let us get them back without injury. And help us find the jewel that will save the Kayapó tribe from certain genocide. In Jesus's name we pray, amen."

"Amen," said Rick and Gary simultaneously.

"Rick, we're only an hour ahead of Destin," said Gary as they were eating. "You should call your crew and get them up to speed. I'll call my pilot and have him take the plane tonight to Destin and refuel for tomorrow."

"You can use the house phone in the kitchen," said Gina.

Gary used his cell to call his pilot and then told Rick the plane would be ready to head south at ten a.m.

After Rick finished his Goat Water, he found the kitchen phone.

"Hello, Nine-Tenths Charters. Johnie McDonald here. How can I help you?"

"Hey, Johnie. It's Rick. You are consistent with the way you answer, I'll give you that."

"What's up, Rick? You okay? Did you make it to Brazil?"

"Yeah, I'm here. I need you and Possum to get packed and be at the Destin airport about 9:30 a.m. tomorrow with Chief and his travel cage."

"What about the charters?"

"Cancel them. I need y'all here."

Johnie hesitated for a moment. "I think I can get my buddy and his first mate to cover all the charters again. We don't want to get a bad name for canceling trips."

"Do whatever you think is best, Johnie. I trust you. Just get your butts here. It's about to get real. Is Possum there?"

"No, he's up at AJ's listening to Black Eyed Blonde. They are rocking tonight."

"Okay, get the passports together and see if you can get Possum away from the college girls early enough to catch the flight. When y'all get here, I'll fill you in on everything. When you land in Tefé, you'll be taken by a private chopper to Fonte Boa. We will rendezvous there tomorrow."

"Okay, Rick, see ya soon. Chief will be thrilled!"

"Me too. Bye, Johnie."

Rick returned to the parlor, finished the last of his drink, and thanked Gina.

"No problem, Rick. Any fried of Gary's is a friend of mine. Hell, family!"

"Where is that scoundrel, by the way?"

"He stepped onto the back deck. He loves it out there. He has a couple of stogies, if you're interested."

"Why not? I'll sleep when I'm dead."

Outside, Gary was clipping the end off of his cigar. "Want one? They're Cuban," he said when he saw Rick.

"Sure. In fact, I was just in Cuba."

"Really? Wow."

"Yeah, it's been kind of a whirlwind."

"Shh, shh, listen. There's something moving a few yards off the deck."

Rick tensed. "What is it?"

Gary didn't answer and pushed his ears out like a rabbit to hear better. Rick listened, too. A low growl could be heard in the distance. A tingle of fear ran down Rick's spine.

"Should I grab a gun?" he asked.

"No. It's definitely a jaguar, but it won't come up to the main house with all the lights on inside."

Gary whistled to get the jaguar's attention and let it know they were there. As Rick stared into the darkness, trying to spot the animal, out of nowhere, a rush of sound headed straight toward the deck. The crash of feet in the grass and twigs made Rick inhale sharply. He looked out and saw two eyes coming toward him, glowing in the dark, that looked nothing short of demonic. The animal's speed was undeniable, and before Rick could turn toward the door leading into the house, it was at the base of the deck.

He stumbled backward in panic, tripping over a lounge chair. Certain death was upon him and he couldn't even get up in time to attempt some form of defense. Rick covered his eyes with his forearm, waiting for the massive cat to launch its attack.

Gary started laughing uncontrollably. After a moment, Rick looked up, his heart still racing, to see the world's largest rodent nuzzling his ankles. Gary was bent over, holding his stomach from laughing so hard.

"What in God's name kind of guinea pig is that?" spat Rick.

Gary struggled to catch his breath so he could speak.

"It...it...it's not a guinea pig. It's a capybara. It's Gina's capybara. His name is Oliver."

Rick scowled at him, getting back to his feet. "You son of a bitch. You whistled at him, knowing he'd rush up on the deck."

"I can't lie. It's not often you get a rare treat like that just handed to you. When I heard the jaguar in the distance, I knew you would think it was rushing the deck. Sorry, bro, I couldn't help myself."

"Paybacks are a bitch!" said Rick, but he couldn't help it; he started laughing too.

CHAPTER FIVE

"Wakey, wakey, hands of snakey. Wake up, Rick!" yelled Gary at six a.m.

Rick jolted awake, unsure where he was for a minute and why his old buddy from high school was waking him up. Then it all came back to him, and he sat bolt upright in bed. The smell of coffee and bacon permeated his nose.

"Good morning, Rick," said Gary. "Ready for breakfast? I made a huge one."

"What, no more Goat Water?" said Rick.

Gary snorted. "If you prefer, I can throw this all out and heat some up for you."

"No, no, bacon will work." Rick threw back his cover and got up. He followed Gary into the kitchen.

"You stoked for the boat ride, Rick? The Amazon is magical. I wish it was under different circumstances, but you'll enjoy the trip nonetheless. I already loaded the SUV with all the gear and my crew is readying the boat. Also, I spoke with my pilot, and the Gulfstream is fueled up and sitting at Destin Executive Airport. He's already contacted your boys and instructed them to meet him in the LYNX FBO lounge around nine. He filed a flight plan with one fuel stop in Caracas."

"Wow, Gary, you're all over this. I appreciate the effort." Rick took a seat and reached for a slice of bacon.

"I'm not doing this for you, dude. I'm doing it for those pink dolphins Juliana looks after." He grinned. "Just kidding. Don't worry, Rick; it's all gonna work out."

"I hope you're right, Gary. I love that girl."

"We all do, man. We all do."

After breakfast, the two of them and Gina loaded up in the Ford Expedition and headed for the boat dock. Gary's Expedition was quite the unique vehicle. It had a three-inch lift and huge 35s all the way around. A blower stuck out through a hole in the hood, and Gary had installed an air suspension that could raise or lower the clearance. Rick thought it was all overkill until he saw the roads leading toward the dock. Holes the size of Volkswagens abounded in the middle of the two track dirt roads, where the only thing marking a car-eating sinkhole was a stick with a plastic grocery bag tied to the top of it. It reminded him of Costa Rica, only even more primitive.

"How much horsepower does this beast have?"

"With all the mods I did and the 650 Huffy, about 1250 HP and a ton of torque."

"That's impressive."

"Thanks. I ordered the engine from the States and had it shipped here in a crate. Hell, ordered all the parts stateside.

You can't get so much as an air filter around here locally. Hang on!"

Gary floored it, and Rick and Gina held on for dear life as the Ford hit a large berm in the road and caught air, jumping a creek and landing cleanly on the other side.

"What do you think this is, *The Dukes of Hazzard?*" cried Rick.

"I didn't want to get my tires wet," replied Gary with a belly laugh.

"Holy shit, this thing is built like a tank!"

"I thought you'd appreciate it, Mr. Ford Guy."

"You got that right. I'm impressed."

They pulled up to the dock, and Rick was about to step down from the SUV when Gary grabbed his arm and pulled him back in. He pushed a button on the sun visor, and a garage door on the catamaran opened up. His crew lowered down a ramp to the dock.

"Ain't many car rentals in Fonte Boa. We're taking ours with us," said Gary.

"Okay, now you're starting to blow my mind. Next thing you're gonna say is it also has a helicopter."

Gary pointed to the top of the three-story catamaran, where the aviation windsocks of a helicopter pad sat. Rick gaped at it.

"I had the whirlybird parked at my estate to bring your boys to Fonte Boa when the Gulfstream gets here."

"But there's no airport here. Where will they land?"

"On my runway. I had a 5,000-foot runway built on the edge of my property," replied Gary.

Rick shook his head, grinning. Wealth suited Gary just fine, and he was happy for him.

Once the Ford was parked inside the pristine garage, they all stepped out and were greeted by the crew.

"Hello, my name es Abai. I chief engineer."

"No, you say, 'I *am* the chief engineer,'" said Gary.

"Thank you, boss. I *am* the chief engineer."

"I hired a tutor to teach my entire crew English. Their families too, if they want. I can't take the time to learn Portuguese, and English will help them all in the future if they ever move on from this job."

"Good man," replied Rick.

"This is our captain, Nicolau—you can call him Nick. And over there is Leo, the first mate."

Leo waved with his head as he coiled a garden hose.

"Welcome, Mr. Waters," said Nick. "Hello, Gina. Nice to see you again."

"Hi, Nick, great to be seen."

They all shook hands, and Gary gave them the grand tour of the catamaran. It was not what Rick was expecting, but based on Gary's other vehicles he was starting to think he shouldn't have been surprised. The first floor was the galley and crew quarters, with the garage taking up most of the stern. Behind the garage at the very end of the stern sat the toys: four Jet Skis and an eight-person inflatable. The second level was where all the glory shined. A massive lounge in the bow had wraparound glass, and a hallway led to six staterooms. At the end was a doorway leading to a huge stateroom, fully adorned with animal skins from the area. Back in the salon, Gary pointed to a circular stairway leading to the cockpit.

"Follow me and prepare to be blown away," said Gary.

Rick followed closely as Gina plopped down on the leather sofa and sipped a cup of tea the first mate, Leo, had made for her. Of course, she had seen it all before.

The cockpit was like something out of a Star Wars movie. Four forty-inch monitors sat in front of the helm. The helm was a joystick, and two more radar screens sat in each corner above them.

"Rick, I have this river so dialed in, I can set the course and never touch the helm. It's pretty much a self-driving catamaran. I have the captain for legal reasons, and he's a great guy and his family needs the money. I could steer it myself, but as you know, I have a tendency to find five o'clock somewhere, sometimes around noon, so I figured it'd be best to have a captain."

"Good move."

A croaking sound came from behind where Gary was standing. Rick hadn't even noticed the back wall yet. There was a huge glass window with a full aviary behind it. Inside was a beautiful toucan.

"That's Tico the Toucan. I got him shortly after arriving. I was so taken with your cockatoo, I decided I wanted a bird too. He was just a baby then, and I hand-raised him. He's very gentle. He and Chief will get along quite well. If for some reason they don't buddy up, I can split the aviary down the middle and they each can have their own space. I designed it that way in case I ever decided to get another bird. So far, Tico is a handful. Wanna meet him?"

"Sure."

Gary pushed a button, and the glass window slowly disappeared into the inner wall.

"Step up, Tico," said Gary as he held his hand out.

Tico hopped onto Gary's arm in one quick leap. Gary stroked behind his ears as he croaked a few more times.

"He sounds like a frog," said Rick with a chuckle.

"I know. Actually, more like a cross between a frog and a pig. They only make two distinct sounds—croaking and a yip sound similar to a small puppy."

"They might get along after all. Chief yips, barks, growls, and makes many dog sounds."

"Well, that's the tour, Rick, unless you wanna see the engine room—I mean rooms. They're identical anyway, so let me show you the port engine room, if you're game."

"Yeah, let's see it."

A door in the floor of the main deck opened up, revealing a stairwell leading down to the port engine room. LED lights lit up the room like a Christmas tree. Rick was taken aback when he saw the motor. He was expecting a Yanmar or Mann diesel, like he had on *Nine-Tenths* back in Destin, but to his surprise it was a Torqueedo Deep Blue 100kW 900i electric motor. Behind the Torqueedo sat a 20kW generator.

"Electric, huh? Having this diesel generator kinda defeats the purpose of going electric, doesn't it, Gary?"

"You would think so, but I've honestly only fired them up a few times. The entire foredeck and roof are lined with solar panels. We're so close to the equator here that I stay fully charged most of the time. I installed state-of-the-art gel cell batteries. The entire boat is green. I had the electrical system designed by a guy in California. You may have heard of him—Elon Musk."

Rick's jaw dropped for the second time that day. "You've got to be kidding me. Elon Musk? How do you know him?"

Gary smiled wide. "Remember when I told you I have a great money guy? Well, anyway, he got me into something called cryptocurrency. I bought one billion Dogecoins. To the moon! To the moon! Elon was also big into Dogecoin, and the word got out that he wanted to meet me, as we were the two largest hodlers of Dogecoin."

"Don't you mean holders?"

"No, hodlers. Apes like me are known as hodlers on Reddit. Never mind, I'll explain it another time. They have their own lingo. Anyway, I flew out to Cape Canaveral where Elon was testing his Falcon rocket, and we had dinner. I mentioned to him that I wanted to build an all-electric river cat, and he got quite intrigued. He's a genius and incredibly motivated. He demanded that I let him design the schematics. What could I say? He's Elon Musk, so I said yes. He put a team on it and when it was done, he came down and did a week on board with his team. There's a photo of me and him."

Gary pointed to the starboard wall, and sure enough, there it was. Gary with his arm around Elon Musk, each of them holding a Skol beer. Rick was speechless.

"Gary, you never cease to amaze me."

"I've had several celebrities on board. This is the premier Amazon cruise and the word's getting out. When you get a chance, look at the guestbook and photo album in the salon."

"Will do, man!"

"Ready to roll?"

"Let's do this."

Gary got on a radio and called for the captain, who arrived within a couple of minutes. He took the helm and steered the cat out of the Tefé River into the mighty Amazon, and they began the journey.

Gary and Rick adjourned to the salon to join Gina. It was a smooth ride, and after a little while, Rick walked to the foredeck to take in the sights and sounds. The river was spectacular, so wide it almost seemed like an ocean. The jungle banks abounded with people going about their daily lives: washing clothes, fishing, and swimming in the muddy river.

Rick grabbed the spotting scope fixed to a tripod on one side of the deck and looked in the trees for exotic birds. It didn't take long to spot a few macaws, toucans, and some green-headed parrots. An hour later, he was still spotting birds he'd never seen before. As he scanned the bank, he saw a man with a gun pointed at a group of what looked like native tribesmen. They were huddled together looking rather terrified.

He ran to the salon and got Gary's attention. "Dude, come fast. Something's happening on the bank. A robbery or something."

Gary ran to the foredeck, and Rick told him where to look through the scope. Sure enough, a man with a gun had four small natives pinned down.

"That didn't take long to get in the soup." Gary grabbed the radio at his waist. "Nick, proceed two hundred yards ahead, hold, and drop the RIB. Have Leo meet us in the RIB with the go-bag. Okay, Rick, you ready for this? We're gonna dock a few hundred yards ahead around that bend, and flank the guy though the forest."

Rick and Gary hopped in the RIB, and Leo motored toward the bank at an angle and found a low spot. Gary tied up the RIB, and they all jumped out. Rick took a .45 and shotgun out of the go-bag, while Gary grabbed an Uzi.

"Leo, stay behind us. I only need you here to communicate with the tribe. I don't pay you enough to get shot at."

"Thanks, boss. I stay back here."

"Leo speaks several native dialects. Those people are probably Kayapó. Hard to tell, but we'll know soon enough."

They slowly trekked through the rainforest, as stealthily as possible. Soon Rick heard a man yelling. They were close. He was yelling Portuguese at the tribe, and they weren't responding. The got closer and could see his back. He was shaking his left hand and cursing at the terrified tribesmen.

"Onde está a jóia? Me diga agora ou eu atiro em você!"

"Leo, what did he say?"

"He say, where is jewel? Tell me or I shoot you," replied Leo.

They moved a little closer, and Rick had him dead to rights with the shotgun, but he didn't want to take a chance at hitting the tribe members.

"Can you speak to him, Leo? Tell him he's surrounded and to drop his gun."

Leo crouched behind a tree and cupped his mouth. They were still out of the gunman's line of sight.

"Você está cercado, solte sua arma!"

The man spun around, searching the trees for the voice. His gun pointed in their general direction. Rick took off the safety of his shotgun and cocked his .45. Gary did the same with the Uzi.

"Quem está aí? Não é da sua conta!" replied the gunman.

"What did he say?" whispered Gary.

"He say, who there? Mind business."

"Tell him police. Maybe he'll drop the gun."

"Polícia!"

The man keyed in on where Leo's voice was coming from and began to fire. Leo ducked as bullets ripped the tree apart and wood shavings flew everywhere. The man continued to fire his M-16, and they had no choice but to return fire.

Rick aimed his .45 at the man and unloaded the chamber, as Gary did the same. The man fell out of sight with a cry.

Silence fell over the jungle. The only sound was the river and birds in the distance.

Gary and Rick waited to see if the man would get up again and return fire. He didn't move. They approached him slowly. The tribesmen ran off in different directions before Leo could speak with them. Rick looked down at the man. Blood pooled around his head; he had taken one in the forehead. He was dead before he hit the ground. Gary spun him over and pulled out his wallet and dug through his pockets for anything else that might explain why he was threatening the tribesmen. Then he grabbed the M-16 and handed it to Leo.

"Help me drag him to the bank. Leo, grab those three big rocks over there."

When Leo brought them over, Gary shoved the rocks into the guy's pockets.

"Shouldn't we call the police?" asked Rick.

"Hell no. This is a third-world country. As far as we know, he might be the police. Let's drag him into the water. The crocs and piranhas will do the rest."

They dragged the man by his feet and shoved him as far into the moving water as they could. He slowly sank and disappeared.

"Let's get out of here. I ain't in any mood to answer questions to whoever shows up here," said Gary.

They vanished back into the rainforest and returned to the cat. They were upstream in no time, as if nothing had happened.

CHAPTER SIX

Rick laid the dead man's wallet on the settee and emptied the contents onto the table. There were a few hundred reals, some scraps of paper, and his ID, but not much else.

"Paulo Silva. That's his name. Paulo Silva. Does that mean anything to you, Gary?"

"Sadly, no. Silva is one of the most common names in Brazil. So is Paulo, for that matter. That basically equates to John Smith in the US."

Rick continued to rifle though the wallet and came upon a folded piece of paper.

"There's a name and number here. John Cunningham, (281) 555-4702."

Rick recognized the area code immediately. It was a Houston number.

"We should call that number and ask for John. I think it's a clue."

"Okay, we can use the sat phone," replied Gary.

He handed it to Rick, who dialed the number. Two rings, three rings, four rings, then a voicemail came on.

"This is John Cunningham with Thomas Antiquities. Leave your name and number and I'll return your call as soon as possible."

Rick hung up. "Do you have Wi-Fi? I wanna look up Thomas Antiquities."

"Yeah, the entire boat is wired into satellite Wi-Fi. The Network is Gary 66 and the password is Crawdads730," replied Gary.

"Clever password, the name of the place you won Powerball and the amount."

"You have a good memory."

"That's not something you forget very easily."

"I guess that's true."

Rick pulled his laptop from his backpack and googled Thomas Antiquities. It was the first site on the first page. He clicked on it and read aloud:

"Thomas Antiquities, premier dealer of precious metals and hard to hard-to-find stones. If you want it, we can find it."

"Do you think there's a connection between the dead man, the sacred sapphire, and Juliana's disappearance?" asked Gary.

"It's hard to say. I do find it rather odd that an M-16-toting gangster was harassing a bunch of Kayapó. It's a strange coincidence, indeed. Is there a phone and Wi-Fi on the plane?"

Gary rolled his eyes, and Rick wish he hadn't even asked.

"Speed dial two on the sat phone."

Rick clicked number two and waited. Soon, the phone rang and a woman answered.

"G-man's plane. How may I help you?"

Rick covered the receiver and shot Gary a look. "G-man, really?"

Gary just shrugged his shoulders and laughed silently.

"May I speak with Possum, ma'am?" said Rick.

"One moment."

"Hello?"

"Possum, it's Rick. How's the flight? Chief and Johnie okay?"

"Yep, we're flying high in luxury, dude. This plane is off the hook! Chief is sitting on top of his travel cage, and the flight attendant is feeding him grapes. I think he's in love. I think I am too. Damn!"

"That's great, man. Listen, do you have something to write on?"

"Hang on." A moment went by and Possum returned to the phone. "Got it."

"Have you ever heard of Thomas Antiquities?"

"Yeah, I actually took that old watch you found there to get it appraised."

"Huh," said Rick. What were the odds of that? It seemed like an awfully strange coincidence.

"I got a bad feeling about the place," continued Possum. "It was in a warehouse, and when I knocked on the door, a guy with a bent nose answered and was in no mood to help me. I peeked in and saw a single desk and a phone and nothing else. To be honest, it looked like a front to me. Why?"

"Get all the info you can on the place, as well as a John Cunningham. I won't go into great detail now, but please just take care of it and you can give me the rundown when we rendezvous later tonight in Fonte Boa."

"Okay, amigo. See ya soon."

After Rick hung up, Gary said, "We'll be in Fonte Boa in a couple of hours. What's the plan?"

"I think we should split up and start asking about Juliana," said Rick. "I'll check her house and hopefully retrieve the backpack she hid. Then, I'll visit the hotel she was last at for clues and see if I can get any info from the front desk. You can check her office where she was studying the pink dolphin, since you know where that is, and I think Gina should see if she can sweet talk any of the locals for info, since she speaks the language. Something's bound to turn up."

"I like it. Watch your six and I'll send Leo with Gina in case she comes in contact with any Kayapó or Yanomami. She's likely to run into Yanomami, since there are so many more of them, and I know they come into town to trade sometimes. I'll also give her a bag full of hard candies. That's better than gold to them. They love it.

"We should eat before we dock. Is fish okay? I have some fresh peacock bass fillets in the fridge. I caught a mess of them off the dock yesterday. They're similar to largemouth but even whiter and flakier. Very firm and not fishy at all."

"Sounds good to me."

Gary had the crew grill and fry some of the peacock bass fillets and serve them with mashed sweet potato and sliced papayas. It was a meal for a king.

The boat docked around two p.m., and the crew offloaded the Ford. Gary had built his own dock a mile from Fonte Boa and offered free shuttle service via several souped-up golf carts just to the edge of the property. They opted to travel together in the SUV and meet up at the Mercearia Ore Com Dogão, the main market in the center of town, no later than five p.m. That would give them a little less than three hours to see what they could find.

Gary dropped Gina and Leo off first at the edge of town and drove to the Mercearia Ore Com Dogão so Rick could find it later, then dropped him at Juliana's last known location. Rick had already gotten the address of her house and would hit that first then double back to the hotel. He wanted to approach her house on foot and not in the SUV. Gary drove on as he pointed at his watch and held up five fingers to Rick, reminding him of their meeting time.

Rick nodded and began to walk toward Jules's house. Anxiety was stirring inside him. It had a been quite a while since he'd seen her, and he was getting butterflies in his stomach at the thought of something bad happening to her. It was a strange feeling and he couldn't shake it.

Her house was modest and up on blocks. He walked past it, glancing sideways at it to see if there was anyone inside or anyone watching him. He passed it and walked another block before turning around and heading back. Bending over to tie his shoe, he checked both sides of the dirt road, then hopped up and walked to the side of the house toward the back.

"Bailey, Bailey, fweet, fweet."

In case anyone approached him, he could say he was looking for his lost dog. He continued to call and whistle until he got to the rear of the house. Trees surrounded the backyard and no other houses were in view, so he let his guard down a bit. He knelt down and tugged at the wooden slat under the house. It popped loose and he peered underneath it. All he could see were dirt and cobwebs. Jules's email had said she hid the backpack in a hole under the crawlspace.

He knew what he had to do. Spiders weren't his favorite encounter, but he had no choice.

Slowly, he wriggled under the house, looking for any sign of fresh dirt. About five feet in, he saw it. A small mound stuck out like a sore thumb. After digging for less than a minute, he felt the strap and gave it a huge pull. The yellow drybag unearthed itself, and he tucked it in his shirt and began to crawl back out. This was what he was looking for, but he still wanted to go inside and see what else he could find. He also needed to dump the contents of the drybag into something else. The bright yellow bag was far too obvious to be walking around with it.

He peered through the cloudy window. It was obvious someone had been there looking for the backpack. The place was a mess. All the furniture was turned upside down, and stuffing from the mattress was strewn everywhere.

He was about to break a window to get in when he decided to try the back door first. He reached for the handle and turned it. Unlocked.

Once inside, he stealthily crouched down and began to look for clues and something to dump the contents of the drybag into. Under the bed, he spotted a backpack. He remembered Jules wearing it before. It was a plain brown JanSport and as common as mosquitoes down here. After righting the kitchen table, he dumped the contents of the bag onto it. Inside of a small tourist book, he found a folded map.

"Bingo!" he murmured.

With his iPhone, he snapped several photos of it in case it was ever taken from him. He held it to the light to see if there were any hidden watermarks. Nothing. It was definitely a map, but it was in code and he would have to break it. In one of the drawers, he found several 2x2-inch photos of Jules he figured she was planning on using for a new passport, so he stuck them in the backpack. Maybe they'd come in handy later. After scouring the house for another thirty minutes, he decided to check out the hotel.

Hotel Eliana was less than half a mile from Jules's house, and he got there in no time. Calling it a hotel was quite an overstatement, but it was where she'd ended up and he needed to speak to someone.

"Excuse me, do you speak English?" he asked the man at the front desk.

"Não ingles?"

"I'm looking for a woman who was recently staying here. Her name is JC."

The man just shook his head, not understanding, and looked down at his computer.

"Her name is JC," Rick said again. "Wait, I have a picture of her."

He pulled out one of the passport photos and pushed it toward the man. He glanced down, then his eyes widened and he pushed it back.

"Eu nunca a vi antes."

Rick pulled out five one-hundred-real bills and slid them toward the man.

"Please."

He shook his head. Then waved at Rick to leave.

"Okay, no problem, buddy. I'll get out of your hair."

I'm not sure what he's saying, but he's obviously lying, thought Rick as he turned away.

The front desk guy walked into his office, and Rick could hear him talking aggressively to what sounded like someone on the phone. Figuring he'd better leave, he walked out the front door and around the side of the hotel. A couple was coming out of another entrance into the hotel, so he caught the door before it closed.

He spotted a maid in the hallway. She was a local. Some tribe. He wished Leo were there to translate, but he knew he had to try to talk to her, so he did his best and approached the woman. He held up the five bills and the photo of Jules. She took the photo and gave it back to Rick as she looked over her shoulder to see if anyone was watching her. Then she crossed her wrists together to indicate Jules had been tied up. She moved them side to side, mimicking a struggle, and then pointed at Rick's skin and made a sign for tall men. Then she held up two fingers.

Rick's stomach churned. He knew exactly what she meant. Two white guys had tied Jules up and taken her. He gave the maid the money and made a prayer sign, thanking her.

It was 4:30 p.m. now, so Rick headed toward the market. He knew he'd be a little early but was incredible thirsty and figured he'd buy a water and wait for the rest of them. At five o'clock on the nose, Rick heard the telltale sound of the Ford's supercharger coming up the street. He hopped in.

"Any luck?" asked Rick.

"No, I didn't get anywhere," said Gary. "You?"

"Yeah. I bribed a maid and she told me Jules was taken by two white men. I really couldn't converse with her, though, and I was hoping we could swing back by with Leo and see if he can talk to her. I found the drybag and the map, but it's coded. I'm gonna need some help with this one. Thank God Possum will be here soon. That's his forte."

"That's great news, Rick." Gary looked around at the street and the market, his brow furrowed. "Speaking of Leo, he and Gina should be back by now. It's after five now and she's always prompt. I hope we don't have to do two rescue operations today. I'll give it until 5:50, then we've gotta go look for them."

They waited and waited. Gary rapped his knuckles on the steering wheel, getting anxious. Rick couldn't blame him. The bad feeling in the pit of his own stomach was worsening.

"Okay, let's go," said Gary. "I'll start where I dropped them off."

He floored the big engine, and Rick's head hit the back of the seat. He rubbed his head as Gary zipped through town, dodging goats and people on bicycles, and came to a screeching halt right where he'd dropped off Gina and Leo. Several men were sitting around playing dominoes at a cantina. They were dark guys, probably from another country working the mines.

"Did you see a guy and girl here earlier?" Gary asked. "The guy is a little taller than the girl, maybe five foot nine, both thin with dark hair. Her hair is shoulder length and he has a short cut parted on the side."

From the back of the lean-to, a voice said, "Polícia."

The man slowly walked into the light. He wore a bandana around his head, and only the top button of his denim shirt was buttoned over a wifebeater undershirt. He looked like a regular chulo from SoCal.

"Ella trató de sobornar a un policía y ambos fueron arrestados," said the man in Spanish as he held out his hand.

"What'd he say, Rick?"

"Basically, he said they were arrested for bribing a cop."

Gary shook his head and gave the guy a couple hundred reals. He strolled back under the lean-to like the whole thing never happened.

"Let's go," blurted Gary.

"Where to?"

"Jail! We're gonna get them out."

"How?" asked Rick.

"We, I mean *you* are gonna bribe them. It's so corrupt here that's all they want. Gina probably just didn't have enough on her, so they know soon enough someone—and by someone, I mean you—will show up with a couple thousand reals."

"Why me?"

"Because you don't live here and I plan on staying for a while, capeesh?"

"No worries."

Gary drove toward the police station and parked a couple of blocks away. He pulled out two thousand reals and handed them to Rick.

"Now just go in there and find the sheriff. Shove this on his desk and point at Leo and Gina. You don't even have to speak. You got it?"

"What if he doesn't take it?"

"Then we have a big problem and we'll have to go to plan B. One way or the other, they are getting out tonight."

"Okay, here goes nothing." He sure hoped Gary was right and this would be easy.

Rick strolled toward the police station. It was tiny, as Gary had described. Maybe one thousand square feet. He opened the creaky front door and immediately saw the room-length jail cell toward the back, with two familiar people inside. Three desks were also in the station, with the largest one separate from the other two. That had to be the sheriff's desk. The man sitting behind it was chewing on a stogie.

Rick winked at Gina and Leo, who stood up when they saw him. He pulled the bills from his front pocket, slid them toward the sheriff, and pointed at Leo and Gina. The sheriff's eyes narrowed in anger, and he reached for his pistol, yelling in Portuguese. Before Rick could get the .45 out of his pants pocket, two deputies tackled him and they all hit the floor. Rick fought with them as the sheriff cocked his weapon, and it was over. They handcuffed him, patted him down, and took his .45 before shoving him into the cell. The sheriff immediately got on his phone and called someone.

"Well, that was a fail. What's he saying?" he whispered to the others.

"He say, I got them all, come get them," said Leo.

Rick shared a grave look with Gina. This day was sure going from bad to worse.

It was seven o'clock, and Rick sat there frustrated, wondering what the hell plan B was. He then heard a whisper from the back window of the jail cell.

"Move toward the front of the cell in one minute."

Oh, this isn't gonna be good.

Rick took Gina and Leo by the arm and nodded for them to follow. They all put their arms through the bars, as convicts often do.

A moment later, the roar of the supercharger erupted outside. A crashing sound came as dust flew and the back wall was ripped out completely. The three of them bolted out of the gaping hole as shots rang out. One whizzed right by Rick's head. The rickety jail began to sway, and they climbed into the Ford. Bullets rang out and without warning, the entire building collapsed into a pile of cinder blocks and tin roofing.

Gary unhooked the chain from the hitch, jumped in, and they sped off into the darkness.

"Are they dead?" asked Rick, exhaling so his heartbeat would return to normal.

"Nah, probably scratched up a bit. The stupid roof of that place was made of aluminum siding. It doesn't weigh anything. That was plan C. I was just gonna have y'all climb up to the top bunk after the jail closed and push your way out. They'll be too embarrassed to come after us, and we have a huge head start. There's no way they even know it was my truck. It was way too dark to see and I turned my rear floods on to blind them."

"Yeah, that was bright. You are one crazy son of a bitch."

Gary flashed him a smile. "Just another day in paradise."

CHAPTER SEVEN

Before they knew it, they were back at the boat. The stainless diamond plate on the rear of the Ford had a bullet lodged in it. Gary had installed the plate for aesthetic reasons, and thank goodness he had, since it had protected them against the gunfire. He pulled the truck into the garage and pulled down the doors.

"It's close to time for the Gulfstream to be arriving in Tefé. I'll shoot the pilot a call," said Gary.

Gary and the jailbirds all sat in the salon to debrief. Rick was excited about going through the backpack and trying to break the code of the map. He knew he would need more eyes on it and was looking forward to showing it to Possum. Rick laid the map on the large dining table in the center of the salon, and they all gathered around it. Gary handed Rick a magnifying glass as he held the phone to his ear with his shoulder, waiting to connect with the pilot. He stepped out of earshot as the others studied the map. Rick read it aloud:

"Take the JR to the right of the Y and copa tana. Once you reach Port S, exit right through the eye of Yucamama to the end is where you'll Biá. Find the devil's cross and walk ten steps south. Inside the cave of tokrãk is where God is swathed."

He sighed in frustration. "Well, that makes absolutely no sense to me."

"I just got off the phone with the pilot," said Gary. "They are in Tefé and loading up the chopper now. They'll be here in an hour or so. Here, maybe these will help."

He handed Rick several local maps and a large scroll chart of the area.

"Can any of you make heads or tails of this map?" asked Rick.

"I've heard of Copatana," said Gina. "It's a small village in Jutaí, deep in the rainforest."

"It's copa tana, two words, and it's not capitalized," said Rick.

"But when you read it, I heard Copatana. Maybe they wrote it that way to throw off whoever read it. Because if I had read it instead of hearing you say it, I would have seen copa tana, which translates to tan cup. You reading it aloud may be the cipher. Sort of. Read it aloud again and I'll see if anything strikes me as odd."

Rick read it aloud three more times. Gina chewed on her lower lip as she listened.

"When you read, '*Once you reach Port S, exit right through the eye of Yucamama to the end is where you'll Biá,*' are you saying where you'll be? It sounded like you said bee-ah."

"It is Biá. Spelled B I A."

"Oh, I thought that was just your Texas accent. I wonder if they are referring to the Biá River. It *is* an offshoot of the Jutaí River."

"Do you think JR stands for Jutaí River?" asked Rick.

"It would make sense," replied Gina with a shrug.

"What about the devil's cross and cave of tokrãk?"

"I have no clue about that. Tokrãk means *to swallow*, but none of that really adds up to anything. Maybe they're clues we have to find once we're in that area. That's some serious rainforest trekking. We're talking days of heavy brush, bot flies, snakes, and many other things that wanna kill and eat you. Not a nice afternoon hike in the woods and definitely not for the faint of heart."

Rick grimaced. "You just had to say snakes, didn't you?"

"Well, I didn't say spiders. Forgot about those. There are over seventeen poisonous snakes in the Amazon basin. Everything from pit vipers to the pygmy black-backed coral snake. I haven't even mentioned the constrictors, like thirty-foot anacondas. Spiders? Let's say there are close to 3,600 species of spiders here. Many are poisonous, and the wandering spider is not only poisonous, but also the most aggressive spider in the world. It's caused more deaths than dengue fever. So, here's a tip. Stay away from banana plants. Their nickname is the banana spider. Remember the song 'Day-O' by Harry Belafonte? Where he sings about bananas and a deadly tarantula? He's really singing about the wandering spider. Its bite can kill a man in less than twenty-five minutes if untreated."

"Ewwww!" Rick made a disgusted face and shook off a shiver as he thought of the spiders.

Gina laughed at him. "Should I make some dinner?"

While she prepared the food, Gary made up a batch of margaritas. "What shall we toast to?" he asked.

"How about freedom? I've been in some bad jails before, and Fonte Boa is right up there with one of the dirtiest," replied Rick.

Gary raised his glass. "*'My country, great and free! Heart of the world, I drink to thee!'* Not sure it pertains to this third-world country, but at least you're not stuck in that cell eating porridge."

They clinked their glasses and took big swigs. They did the *ha-ha clink-clink* all through dinner and wondered aloud how mad the sheriff was, and if he planned to search for them or bury his head in the rubble. Maybe it was all a scam to get money in the first place. Then Rick remembered the phone call.

"Wait, why didn't he just take the money? And who did he call and say, 'Come get them'?" asked Rick.

Gina frowned. "That's a good question. Who would possibly know we're here and looking for Juliana?"

"I think I know," said Rick as he slapped the table. "When I was at the Hotel Eliana, the front desk guy was indignant and didn't go for the bribe. He asked me to leave, then got on the phone and started yelling at someone in Portuguese. I assumed he was talking about me. The hotel was the last place Juliana was known to be. I think he was in on the kidnapping. He was probably giving them a heads-up that someone was asking about Juliana."

"Since he couldn't be convinced with a bribe, maybe we can coerce him another way," said Gary.

"Like how?" asked Rick.

"You know, the old-fashioned way. We'll beat him until he spills his guts."

"That could work."

"We can take the golf cart into town. The Ford is too high-profile right now until we find out what the sheriff plans to do in retaliation. We'll take Leo with us to translate. Gina, you can stay here. This is just a two-man operation."

Gina reluctantly agreed. "Be careful, you guys."

Rick, Gary, and Leo climbed into the six-person golf cart designed to look like a '57 Chevy and headed back to Fonte Boa.

"Don't you think this will stick out like a sore thumb?" asked Rick.

"It doesn't matter. I have four of these, all the same color. Three are rented right now. The townspeople are used to seeing them all the time. Besides, I'll park a few blocks from the hotel and we can walk up."

Gary parked by a small tavern on the side where a few other golf carts were parked. They made their way to the hotel and cased it for a minute. Very few cars were around.

"Okay, let's go to the entrance. Rick, you peek in and see if it's him behind the desk. If it is, stay back. Leo and I will approach him and distract him, and you can come behind and block the exit door. Got it?"

They slowly approached the front of the hotel. Rick crouched down and raised his eyes to the glass of the front door. The same man was working behind the front desk. He signaled to Gary and moved to the side of the door.

"Now, when I take off my ball cap and rub my hands through my hair, you come in and block the door."

"Got it."

As Gary began talking to the front desk guy, Rick watched intently for the signal. As soon as he saw it, Rick swung open the door, catching the man's attention. He ran to the office, trying to evade what he knew was coming. Gary was on him like a flash of lightning, slamming him against the door jamb. He moaned in pain as a loud crack was heard. The man swung desperately at Rick, who ducked his fist and connected with the side of his ribs, leaving him breathless.

"Conte-nos sobre Juliana!" demanded Leo.

"Quem?" replied the out-of-breath man, trying to get his air back.

"You know who I'm talking about! Juliana!" said Leo, slipping into English again.

"I don't know Juliana!" said the man.

"So, you do speak English, you son of a bitch!" yelled Rick.

He pulled out the photo and shoved it in the guy's face.

"Who took her? If you don't tell me now, I swear, I'll blow your damn head off!"

Rick pulled out the nine-millimeter he'd tucked in the back of his waist before they left. He had no intention of shooting the man but thought the sight of the gun might revive his memory a bit.

"Okay, okay, I'll tell you. Please don't shoot me. I have a family," the man pleaded.

Rick lowered the gun. "Then talk. Now."

"Two men paid me a thousand US dollars to make a key to her room. She was checked in under the initials JC. They gave me a phone number and said to call them if anyone came around asking about her. That's all I know."

"What did they look like? Describe them!"

Rick cocked the nine-millimeter for dramatic effect.

"They were light-skinned and tall. They had British accents. That's all I know. I swear."

"Where's the number?"

The man held his hands up and slowly walked to the front desk and opened a drawer. He pulled out a notepad with a number on it. It was just a number. No names.

"We're gonna leave now, and you pretend we were never here. If you call anyone or tell anyone, we will return, kill you, then kill your entire family, capeesh?" snapped Rick.

"I understand." He made the gesture of locking his mouth and throwing away the key.

Rick ripped out the page with the number on it and threw the notepad onto the front desk. They all strolled out, made sure the coast was clear, then headed to the golf cart.

"Wow, Rick, come back, kill you, and your entire family? That sent chills down *my* spine," said Gary.

"I know. I saw it in a movie once. Some gangster film— maybe *The Godfather* or *Goodfellows*, can't remember."

"Your acting skills are impressive!" Gary threw the golf cart into drive and laughed.

Back at the catamaran, Rick took a quick photo of the number so he'd have it for later.

"Should we call it?" asked Rick.

"No, let me see it. I'll look it up online and see if it's a landline or cell. If it's a cell, I have an app that can triangulate a cell down to the street. It uses advanced forward link trilateration and is extremely accurate. It depends on how many towers are in the area, and the phone has to be on."

Gary typed the number into Google.

"We're in luck. It's a cell phone. Let me open the app on my iPad and put it in."

They all hovered over Gary's shoulder, looking at the iPad. After a minute, an error message appeared. *NO PING DETECTED.*

"Dammit," said Rick.

"That's okay. That just means the phone is either not near a tower or it's turned off. I'll keep trying."

Gary rang the pilot. When he frowned, Rick knew something was wrong.

"That's strange; he always answers," said Gary. "Can you call Possum? Maybe there's something wrong with the pilot's headset."

"Sure."

Rick took the phone and dialed Possum's cell. It just rang and rang, no answer. His heartbeat picked up.

"Nothing," he said.

"They're probably out of cell range," said Gary lightly. "I know the route he takes. I've done it a hundred times. He just hugs the river. It's almost a straight shot here from Tefé. If they went down, we'll find them. Don't worry, Rick. He's a good pilot and has lots of experience. Billy flew Apaches in Iraq. Leo, lower the inflatable and mount the spotlight on the bow."

"You got it, boss," said Rick, but his mouth was dry.

"Enough excitement for one day, eh?"

Rick just took a deep breath and nodded. He was trying to stay calm, but he was close to having a panic attack. His best friend, first mate, and Chief were all on that chopper. He couldn't hide his anxiety. Gary patted Rick on the back and gave him a reassuring look.

Gary steered the boat toward Tefé, as Rick scanned the bank for any sign of the chopper and his crew. They continued downstream, checking the right side of the bank. If they didn't have any luck, they would cross over and search the other side.

After forty-five minutes, Rick was getting frustrated and worried. He inhaled deeply and smelled smoke. It wasn't a wood fire and had a hint of fuel in it. His fear swelled as he pictured the worst of all possible outcomes.

They approached a turn in the river, and a fire came into view about five hundred yards ahead on the right side of the bank. Rick shined the spot on it and there it was, the helicopter, on its side and on fire. The tail was still intact and debris was strewn across the bank.

Rick held his breath, praying his friends weren't trapped inside the wreckage.

As they got closer, he saw someone about twenty-five yards away from the chopper, waving his arms. It was Possum.

Oh, thank God.

"I see Possum!" shouted Rick.

Sitting beside him, holding his arm, was Johnie, and lying in a makeshift stretcher was the pilot, but no Chief.

They slammed onto the bank, and Rick leapt from the boat onto the shore in one giant stride.

"Are you okay? What happened?"

"I'm fine, Rick," said Possum, forcing a smile. "Not a scratch. I got a small bump on my head but that's it. I was sitting beside the pilot chatting away about the catamaran and how much we were gonna like it, and suddenly he started slurring his speech. I looked over at him and the side of his mouth was drooping down. I knew immediately he was having a stroke. His hands slipped from yoke and the chopper started spinning. We weren't very high over the water, as he was using his spotlights to show us crocs. I grabbed the yoke and tried to get control. There was nothing I could do; his feet were controlling the pedals and they slipped off. Before I knew it, we were spinning closer to the bank and we hit that tree"—he pointed at it—"and came to a sudden stop when the top rotors broke off. We hit pretty hard, but the chopper is still intact mostly. The doors flew off and Johnie landed on his shoulder in the mud."

"Where's Chief?"

Possum gave him a solemn stare and didn't say anything.

Rick grabbed a flashlight and sprinted toward the burning chopper, never even considering it might blow up. He was ten feet away when he saw it—Chief's travel cage was lying on its side near the water, and feathers were stuck in the mud. His throat tightened. *No, no...*

"Chief, Chief, where are you? Come on, boy!" yelled Rick repeatedly.

Possum and Gary caught up to Rick and helped him search. Rick climbed into the smoldering aircraft and frantically pulled up the seats, looking everywhere and calling Chief's name. He ran to the bank and shined the light down the river, fearing the worst. Chief wouldn't last two minutes in that water and would already be in the belly of some predator.

"Wait, stop. Everybody listen. Be quiet and listen."

Gary had already put out the flames of the oil fire on the chopper, as smoke continued to slowly rise.

"Be perfectly quiet."

Ruff, ruff, ruff. Rick barked, imitating a dog, then fell silent again. He did it two more times.

Suddenly, he heard it.

Ruff, ruff.

They all looked up together as Rick shined his light into the tree above. There on a long epiphytic vine sat Chief, preening himself and barking away. Rick's heart almost skipped a beat, and he took a deep breath and sighed with relief.

"Come here, boy! Come here!"

It took a little coaxing, but eventually Chief half flew and half fell into Rick's arms.

"Thank God you're okay." Rick snuggled with him and then put him back in his travel cage.

They gathered all the luggage and placed the pilot across the bow. They were closer to Tefé than Fonte Boa, so Gary raced as fast as he could to the dock. He called ahead on his sat phone, and an ambulance was waiting when they arrived. Once the pilot was safely in the ambulance, Gary came back.

"The paramedics said he's stable," he told them.

They motored past the wrecked helicopter and all gave each other looks that were undeniable. *We are some lucky mofos!*

CHAPTER EIGHT

Chief sat on the dining room table and nibbled on grapes as Rick got Possum and Johnie up to speed. Johnie had suffered a light shoulder socket injury but would be fine after a few days. They all knew they were incredibly lucky. It could have been a lot worse.

"I did some research on the flight about Thomas Antiquities and John Cunningham," said Possum. "Thomas Antiquities specializes in rare gemstones. That in itself is not all that interesting. I dug deeper, though, and it turns out Cunningham's former last name is Adams and he is from the town of Salisbury on the outskirts of London. He was tried but never convicted of manslaughter, and was questioned about a few other murders in the Houston area. He has ties to the Gillich family, who are of Croatian descent, and he's associated with what is known as the Dixie Mafia out of Biloxi, with fingers in Dallas and Houston. So, yes, your instincts were right. He's basically a soldier and probably a hit man for the Houston syndicate."

"You are amazing, Possum. I don't know what I'd do without you."

"All in a day's work, my man!"

"Take a look at this map," said Rick. "We believe this is where the Sacred Jewel of Orinoco is hidden. We have the only map, but they have Juliana. So, it's a Mexican stand-off. Don't you think we should try and get Juliana first?"

"Yes, if we can find her. Any idea where she is?"

"No, but we have a phone number and Gary thinks he can triangulate her location as soon as they get near a tower or turn on the phone."

"Here's what I think we should do. Since they're after the jewel, and we have the map, we have an edge. If we just give them the map, there's nothing to stop them from killing Juliana. But if we get the jewel, we can do an in-person swap. It's our best bet. So, I say we find this jewel."

"Let's not forget that if we don't find the jewel and return it the Yanomami, they will decimate the Kayapó," interjected Gina. "The jewel is the key to it all."

"You're right, Gina," said Rick. "Can you set up a meeting with the leader of the Yanomami and explain to him that we plan to return the jewel to him as soon as possible?"

"Yes, he is attending a conference for the rainforest in Rio. I think I can get to him and persuade him. I'll bring a picture of the map and show him alone. He won't understand it well, but it might instill confidence and give us some more time. Both tribes are special to me, but the Yanomami are the fiercest fighters, and the small Kayapó don't stand a chance against their numbers. Can you arrange the jet for me to fly to Rio in the morning, Gary?"

"I'm on it. I'll take you to the jet in Tefé myself, at five a.m. in the dinghy. When I get back, we can begin our glorious hike into the vast green jungle. Should be fun!" said Gary sarcastically.

Possum and Rick studied the map as Johnie sat on the plush leather sofa, resting his shoulder. Chief was in the aviary getting to know Tico but separated by a partition. They'd decided it would be best to leave them separated, since they didn't seem to be bonding well.

"We think JR stands for the Jutaí River," said Rick.

"Makes sense."

Possum used a highlighter to trace a route from Fonte Boa to what seemed to be the end of the line. Rick explained that copa tana was most likely supposed to be spelled Copatana and was clearly in the right direction.

"Hmmm, Port S...?"

Possum ran his finger down the river and came upon Porto Seguro. It made sense. Continuing to follow the river, he came to the end and split. One way went on miles and miles, almost to Peru, but the other one fingered off and stopped at the end of Biá River.

"If I was a betting man, and you know I am, I would say that *where you'll Biá* is actually the end of Biá River," exclaimed Possum.

"I have to agree," said Rick, and the others in the room nodded. "You just sealed the deal."

Exhaustion seemed to hit them all at the same time, and tomorrow was going to be a big day. They all went to bed.

In the morning, Gary headed off to shuttle Gina to the jet in Tefé. Johnie would stay behind with the captain. He would return to pick up the crew bound for the Biá River. Only the captain and Johnie would stay behind. Johnie would slow them down, and Rick figured it would be useful for him to stay back at base in case they needed him to make a run to Tefé for anything. He could use the second dinghy that always stayed at the dock in Fonte Boa. It was more of a work dinghy but could easily make it down the river.

Leo would join their group in the jungle to be their interpreter. He spoke fluent Portuguese and could communicate well enough with the local tribes to be helpful. Gina was more fluent in the dialects, but her trip to Rio was just as important.

Gary had brought lots of supplies for them to take, including enough ammo to start a small war, as well as snake and spider antivenom. They would all have machetes and sidearms, and Rick planned to bring along a bull whip for good luck. Based on the movie *Romancing the Stone* and the Indiana Jones franchise, they were necessary tools and he was superstitious.

"Rick, you up?" asked Possum.

"I've got coffee and pancakes going."

"Of course you do, amigo. I'll be right there."

Johnie was half asleep on the couch and super groggy from the meds Gary had given him.

"You can take room five after we leave, Johnie," Rick told him. "I tried to get you up last night, but you were dead to the world, so I let you sleep."

"Thanks, man. I'll feed Chief and go back to bed after y'all leave."

"Already done, bud. Just chill. I need you to heal up. You may need to come save our asses."

Before breakfast was finished, Gary returned as chipper as a jaybird.

"Gina's already on her way to Rio. I stopped by the hospital and the chopper pilot is gonna make a full recovery. It's gonna take some time, but he's strong and he'll do fine. I'm paying him his full salary and all his medical bills while he's out too."

"You're a good man, Gary. What will happen to the chopper? Do you have to pay to have it removed?" asked Rick.

"Nah. That's the beauty of it all. I got a sweet deal for it at an auction and insured it for twice what I paid for it through Lloyd's of London. I'm actually making money on the deal, and the next auction is in a month. I'll just grab another one. Maybe bigger this time."

Rick chuckled. "You're something else, man."

"Y'all ready? Got your skeeter spray on? The dinghy is already loaded and fueled. I strapped on two more full cans as well."

"Let's roll!"

The first part of the trip was monotonous. They motored down the mighty Amazon to the entrance to the Jutaí River, about forty miles from Fonte Boa. Once in the Jutaí, the river began to get narrower with each passing mile. They made it to the split near Porto Seguro and stopped to see if they could get more fuel, just in case, and to get off the river and stretch their legs. It was an utter waste of time. Unlike the Porto Seguro on the Atlantic coast, this was just a blip on the map and uninhabited.

They pulled the dinghy to the bank and ate some sandwiches from the supply cooler. After about a half an hour, they returned to the river, heading deeper and deeper into the rainforest. They occasionally saw local tribes doing laundry or fishing, and Gary would stop and give them hard candies as a token of goodwill. Even though they had no cell phones or other technology, word would travel fast if there was a bad white man on the river. Gary took no chances getting that reputation.

Near sundown, they decided to set up camp for the night. They made it to the split where the Jutaí and the Biá met and found a high, dry spot to put up the tents.

"Rick, yours is the red one," said Gary as he tossed him a dry duffel with a flat bag inside.

"How do I set this up? I've never seen one like this."

"Here, let me show you."

Gary unzipped the tent from its carrying case and flung it like a Frisbee. It opened in midair and landed fully set up.

Rick laughed aloud. "That's the coolest thing I've ever seen!"

"Just wait and check out my tent."

Gary pulled out an odd-looking tent and loaded a small pistol with a ball attached to a stainless-steel cable. After taking careful aim, he pulled the trigger on the pneumatic pistol, and the ball shot up over the top of a large tree branch and back down, where Gary caught it. He removed the ball and connected the cable to a small hand ratchet, raised it about four feet, and secured it tightly.

"It's called a Tree Pod. I'm not sleeping on the ground. Things slither and crawl around here at night. I'd rather be up in the air."

Rick put his hands on his hips in protest, as Gary almost fell over laughing, then threw Rick his own Tree Pod.

"Don't worry, bud, we're all sleeping in the air. I was just busting your balls. It takes a great prop to make a great joke!"

Rick just shook his head, but was almost giddy to shoot the pneumatic pistol over his own branch. Once camp was set up, they all gathered firewood and created a ring in the center of the tents. They got enough to burn all night.

"These Tree Pods will protect us from most creepy crawlies, but they ain't shit against a jaguar. The fire will keep them at bay," said Gary.

As darkness settled over the camp, the rainforest got louder and louder with howler monkeys and insects of every variety. It was almost deafening. Rick was glad he found his noise-cancelling headphones, buried in his bag, at a full charge. He had to give Gary credit. He thought of everything. Not only did he have small solar panels for charging all the devices, but he also had a micro-hydro generator. It was a plastic disc with props and a weight connected to a float and a long electric cable. Once thrown in the river, the current would spin the prop, generating power that Gary hooked to the four lithium-ion batteries secured in the stern of the dinghy. Even without sun, they would always have power.

Rick was restless in his tent. The humidity and heat from the rainforest didn't let up much after the sun set, and the smoke from the jaguar fire was bothersome. But mostly, he was worried about Jules. He prayed that she was okay and that her kidnappers hadn't hurt her or taken advantage of her. She was a fighter though, and if they tried anything, they would take a beating. She wouldn't give up easily.

He finally dozed off around midnight. The sounds of the ocean played though his headphones, and he dreamed of being on the beach with Jules. Then he was whisked away to the Voodoo den where the giant spider had crawled up his zombie-like body. He remembered being able to see it but not feel it, but in his dream, he felt everything. Suddenly, the spider opened its poisonous jaws and clamped down on his arm.

Rick was jolted awake and screamed loudly when he found a real spider chomping down on him. He slammed it with his hand, but it was too late. It had already injected its venom into his forearm.

"Dammit!"

"What happened? Are you okay, Rick?" shouted Gary.

"Spider bite! Lots of pain."

The dead, half-crushed spider lay on the bottom of the tent.

It had crawled down from the tree branch, into a tiny opening in the zipper door that Rick had left to let in some breeze. Big mistake on his part. His arm writhed in pain, and the area where the spider bit him was turning black. He was losing consciousness.

Gary jumped down, unzipped the tent, and used his flashlight to examine Rick's arm. He quickly tied a tourniquet above Rick's elbow to slow the flow of poison. Gary shined his light on the spider. He hissed through his teeth.

"Dammit. That's no spider. It's an Amazonian giant centipede. I don't have centipede antivenom. Stay calm, Rick, and try to slow your breathing. I'm going to find a shaman."

Rick lay there as the pain consumed him. He was half-aware of the sounds of Gary and Leo zooming off in the dinghy.

Possum's voice came from nearby, trying to calm him down by talking softly, reminding him to slow his breathing and not get anxious. Rick could barely move and his body was beginning to stiffen. He was entering paralysis. All he could do was laugh inside because his dream was becoming a reality. He was becoming a zombie again.

"It's gonna be okay, Rick. They'll be back soon. These tribes have been living here for thousands of years without the benefit of modern medicine."

"Not a great way to start," muttered Rick, barely loud enough for Possum to hear.

"It's okay, buddy. You're gonna be fine. Just a little setback."

Soon, Possum could hear the motor of the dinghy returning. The silhouettes of three people stepped off onto the bank. Once they got closer to the fire, he spotted a very short dark man with a painted face and a parrot feather through the septum of his nose. He began to speak to Leo, who translated.

"He wants us to gather long limbs and banana leaves."

They all grabbed their machetes and began to chop.

"Be careful for wandering spiders. Use your head lamps. All we need is another bite tonight," yelled Gary.

They gathered several long branches, and the shaman instructed them to place them like a low-profile tepee over the fire and cover them with banana leaves. He was making a makeshift sweat lodge. Gary and Possum carried Rick's body into the sweat lodge, and the shaman went inside as well. He gave Rick, who had slipped into a coma-like state, a mix of herbs and liquid from a gourd and began to chant. Waving feathers over Rick's body, he continued to chant for hours. Periodically, he would add wood to the fire and run a black liquid over Rick's bite.

The sun began to rise and the shaman climbed out of the banana leaf structure. He spoke to Leo for a few minutes and began to walk toward the dinghy. Gary followed him, and the others watched as the two motored out of sight.

"What did he say?" asked Possum.

"Him say all can do. Now wait," responded Leo.

Soon Gary returned and they all stood around the sweat lodge, praying in silence. Suddenly, a Harpy eagle swooped down inches from the tent and whistled its lonesome cry. At the same moment, Rick climbed out of the tent.

"I'm parched. Got a beer?"

Gary moved toward Rick and examined his arm. It was no longer black, and only two small slightly red puncture marks were visible.

"How do you feel?" asked Possum.

"I feel great. What happened? Why was I in that tepee?"

"You don't remember?"

"I don't remember anything. I had a crazy dream about an eagle flying over me all night and I was walking on the river like Jesus. It was freaky. Then I woke up and climbed out. What happened?"

Gary and Possum just looked at Rick in astonishment.

"Go look at the bottom of your tent," said Gary.

Rick strolled over to the Tree Pod and unzipped the door, then nearly fell backward trying to get away.

"What the hell is that?"

"That's a giant centipede. One of the most poisonous insects in the rainforest. Look at your arm."

Rick glanced down at his arm as Gary pointed out the two puncture marks.

"He got you last night, bud. We nearly lost you. A shaman saved your life. You and him were in that sweat lodge all night."

Rick looked like he was trying to comprehend what they were saying, but it just didn't compute. Gary made some coffee as Rick continued to elaborate about his dreams.

"They weren't dreams, Rick. I think you died last night and crossed over. The shaman brought you back. You went on a shamanic journey," said Possum matter-of-factly.

CHAPTER NINE

Steamy mist rose from the slow-moving river as the sun appeared above the dark green canopy. The rainforest was alive with hoots and screeches of macaws, parrots, and white bellbirds, which sounded like a car alarm going off. Rick had already packed up his Tree Pod and was eager to get going deeper into the jungle. The rest of the crew was dragging. While he'd been given a fresh start and a renewed burst of energy, the other guys had been awake all night milling around the sweat lodge, worrying and praying for Rick's recovery. Rick was on his fourth cup of camp coffee, restless. Slowly, the gang got packed up and he extinguished the fire.

"Let's roll, boys," hollered Rick.

"Yeah, yeah, we're coming," moaned Gary with a yawn.

Once they were all on board, Gary fired up the outboard and motored downstream. Several crocs swam lazily by, and bullfrogs chirped. Rick had his binoculars out and was spotting birds—a pair of toucans, a cotinga, several kingfishers, and a flock of herons. It was a glorious morning.

The farther down the Biá River they went, the narrower it got. After four hours, the outboard was starting to kick up mud as the river became shallower. Soon it would be too shallow to continue. They still had about five miles left until the river's end, and the outboard was already tilted as high as it could go to continue forward progress.

"What are we gonna do?" asked Rick.

"Just wait. You'll see shortly," replied Gary.

As they approached a large bend in the river, Rick saw a wide, flat bank strewn with dugout canoes. Several tribesmen stood there, waving. Gary motored to the side, and the men helped pulled the dinghy ashore.

"We switch boats here," said Gary. "I arranged with the shaman who brought you back from near death to set up guides and canoes for us for the final leg of the river journey. Leo interpreted and we paid them in hard candy. You'd be amazed what a five-pound bag of Werther's will get you."

Rick raised an eyebrow, impressed. "I guess you got it all figured out. I'm glad you're so prepared."

Possum interjected, "Do the Kayapó know that we're trying to save the tribe from total massacre by the Yanomami? Because if they don't know, why they are helping us? I'm not comfortable with this."

"They will know. Leo helped me explain the importance of our trip to the shaman, and now he's explaining to the Kayapó what's at stake," replied Gary.

Leo spoke to the Kayapó men and showed them on the map where they wanted to go. They didn't understand the map very well, but when Leo said *tẽ kato Biá*—loosely translated to mean "end of the river"—they all chanted in agreement and nodded. The men wore brightly colored headdresses made from a mix of feathers and beads. They had wide beaded neckbands and bracelets, and were tattooed vertically with jagua ink, which Rick later learned was similar to a henna tattoo and lasted four to six weeks. Each man had a spear and a machete as well as a bow and arrows. Their average height was five foot two inches, yet they appeared quite intimidating with their painted faces and colorful headdresses.

There were five dugout canoes—a canoe for everyone in the crew plus one for supplies. Each man would be teamed up with a Kayapó man and assist in paddling the heavy canoes. At this part of the river, the flow was almost stagnant and five miles would be quite a workout. Rick was up for the challenge. All he could think about were two jewels: rescuing Jules and finding the Sacred Jewel of Orinoco, which would rescue the Kayapó from certain annihilation.

Once all the canoes were loaded, each man on the crew joined a tribesman and began to paddle. Rick was teamed up with Xãn, which Leo told him meant *cat*. Xãn shared Rick's enthusiasm for birdwatching, and pointed out birds to Rick over and over with childlike amazement. Although Rick couldn't communicate to Xãn with words, they seemed in sync and able to work together. Rick wasn't sure what had happened with the shaman, but he felt a connection to the rainforest that he hadn't felt before. He felt in tune with the trees, plants, and animals all around him. He assumed this was exactly how the indigenous tribes felt as well. He also felt connected to Xãn on a spiritual level, almost as a brother, even though they had only been in the same canoe for a little over an hour. It was a strange but welcome feeling.

From upstream, Gary called out, "Rick, look to your left on the next bend!"

Rick pulled out his binoculars but was still too far away to see what Gary was going on about, so he paddled faster, and Xãn pitched in as well. As the bend approached, a family of capybara appeared, rooting around in the mud at the edge of the bank.

"Better run, Rick. Those guinea pigs are gonna get ya!" shouted Gary, grinning.

"Ha-fucking-ha!" replied Rick.

Rick snapped a couple of pics of the giant rodents. They were only a few feet away from the canoe and seemed uninterested in the men, not the least bit scared. Rick's boat caught up to the one carrying Gary, who had slowed down to tell him something.

"Rick, I tried to triangulate the cell number we found several times using my satellite Wi-Fi. Still no luck, I'm afraid. I hope it wasn't a burner phone. I still wanna hold off on calling it, because they might ditch it if they see a number they don't recognize."

"That makes sense. Just keep trying, I guess. How much longer until the end of the river?"

"I'd say only about an hour left. We got a decent start, so I think we should set up base camp at the end and prepare for the overland part. The tribesmen will join us for the journey. It's a blessing we have their help. They know the rainforest well, and the extra machetes will come in handy. The bush will be thick and there aren't any trails, so we'll have to chop our way through. It's gonna be slow going. Keep applying that insect gel I gave you. This area is known for bot flies and that's the last thing we need. Are you familiar with them?"

"Bot flies?" Rick frowned. "I've heard of them but no, not really."

"They're nasty buggers and my worst nightmare. They implant their eggs into a host, usually cattle or hogs, but humans can also be a host. Trust me, you don't want to be one. Once the egg is in your skin, the larvae grow, causing a rise in the skin, and eventually an antenna will appear as the maggot continues to grow until it finally hatches through the skin. It's the stuff of a horror movie, man!"

Rick rushed to rub on more of the gel comically as Gary spoke, making him laugh. They continued to paddle and were nearing the end of the Biá River when Rick spotted something—a flash of light reflecting off something in the trees. He yelled at Gary to stop.

"What's that?" asked Rick, pointing at it.

They both grabbed binoculars and saw a large shiny object through the trees and brush.

"Let's check it out."

The pulled all the canoes to the bank and began to chop through the brush. As they got closer, a stench filled Rick's nose. A smell he was all too familiar with: the smell of death.

Twenty yards ahead of them lay a crashed bush plane. Rick could soon make out the decomposed body of a pilot draped over the steering controls. The plane was on its side and had lost its tail, and was easily accessible from the rear. Two more badly decomposed bodies lay inside. Rick, Gary, Possum, and Leo covered their noses with their shirts and moved closer. The tribesmen stayed back.

"Could this be the plane Jules wrote about in her email?" Rick wondered aloud.

"Let's see what we can find," said Gary.

Rick climbed in and started pulling debris away and tossing it out the rear. He came upon a small duffel bag. After unzipping it, he dug through the bag and found what he needed—a passport.

"Kevin Randall Clizby," read Rick aloud. "It's the plane. Jules told me Kevin Clizby gave her the backpack with the map inside. I can't believe she was this deep in the rainforest. She's a rugged girl, but damn!"

"Well, with boats and a guide, this area isn't all that bad when you think about it. Going any farther is where it gets real hairy."

"I guess that's true."

Rick and Gary rummaged through the aircraft, trying to find anything that would help them, but came up short. All they found were a few passports and a mountain of scientific papers. They were about to quit when Rick came across a manila folder tucked in the rear of a seat on the plane. When he opened it, he found a crude drawing with the words "Yucamama Eye" written across the top. It looked like an eye with a mean frowning eyebrow above it. He snapped a photo of it with his phone, showed it to Gary, then folded it up and stuck it in his pocket. He was sure it would come in handy, as the Yucamama Eye was mentioned in the treasure map. Hopefully, it would shed some light on the hiding place of the sacred jewel. They trekked back to the canoes and began to paddle again. After a short while, they came to a flat spot on the bank where the river ended and disappeared beneath the heavy canopy.

"We can set up base camp here," said Gary. "We've only got about an hour until sunset. Seems smart to rest and get a fresh start in the morning, instead of starting into the brush now and risking it getting dark on us."

They all enjoyed taking turns shooting the pneumatic gun onto the trees to hang their Tree Pods. Rick let Xãn shoot his. It took him a couple of tries, but he finally got it over a large limb. Rick scoured the ground for centipedes and zipped up his hanging tent tightly in case one wanted to sneak in while they prepared dinner. The tribesmen collected banana leaves and made beds out of them on the ground. They all assisted in getting wood for the fire. They worked as a team, and few words were spoken. It was as if they all knew what job they were supposed to do and language was not a barrier.

The fire was soon roaring, and two of the tribesmen returned with a forty-pound wild pig known as a collared peccary. They skinned and gutted it, and hung it upside down from a long stick. The men laid it down near the fire and began to hit it with large rocks repeatedly. Rick assumed it was some sort of ritual, but Leo explained they were merely tenderizing the light pink meat. They then rubbed something on the carcass that came from a leather pouch one of the tribesmen had on him, and wrapped it up in banana leaves. They placed it directly on the fire. Rick thought to himself, it was just like an old-fashioned pig roast, which he'd been to many times in Texas. He was ready for some BBQ!

"How about a drink? Just because we're on an expedition doesn't mean we have to suffer, right?" asked Gary.

Gary pulled out a collapsible water bottle inside one of the drybags and set some glasses on a foldable rollup table. He poured the brown liquid into the glasses, and Rick was about to reach for his when Gary stopped him.

"Uh-uh, just a second."

Gary opened a box, pulled out some perfectly round large crystal ice cubes, and plopped them into Rick and the others' drinks.

"Where in God's name did you get clear ice balls in the jungle?"

"I made them in that freezer." Gary pointed at a small stainless-steel box with cables running to the battery bank, hooked to solar panels on the cargo canoe.

"Dude, you are too much!" exclaimed Rick.

"Enjoy it while you can. Tomorrow we'll be going on foot, and we'll have to leave all this behind."

The four men picked up their glasses, and Rick made a toast.

"Here's to a safe expedition and the return of two jewels. My Jules and the Sacred Jewel of Orinoco."

"Cheers!" said everyone in unison.

Even the tribesmen seemed to understand what was going on, as they sipped from coconut cups some liquid that came from a gourd. Everyone seemed to be at peace and harmony with the rainforest as the sun began to set.

Gary finished his second drink and began to offload the gear from the cargo canoe in order to get it all together and hang it from a tree out of harm's way. He was bending over to pick up a line he had dropped when a whooshing sound went by his ear and then, *thunk*, an arrow buried itself into the dugout canoe behind him. Gary spun around, and Rick followed his gaze. Several more arrows were headed his way.

One of the Kayapó men yelled, "Himarimã!"

"Take cover! Ambush!" yelled Gary.

A large group of Himarimã warriors appeared just beyond the clearing. One of the arrows sliced through the shoulder of one of the Kayapó, and blood dripped down his arm. It was a superficial wound, and he returned an arrow with deadly accuracy. Rick and Gary scrambled to turn one of the dugout canoes on its side for cover, as Leo and two of the Kayapós dove behind it. Possum was on the other side of the clearing, and ducked down beneath some tall grass out of sight.

"What do they want?" Rick yelled to Leo.

Leo was speaking to one of the Kayapó as the sound of arrows echoed off the canoes.

"They want take our supplies! They kill for food!"

The guns were all in a drybag, except for the .45 Rick had tucked in the back of his pants—and the shotgun that was just out of reach, leaning against one of the other canoes. Gary had been cleaning it, and a fresh box of double-aught buckshot sat beside the stock.

Rick looked at Gary confidently and passed him the .45. He had to get the shotgun. As a third shower of arrows hit the canoe, he dove for it, grabbing the gun and ammo together and rolling behind another canoe. It was too heavy for him to tip by himself, so he lay low just below the highest point. An arrow missed his head by inches and ricocheted off of a rock near the water's edge.

"Gary, come closer. I'm gonna throw you the shotgun loaded."

Rick quickly loaded five shells in the long gun with the plug out. He made sure the safety was on and counted.

"One, two, three!"

He tossed the gun barrel-first toward Gary, who caught it in midair.

"Cover me!"

Bam, bam, bam! Gary fired the shotgun in the direction of the Himarimã, who were out of range, but took cover as Rick bolted back to the first canoe and grabbed the .45 again. Its bullets could reach the warriors, but every time he tried to get off a shot above the canoe, an arrow whizzed by his head.

"Give me the shotgun."

Rick took the shotgun and placed the barrel an inch from the inside bottom of the canoe. *Blam!* Wood splintered everywhere as he blew a three-inch hole in the canoe. From this vantage point, he could see the warriors crouched down. Carefully, he took aim as one of them pulled back on his bow.

Bam! Rick fired through the hole in the canoe. The warrior fell backward from a direct hit to the chest.

"Got one!"

The Kayapó were huddled together, most of them crouched down behind a tree near the bank. They started a war cry, and without notice bound together side by side, bows and arrows firing in unison at the Himarimã. Two went down as well as one of the Kayapó. He had taken an arrow in the leg and rolled to the ground in agony. Ripping the arrow from his leg, he bounded up, waving his machete wildly in the air, and ran full speed toward the attacking tribe.

Rick and Gary came out of hiding too, flanking the warriors on the same side where Possum was hiding. Since he had no visible weapon, Rick waved at him to stay down.

"We're coming, you sons of bitches!" yelled Rick.

Firing his .45 rapidly into the group, he hit one, who fell. Only three remained as the Kayapó descended upon them, throwing spears and arrows at the tribe. Gary blasted the bushes with the shotgun, taking out one. The gunshots ended as the Kayapó stabbed and kicked at the warriors on the ground, finishing them off. Bodies lay strewn in the high grass as Rick approached. One of the Kayapó was among them. He had sacrificed his life to save Rick and the gang.

"Aye, ya, ya, ya, ya, aaaaaaaaaaaaa!"

"Look out!" yelled Rick toward Possum as the only remaining Himarimã leapt into the air behind him with a spear in hand, ready to drive it into his back.

Possum spun around just in time and pulled the buck knife from his side. The warrior's body fell onto Possum with a loud *thud*. The silence was deafening.

Rick ran toward Possum, his eyes wide with worry.

"Possum, Possum, are you okay?"

Possum shoved the warrior off of him, revealing the knife buried deep in the man's chest. The spear was lodged in the ground inches from Possum's head. Rick exhaled in relief.

As quickly as it had happened, it was over.

The gang worked together to bury the bodies of the Himarimã, as the Kayapó used their machetes to build an above-ground funeral pyre for their fallen warrior. They chanted and danced around the fire until sunrise. He'd died a hero.

CHAPTER TEN

The next day began on a somber note. The smoldering embers of the ceremonial pyre where the fallen Kayapó warrior was laid to rest were a harsh reminder of the battle they had all been through.

Gary packed up all non-essential gear, bound it together, and raised it high in a tree, concealing the rope with tree branches. He would have to retrieve it at a later time. If any tribe stumbled into the area, they'd never know there was thousands of dollars' worth of battery banks and solar panels. The journey would now be on foot. Gary brought several roll-up solar panels, just enough to keep the sat phone charged up. It was their only connection to the outside world.

With the Kayapó leading the way, they began the trek on foot into the deep thicket of the rainforest. Having to hack their way through the bush made for a slow journey. Foot by foot, yard by yard, they moved forward. In a little under three hours, they had only gone about a mile and still had several more to go to get to the devil's cross. Rick still wasn't even sure what that was, but they had to find it one way or another.

By noon, he was sweating like a pig. It was clear everyone else was feeling the effects of the heat and humidity too, plus their stomachs were rumbling.

"Let's break for lunch," said Gary.

Rick and Possum both took turns chugging water from one of the collapsible bottles as Leo prepared lunch. Beef stew was the meal of the day. Gary had frozen individual portions in Ziploc bags and kept them frozen until today. They had two days' worth of meals, but today would be the last of the perishable entrees.

"So, what do you think, Rick?" asked Gary. "Spicy enough for ya?"

"Yeah, you must have used some TexJoy Spicy Steak Seasoning, I assume?"

"You know it!"

"What kind of beef is this? Angus?"

"Nope, believe it or not, it's emu. I invested in an emu farm and they send me cuts on a regular basis."

Rick raised an eyebrow. "Wow, I never would've guessed that. It looks and tastes a lot like beef."

The sat phone rang, and Gary quickly grabbed it.

"Go for Gary. Oh hi, Gina. How's it going in Rio?"

Hearing Gina's name, Rick scooted closer so he could listen in on the call. Gary shared the phone with him.

"I met with Davi Kopenawa, the leader of the Yanomami," said Gina, her voice a bit muffled. "He speaks fluent Portuguese, which surprised me, but that's helped move along negotiations. They're in a bitter battle to stop the new Belo Monte dam. They're also facing struggles with illegal gold miners invading the Yanomami territory. He needs an ally in this battle. I've advised him of your quest to find the sacred jewel. He has agreed to give you two weeks to return it, or they will massacre the Kayapó. You have to find it, Gary."

Gary and Rick shared a grim look, and nodded to each other.

"We've made great progress," Gary told Gina. "And I think by this time tomorrow we'll be in the area suggested on the map. With a little luck, it will all come together."

"Great! Davi has authorized me to fly to New York and Washington in order to raise more funds for their battle. I have meetings set up with the American Museum of Natural History in Manhattan, as well as the Smithsonian in DC. The plan is to start a bidding war for the jewel. If I can pit each museum against each other, I think I can get a much higher price, so the Yanomami can have the funds they need to lead a strong battle against Belo Monte."

"Keep up the good work, Gina. We'll do our part on this end. Check back with me tomorrow. When are you heading to New York?"

"I'm on an eight o'clock flight tonight. The private jet is in São Paulo for scheduled maintenance, so I'm flying commercial."

"Okay, just keep all your receipts and I'll reimburse you."

"Thanks, Gary. Y'all be safe and tell everyone hello for me."

Gary put away the sat phone, and he and Rick continued their lunch. This would be their last hot meal for a few days, and they savored every morsel. The rest of the journey would consist of freeze dried pre-prepared meals. Rick reckoned none of them were looking forward to those. Especially not Gary, given what a foodie he was.

"Hey, Rick, remember that time I called you from New Orleans when I had to go there last minute because I had some points that were about to expire?"

"Oh, yeah. I drove over from Destin and met you at the Gumbo Shop. Damn, that was some good chow!"

Gary chuckled. "I don't think we slept for two days. It was a nonstop food and drink fest."

"The good ol' days for sure."

The Kayapó made funny faces while eating the stew. Rick asked Leo about it, and he explained that they rarely used seasoning and the spiciness of the food was hard for them to handle. But they managed with the aid of lots of water. Water was the one thing they didn't have to worry about. The Kayapó drank straight from the river. Their bodies were used to the bacteria in the water. The rest of the crew also drank the river water, but it was filtered through a multi-stage filtration system Gary had brought. It was only about the size of an aerosol can but had five layers of filters and used batteries to push water through the microscopic membrane, turning the brownest of water crystal clear. It was from another company Gary had invested in. He had become quite the venture capitalist since winning Powerball.

With all the gear repacked in the rucksacks, they began to hack their way forward. Every step was arduous as they chopped the high grass and vines to clear a path. They were lucky the Kayapó were masters of the machete. As isolated as the tribe was from the outside world, they had adapted to some changes and were skilled with many weapons and tools.

The heat was unbearable, and they all had to break every forty-five minutes and hydrate. They were approaching a ridge, and the terrain suddenly changed, opening up more with taller trees and less thicket. The canopy above nearly blocked out the sun. Howler monkeys and groups of marmosets mocked them with every step, warning the rest of the jungle of their presence. As the terrain began to change, the ground became more and more wet, until they were trekking through knee-deep marshland. It reminded Rick of a swamp in Texas he used to frequent as a boy.

Gary took the lead from the Kayapó and slugged through the murky, grassy water. The water level rose with each step. Out of nowhere, Gary took another step and disappeared with a shout.

"Gary?" called Rick with worry, struggling to catch up to him.

He popped up again a moment later, waving his arms and yelling. "Son of a bitch! I fell into a damn sinkhole or something."

One of the tribesmen quickly cut a vine and used it to pull Gary out of the hole into shallower water. Gary stood up, and the looks on the crew's faces made him stop in his tracks.

"What?!"

"Dude, look at your arms!" said Rick.

Gary looked down at his exposed arms, which were now covered in leeches. He started ripping at them as blood trickled from his arm. One was stuck to his neck as well. "Argh, get off me!" he shouted.

One of the Kayapó stopped him and pulled out a leather pouch. He took a salve and touched each leech. Within minutes, they released from his skin and fell to the ground. Only a couple that he had swatted caused minor cuts. To avoid infection, another salve was applied to his bite marks. The Kayapó had remedies for everything.

The water bog was a major setback, and the Kayapó spoke to Leo and began to lead them down a new route. It would take them around the bog but cost them more time, as the journey was longer.

"I don't care how long it takes," said Gary with a huff. "As long as we don't run into any more leeches."

Six hours later, they came to a high, dry spot and decided to set up camp. The trees above were perfect for the hanging tents, and they each set one up as the Kayapó gathered wood and started a fire. Gary had lighters, but the tribesmen were so efficient with a flint and dry leaves, they got it started before he could offer them any. e gbagHe

Rick, with the help of Leo, got creative with machetes and designed some crude stools out of bamboo and thin liana vines. It was good to get off of their feet. Each man removed his socks and boots and dried them by the fire. Jungle rot was a real potential problem, so they didn't take any chances.

Gary poured some cognac from one of the flexible bottles and shared it with the Kayapó. They in return gave each man a sip of something they called Cauim. It was a fermented starch and a traditional drink of the tribesmen. The starch was usually made from corn and mixed with berries for flavor. Upon tasting it, Rick nicknamed it Jungle Juice. Without many words being spoken, they did the *ha-ha click-click* native style, and grinned at each other. A common respect was gained, creating a stronger bond between the tribe and the crew.

As the night grew darker, howler monkeys competed with bell birds for who could make the loudest noise. The only bonus was that the drone of cicadas ceased after dark. Mixed in with the nature sounds was the beating of drums from a nearby tribe. The Kayapó listened intently and reassured Leo that the tribe was celebrating and not planning a battle, based on the drumbeats.

The drums and animal sounds continued late into the night as everyone climbed into their Tree Pods and the Kayapó made their beds down on the ground near the fire. They took it upon themselves to keep the fire stoked.

Rick couldn't sleep with the racket going on around him. "Gary, you asleep?" he whispered.

"No, I'm trying, but it's so freaking loud. Next time, we're all bringing noise-cancelling headphones! I'm sure you're worried about Juliana. We have to do whatever it takes to save her, not to mention what this entire thing means to the Kayapó," said Gary.

"Let's not forget her roommate too. That's what started this crazy thing. I don't know her, but she must be a good person if Jules got involved to help her. I'll be honest, man, since Jules took this job down here, I have worried about her a lot. She's from South America, but it's so primitive down here and she's so delicate, to me anyway. She would argue that she's tough, and I know she is, but I can't help but worry about her." Rick sighed. "All I know is that we are under the gun on time, and getting the sacred jewel back will save a lot of lives and be a good bargaining chip for us to rescue Jules and her roommate."

They continued to chat for an hour and eventually drifted off to sleep.

Rick was awakened by a familiar growl. Most of the jungle sounds fell away as he focused in on the sound, and his whole body tensed. Slowly, he climbed out of his Tree Pod and crouched near the fire. He could sense the jaguar was close, and hear movement in the nearby trees, but he couldn't yet see where the beast was hiding.

Two of the tribesmen awakened and said, "Hop Krore!" in unison. They woke the other men and made a circle with their backs to the fire. They began to chant.

"*Hop krore, wapĩja mêtch. Hop krore, wapĩja mêtch.*"

"Leo, what are they saying?" murmured Rick.

Leo listened and thought for a second, then said, "They say 'beautiful black jaguar.' The jaguar is sacred and the black jaguar is most sacred. They pay homage to him in hopes that he will leave."

The jaguar continued to circle the camp, staying just out of sight of the firelight. Occasionally, its eyes would appear for a second, then vanish again in the darkness. Swallowing hard, Rick joined the tribesmen and the rest of the crew, and began to chant along with them.

"Look, Gary," said Rick, "I know this cat is sacred to the Kayapó, but if that bastard attacks, it's getting one between the eyes."

"I agree, but will it anger the Kayapó?" asked Gary.

Leo said they had and would kill a black jaguar if necessary. But only if it attacked. Then, they would consider it no longer sacred. Rick exhaled deeply through his nostrils to stay calm, hoping Leo was right.

For the next hour, the stealthy cat circled the camp, getting closer then retreating again. The tribesmen stoked the fire and continued to chant. Possum's hands were visibly trembling as the jaguar silently stalked the men, and his wide eyes showed his fear every time it growled again. Rick noticed him starting to lift his weapon and quickly grabbed his arm to stop him, reminding him how sacred the cat was to the tribe.

"We only shoot if it attacks."

The sun began to lighten the sky, and the darkness shifted into a hue of reds and oranges. The cicadas began their wave like drones, drowning out the more frequent growls of the jaguar. With the sun coming up, Rick figured they had a better advantage over the jaguar than in the darkness of night.

Sure enough, the jaguar soon retreated. With only a few hours of sleep, everyone was dragging. But time was against them and they needed to keep going.

As they moved through the rainforest, the trees became sparser, giving way to high grass and bamboo. Rather than spend all day hacking the grass, they simply moved it aside to create a pathway. A clearing up ahead was a welcome sight as they completed their leg through the river of grass.

One of the Kayapó men ran ahead to scout the area and look for the next route to the devil's cross. He was about fifty yards ahead of the group when he turned and began running back as fast as he could. Like a flash of black lightning, the jaguar was upon him. The great cat leaped at the man, who tripped and fell forward. The cat missed him by a foot and spun around. Quickly, the tribesman grabbed his spear and raised his arm to throw it, but it was too late. The cat ripped his shoulder with its massive claws.

Rick fired off a shot with his .45 in the air to try to scare off the cat, but it was as if the beast didn't hear it. The tribesman screamed in pain as the jaguar bit hard into his leg and began to pull him away.

"I've gotta take a shot!" yelled Gary.

Pulling out his sniper gun, Gary aimed it at the cat. The Kayapó man was in the same line of fire, and Gary hesitated before pulling the trigger. As the cat let go to get a better grip, Gary took the shot. The spinning bullet came out of the rifle, and before the sound of the blast hit their ears, the jaguar rolled as if hit by a car. A blood-curdling scream erupted from the cat as it wriggled and then fell still. It was a perfect shot straight through the heart.

All the men raced toward the injured Kayapó tribesman. His shoulder had a huge gash in it, and blood was pumping like a fountain out of the holes in his legs. Rick grabbed a shirt from his rucksack and ripped it into long pieces, making a tourniquet. He wrapped the bleeding man with tight pressure.

"He's not gonna make it. He's lost too much blood," said Rick.

Gary grabbed his sat phone and called the boat. Johnie answered on the third ring.

"Johnie, it's Gary. One of the tribesmen was attacked by a jaguar. He's lost a ton of blood. I need to have him medevaced out of here. Go into my office and find the number for the medevac in Manaus." Gary grabbed his handheld GPS and fired it up. As soon as it found him, he said, "Take down these coordinates: *4°29'36.7"S 67°29'06.9"W.*"

"Got it!" said Johnie, loud enough Rick could hear his voice.

"Now, call the number for Manaus Medevac in my address book in the top drawer of my desk," said Gary. "You find it? Good. They'll be reluctant to fly into the rainforest. Tell them we're in a large clearing and I'll pay for any expenses. I have a flare gun and colored smoke."

Gary hung up to let Johnie make the call. After a couple of minutes, Johnie called him back.

"They are en route. They said it could cost as much as $350,000."

"I don't care. This man may have saved our lives, and I plan on saving his. Stay by the phone and pray!"

After hanging up again, Gary explained that the flight from Manaus would take roughly four hours. The Sikorsky chopper had a regular range of 275 miles, but the one in Manaus had external fuel tanks that gave them double that. They could fly all the way without stopping but would most likely have to refuel in Tefé. Rick took in the sight of the tribesman and tried to have hope, but it would be a miracle from God if he survived after losing so much blood.

As they waited, the shaman of the group cut off the right paw of the jaguar. Then he rubbed a potion on the critically injured man's head, and laid the paw on his heart, claws facing the sky. His breathing was shallow, but they had stopped the blood loss.

The faint whirring of chopper blades became audible in the distance. Rick took the flare gun and fired it high into the sky. Gary pulled the cord on the bright orange smoke canister. The helicopter landed, and two EMTs jumped off with a stretcher. As quickly as they landed, they were off again. Gary could see an IV bag being held by one of the EMTs just as the chopper turned and headed back to civilization.

"It's in God's hands now," said Gary, his voice solemn. "All we can do is pray."

CHAPTER ELEVEN

Gina's plane landed at LaGuardia a little after eleven p.m. She shuttled to Arthouse Hotel on the Upper West Side. It was only a couple of blocks from the Museum of Natural History just off of 81st and Central Park West. Her meeting was scheduled for 9:15 a.m. with the curator, and she wanted to be well prepared. Before calling it a night, she sipped on vodka from the mini fridge and studied the notes she had taken from Davi Kopenawa, the spiritual leader and spokesman for the Yanomami tribe. He had given her the green light to begin negotiations between the two museums. The curator in New York had no idea what was about to happen, let alone any idea that the Smithsonian was interested in acquiring the Sacred Jewel of Orinoco. Taking him by surprise would give her an advantage, and she hoped his ego would do the rest.

Jason Hillcrest had received his PhD in 2002 and was one of the youngest curators of a major museum in the world. His youth and immaturity would certainly help favor

Gina in the negotiation. Jason had developed a reputation as somewhat of a playboy in the New York socialite scene. He had dated several models, and been arrested but never tried for a DUI. His daddy's money got him out of trouble time and time again. The only thing he took pride in was the museum. Jason had brought it back into the limelight with his exquisite rotating exhibits, and soon one of the rarest jewels in the world would have its own hall. e has ddated se

"Good morning. I am here to see Mr. Hillcrest. I have a 9:15 meeting scheduled," said Gina to the receptionist.

"Please have a seat and I'll let him know you're here."

Several minutes went by as Gina thumbed through her notes and several 8x10s of the jewel that were taken several years back by a photojournalist from the *National Geographic* magazine. She'd had them photocopied and enhanced with more saturation to make them eyepopping.

"Mr. Hillcrest will see you now," said the receptionist.

Gina stood up and grabbed her things, then followed the receptionist down a long hallway to an office at the end.

"Mr. Hillcrest, this is Gina Russo for your 9:15 a.m. meeting."

"Ah, hello, Ms. Russo. Nice to meet you."

Jason was a handsome guy—tall, muscular and confident. He didn't look like a guy who would be in charge of a museum. He looked more like an athlete and exuded an air of arrogance, or maybe just strong virility, as he entered the room.

"Please call me Gina. We don't need such formalities."

"In that case, call me Jason. Please have a seat." Once Gina was sitting across from him, he said, "So, I understand from your email that you are here representing the

Yanomami tribe and the transfer of the Sacred Jewel of Orinoco."

"Yes, I have a power of attorney for Davi Kopenawa, the leader of the Yanomami. As you know, he is seeking one million dollars in exchange for the jewel to aid them in the battle against the building of the Belo Monte Dam, which would destroy thousands of acres of Yanomami land."

Gina handed him the photo of the jewel. His eyes widened as he gazed at it.

"Where is the jewel now?"

Gina thought for a second and then said, "It's in a safe in Rio, and I have arranged for armed transport for it to the museum upon clearance of the funds."

"We have acquired the money from one of our philanthropists and the check has been written," said Jason. "I just need to know who to make it out to."

Gina was about to mention that the Smithsonian was also very interested—in fact, she had a meeting already set up with them for Thursday. But she held off. She decided having the check in hand would make it easier to negotiate. Her tactics might have been a little unethical, but she viewed it more like two couples in a bidding war for a new house on the market. She could always return the check to New York if the famous DC museum decided to go for the two million dollars.

"Make it out to Regina Russo. I have an escrow account established in Rio for the Yanomami tribe. I can have the jewel on your desk in two weeks."

She had faith in Gary and the crew that they would acquire the jewel. It would at least give them more time to try to find it. Jason signed and put the check in an envelope and handed it to Gina.

"Pleasure doing business with you, Gina. I have some papers for you to fill out. Let's see, today is Tuesday the 13th. I'll put the 30th for delivery of the jewel. Will that work for you? It'll give you an extra few days for travel and the check to clear."

"That's perfect." She smiled at him. "You are doing the Yanomami a great service. Hopefully, one day you can meet Davi Kopenawa. I'm sure he'd be thrilled to see the jewel on exhibit."

After leaving the museum, she returned to her hotel and confirmed her flight for Wednesday instead of Thursday. She wanted to get to DC early so there was no chance of a delayed flight. She was nervous she might lose the check, though. Instead of depositing the money in the escrow account, she would put it in her savings at Chase. There was a Chase on every corner in New York.

Gina snapped a photo of the check and then took a cab to the closest Chase on 86th and made the deposit. To her surprise, the check cleared immediately. Apparently, the museum used the same bank. When she opened her Chase app, she saw the funds in her savings: $1,049,987.32. It made her $50,000 look puny. To celebrate, she strolled into Central Park and had lunch at the famous Tavern on the Green. She pulled out her cell phone to update Gary. She called, but the phone never connected.

Rick, Gary, Leo, and Possum, led by the remaining three Kayapó tribesmen, had entered an area of the rainforest known as the Jutaí-Solimões. The canopy was so thick that it almost seemed dark under the massive trees. Rick pulled out the map again and read it aloud, hoping something would spark an idea.

> *Take the JR to the right of the Y and copa tana. Once you reach Port S, exit right through the eye of Yucamama to the end is where you'll Biá. Find the devil's cross and walk ten steps south. Inside the cave of tokrāk is where God is swathed.*

"Rick, I think I get it," said Possum, looking at the map over his shoulder. "I was reading a book I got on the Yanomami, and I found a passage about the eye of Yucamama. At first, I thought you said 'Yucamana' with an N, which means 'spirit of the tribe,' but when I read it and double-checked it against the map, I realized it was 'Yucamama' with an M. That means 'serpent.' I was trying to figure out how the hell we would spot the spirit of the tribe bit. Now it makes sense. Eye of the serpent. Look there!"

Rick and the crew looked where Possum was pointing. It was a large rock formation at the edge of a stream. The stream was the end of the Biá River. When Rick covered one eye as Possum was doing, he saw them: two large brown rocks with a dark black rock in the center. If he squinted, it did indeed look like the eye of a snake.

"The only reason I found it is because I got a bug in my eye," said Possum with a laugh. "I was looking at the rocks and when I rubbed my left eye to get the bug out, it appeared. That damn gnat is a miracle."

"We are close, boys!" yelled Rick.

"Now all we need to find is the devil's cross," replied Possum.

They walked directly to the eye of the serpent. Looking 360 degrees all around them, nothing resembling a devil's cross could be seen.

"What is a devil's cross?" asked Rick.

"Well, according to ancient folklore and stuff I've read about Satanists, it's the opposite of the cross for Jesus, like a pentagram or an upside-down cross. It's highly unlikely that we'll find a pentagram in the jungle. So, I lean toward an upside-down cross," answered Possum.

Rick climbed on top of the serpent-eyed rocks and stared out at the vast expanse of a clear-cut field. Gold diggers legal and illegal had used the slash-and-burn technique with large machinery they brought in from Porto Velho. A lone tree stood at the bottom of the clear-cut field at what looked like the edge of a drop-off. There weren't any people in sight, but several large earth-moving vehicles were parked at the edge of the forest. A massive bulldozer was backed into the bush a little ways, exposing only its shiny blade. Rows and rows of trees were piled up to eventually be burned, and huge boulders were scattered all along the tree line. Rick hated to see the clear-cutting of the beautiful rainforest.

"Toss me your binoculars, Gary," shouted Rick.

Rick scanned the area, looking for any sign of people. He knew whoever left the moving equipment might still be in the area. Not seeing anyone, he focused on the lone tree, and could only see the top two-thirds of it, as the bottom of it was below the ledge. "Let's check out that tree," he said.

They all hiked toward it. The closer they got, the more of the tree they could see, as the ground slanted upward toward the ledge. Suddenly, Rick stopped in his tracks.

"Look!" He pointed at the tree.

Two fat branches just above the base of the tree stuck out of each side, forming a cross—an upside-down cross.

"That's it!" yelled Rick.

He began running toward the tree. The tribesmen and crew were right behind him.

"That has to be it."

"It certainly looks like an upside-down cross," replied Possum.

Out of breath, Rick slowly climbed down the ledge to the base of the tree and pulled out his compass. He pointed due south and began to walk. He didn't see a cave.

Rick frowned. "I don't get it. I don't see any caves. How can we find the cave of tokrāk? A cave that swallows you?"

The group kept walking around, studying the area for clues or any sign of a cave. Rick was getting more and more frustrated when Possum called out from behind him.

"Rick! Those are puffbirds."

Rick glanced back and saw Possum was using his binoculars to zoom in on a flock of birds nesting in burrows a few yards down from the tree. He'd picked up the bird-watching hobby from Rick, but he'd taken it to the next level and always carried a birding book with him. The book was flipped open in one of his hands right now.

"Nice. Possum, can we focus on finding this cave please?"

"Amigo, you're not getting it. They are puffbirds, actually swallow-winged puffbirds. Get it? Swallow! Look down at the bottom of the ledge. It's a swallow cave, not *to swallow*, swallow as in birds. Plus, it's down at the bottom, aka south. You're pointing due south from the tree, but south can also mean below."

Rick slapped his own forehead. "Possum, you're a damn genius!"

He practically rolled down the hill, knocking rocks down the ledge and making the birds fly out in protest. When he got to the bottom, he saw something out of place. Several cut branches were laid across an opening in the ledge. It took him a few minutes to clear the branches and when he did, he saw the cave. It wasn't very large, just big enough for a man to crawl into, but it was a cave. He pulled off his sidearm, canteen, and backpack.

"Toss me your light, Gary."

Gary had brought several LED tactical flashlights, and passed one to Rick from his rucksack.

"I'm going in. Cross your fingers."

Slowly, Rick wiggled into the cave. The small opening went back about ten feet and then opened up to a large room. From that room, several more caves went in different directions. A small trickle of water ran through the center of the room and disappeared behind the wall. As Rick opened up the light, he saw thousands of holes in the walls, each one filled with birds. He was mostly relieved that they weren't bats.

"Y'all come in," yelled Rick. "Put all the gear in a pile beside the cave and come in one by one. I need your help to search. This is definitely swallow cave."

One at a time, the men climbed inside. Gary had three lights and gave one to Possum. The tribesmen were the last to enter and looked fearful of their surroundings. Leo spoke to them and reassured them they were all safe. Their anxiety finally subdued, and they began to help the others search.

"We're looking for something manmade, I think," said Rick.

"Like this?" replied Possum as he pulled a leather pouch from eye level of one of the swallow's burrows.

"You found it!" yelled Rick.

They all gathered around as he slowly unwrapped the pouch. Rick was shining his light directly on it, and as Possum pulled it out, the brilliant blue sapphire shined brightly and reflected its hue on the top of the cave. It was nearly as large as Possum's hand and similar in size to the Star of Adam, the world's largest known sapphire found in Sri Lanka. The Kayapó men immediately fell to their knees and began chanting. To them, they were staring at God himself. The crew all took turns holding it.

Possum whistled. "You realize this thing is nearly as big as the Star of Adam? That recently sold for $300 million."

"But the Yanomami are only getting a million for it," replied Rick. "I think Gina needs to up her negotiations."

"I agree," said Gary.

The ten-foot hole they'd come through suddenly turned darker, as if a shadow had crossed over it.

"What the hell?" said Rick.

"Thanks for finding it for us," yelled a man with an English accent.

"Who's there?" demanded Rick.

"Never mind who I am. What's important is, we have guns on you and you have our gem!"

"I know it's you, Evan. I'll give you the gem—if you release Jules and her roommate."

Silence fell. Evan finally spoke again.

"I'll make a deal with you. I'll give you the address of where the girls are in exchange for the jewel."

"How do I know they're still alive and safe?"

A minute passed by and then Evan lowered down a sat phone tied to a piece of cord, with the speaker on, to the edge of the cave opening. It echoed through the cavern and Rick heard a familiar voice. Exhaling in relief, he moved toward the sound and picked up the phone.

"Hello, Rick? It's Jules."

"Jules, yes, it's me," said Rick in a rush. "Are you safe?"

"Yes. We're both safe. We're being held in a hangar near the border of Peru. There is plenty of food, but we are locked in and cannot escape. Please help us."

Kevin ripped the phone out of Rick's hands and hung up.

"See, I told you. They're alive and safe, and all I want is the jewel."

"Evan, you son of a bitch, if you harm one hair on her beautiful head, I will personally kill you with my bare hands," snapped Rick, scowling at him.

"Listen, I'm a businessman, not a murderer. All I want is the jewel and I will give you the address. I have a buyer in Rio and he is getting anxious."

Evan threw the small cord down into the cave with a note wrapped around a rock on the end of it. Rick unraveled the papers. Inside was a photo of Jules and a woman who had to be her roommate, along with an address:

R. Perimetral Norte Dois, Tabatinga - AM, 69640-000, Brazil

"Tie the jewel to the rope and we will leave. You can go get your girls after we're gone. You have my word."

"What do we do, Rick?" asked Possum in a low voice. "If we let him take the jewel, then you know the Yanomami won't be happy—"

"I know. Let me think." Rick paced back and forth, rubbing his head. "I don't think we have a choice right now. I've gotta save Jules. We have to trust this guy." They'd find a way to get the jewel back once they were out of this mess.

Rick could hear a diesel engine running just outside of the cave.

"Okay, I'm tying up the gem in a leather pouch," he called out.

He gave the rope three tugs to let Evan know to pull it out. Evan untied the jewel and began to laugh.

"Hey listen, mate, I'm afraid I'm gonna have to throw a spanner in the works."

Suddenly, the diesel engine fired up and the hole went black again. Rick crawled as fast as he could, clawing his way toward the exit, but it was too late. The hole was blocked by a massive boulder pushed in by a bulldozer. They were trapped.

"Dammit!" Rick wiggled backward into the main cave, seething through his teeth. "That diesel engine wasn't their getaway truck, I'm afraid. It was a bulldozer. We're trapped."

Panic began to creep up the necks of the men. Claustrophobia was setting in fast.

"What are we gonna do?" asked Possum in a desperate voice.

"We're gonna get the fuck out of here! That's what!"

CHAPTER TWELVE

Possum and Rick studied the cave carefully. There were two other caves leading somewhere near the back of the large room, but they didn't know where they led.

"Is there any way we can move that boulder?" asked Possum.

"I don't think so. I pushed on it and it was dead weight," replied Rick grimly. "Even if all of us pushed at the same time, I doubt it would budge. Besides, only one man at a time can fit in the hole. It's a lost cause."

"Then our only hope is to find another way out," said Gary. "These flashlights will only last so long, so we need to work fast."

Leo translated what the crew was saying to the Kayapó men. They looked on the ground for something. They flipped their spears around and began to tightly wrap the ends with vines from the swallow's nests. Each swallow took pride in decorating the doorsteps to their burrows. It was a common trait among all swallows in the Amazon.

"How do we know which cavern to try?" asked Possum. "They could go for miles underground and have more passages along the way. Getting lost is a bad idea!"

"You're right, but at this point it's a flip of a coin, I guess."

One of the Kayapó men started waving his hands up and down like a bird flapping its wings. He pointed at the cave wall and indicated for them to watch. They all did so, and soon one of the swallows flew from its burrow to the cave on the right. A few seconds later, two swallows flew into the main room from that passage.

"That's it!" hollered Rick as he patted the tribesman on the back.

In single file, they began to hike into the passageway. Rick led with his flashlight pointed straight ahead. An occasional swallow would whizz by his head, coming or going. The cavern winded and twisted for several hundred yards. It was pitch black in the cave without their lights on. They came to a Y in the path and were unsure which way to go. They waited for birds. Nothing.

One of the Kayapó men joined the front of the pack for a better view. Suddenly, his flame flickered and was blown to the left. A small gust of wind came from the right-side cavern.

"This way," said Rick.

They continued to hike as the breeze grew stronger. Then as they turned a sharp corner, a small flicker of light appeared at the end of the cavern. A swallow came flying by and disappeared through the light. Rick ran toward it. The hole to the outside world was only three inches wide.

"No one can fit through that!" he yelled, throwing his flashlight in anger.

It hit the edge of the hole, and the hole got an inch larger. Rick ran to the hole and stuck his hand through it. It was dirt.

"Help me dig!"

Possum and Gary flanked Rick as they dug with all their might. Soon the hole was twelve inches wide. Within fifteen minutes, Rick was able to squeeze his torso out. He looked to his right. The bulldozer was still there, lodged up against a seven-foot-round boulder some two hundred yards away. He helped each man out of the hole and thanked God repeatedly for saving them.

"We have to beat them to Jules. If he was willing to let us die in that cave, there's no way he's gonna leave any loose ends. He's gonna kill Jules and her roommate, and we have to stop him."

"But Rick, you know that address is bogus," replied Possum.

"Of course, it is. But Jules said she was in a hangar in a small town near the border of Peru. Plus, I memorized the number from the sat phone. Gary, can you use that triangulate app on your phone synced to your sat phone data?"

"You bet your ass I can."

He hooked it up and dialed. It took only three minutes for the app to ping.

"Got it. Let me put the lats and longs into my map. That call was made from San Sebastian, Colombia. It looks like an airport. Alfredo Vásquez Cobo Airport, to be exact. It's right on the border between Colombia, Peru, and Brazil."

"We have to beat them there. They have a jump on us. It will take days to hike out of here. How are we gonna get back?"

"Hold that thought," said Gary

He dialed his sat phone again.

"Bucky, it's Gary. I'm in a bind and need some help."

"Hey, Gary. What's up, bud?" answered a voice Rick didn't recognize.

"Are you still good friends with that guy who flies that V-22 Osprey out of Air Force Command in Tabatinga?"

"Yeah, why?"

"We are in the rainforest in a clearing near the end of the Biá River, and we need a ride to Alfredo Vásquez Cobo Airport. Do you think he can pull that off?"

"It's gonna have to be considered a rescue mission. Is there anyone injured?"

"Yeah, we're all injured—mentally injured, catch my drift? Let me send you the lat and long."

"Okay, let me see what I can do. Stay by the phone."

Fifteen minutes went by and the sat phone rang.

"Go for Gary."

"Dude, you are the luckiest sombitch I know. I got ahold of central command and they are on maneuvers only fifty miles from where you are. They are en route now. Do you have a flare?"

"Yes, I do. Several. We'll be waiting with bells on. I owe you one, big time!"

"Yeah, you do. One of you better have a busted leg when they arrive. Catch my drift?"

"Gotcha, Gary out."

Gary bent over and picked up a long branch.

"Hit me, Rick, right here in the side of my left shin."

"Are you nuts?"

"Some say yes, but we're getting a lift from the Brazilian Air Force and one of us need to be injured to make it a rescue mission. I'll take one for the team." Gary stuck his leg out at an angle. "Do it hard enough to leave a huge welt, but don't break my damn leg."

"Are you sure?"

"Well, I can hit you, if you prefer."

"Uh no. Okay, on three... Are you ready?"

"Ready."

"One...two..."

Bam! Rick swung on two and broke the branch across Gary's shin.

"Dammit, you said three!" Gary fell to the ground, rubbing his leg.

"I didn't want you to flinch."

Gary rolled up his pants leg, revealing a huge red mark. The surface of the shin was scraped and began to bleed a little.

"Perfect! Now I just gotta make some crutches."

He took his machete and cut two branches armpit long, and tied another two branches across the tops with some cord from his rucksack.

"Now we wait. Here, hold these flares. I'm injured, remember?"

Rick grabbed three short branches, ripped a handkerchief into several strips, and created a tourniquet for Gary to sell the injury even more.

"There, now all you need is a medic!" said Rick with a grin.

The roaring sound of the approaching Osprey's twin turboprop Rolls-Royce engines could be heard before it approached. The Osprey was an amazing aircraft. Part air-plane, part helicopter, it had the ability to take off and land vertically, allowing for access to areas without runways. The massive plane slowed to a hover as the engines pivoted upward, allowing it to land thirty yards from the men. Two airmen carrying a field stretcher sprinted down the rear door's lowered ramp. They quickly assessed Gary's leg and gently lifted him onto the stretcher and into the Osprey.

Rick shook the hands of all the tribesmen and gave them the remaining hard candy, and each one a flashlight, which they were amazed by. Waving goodbye, the Kayapó men began their hike back to their village. Rick watched from inside the aircraft as they disappeared into the rainforest.

The Osprey lifted off, bound for the base in Tabatinga. It was only a few miles from the base to Alfredo Vásquez Cobo Airport.

"How are you feeling, Gary?" asked Rick.

"I'm better, thanks."

The medics had cut his pants leg off, cleaned, and wrapped his leg. Gary's cheeks were a bit flushed, and Rick could sense he was feeling a little guilty for getting so much atten-tion for his self-inflicted wound. But they both knew it was the only way to get to the hangar.

The plane touched down, and an awaiting ambulance whisked Gary to the local hospital. He had no choice but to follow through with the complete exam and X-rays.

"Go save the girls! I'll catch up," yelled Gary as they pushed him into the ambulance.

Rick, Leo, and Possum ran to the baggage area and out to the street to find a cab. There was no time to waste. They flagged down an open-air tuk-tuk and climbed in. Leo told the driver where they wanted to go. It was across the border in Leticia, Colombia. The borders of Colombia, Peru, and Brazil all met in Tabatinga; the city sprawled across Colombia and Brazil, with Peru separated by the mighty Amazon River.

Rick paid the driver and they scouted out the airport. The main building housed the terminals for all international flights. A single 6,200-foot runway sat behind the buildings. Rick walked around the east side of the terminals and pulled out his binoculars. Near the end of the runway sat two blue Quonset hut-styled hangars. The girls had to be in one of them.

As they approached, he saw one of the hangars was wide open and a small private plane was inside, mostly likely getting serviced, as its engine cowlings were open. No one was in the building. Stealthily, they approached the second hangar, which was closed and padlocked with a huge chain. The buildings were made of steel. Rick looked around to make sure no one was watching them and banged on the door with a wrench left nearby.

"Jules, are you in there? Jules!"

"Rick, is that you?" came a muffled voice.

"Yes, Jules. We're gonna get you out of here."

"Please hurry before they return!"

Rick ran to the other hangar and spotted an acetylene torch on a cart. He quickly wheeled it over to the chained door. Sparking the handle, he began to burn through the heavy chain. Within a minute, the chain fell apart, and Rick and Possum muscled open the heavy door of the hangar. Jules bolted out and jumped into Rick's arms, wrapping her entire body around him and almost knocking him to the ground. Her roommate also ran out and began to hug both Rick and Jules together.

Jules kissed him all over his face, openly weeping with joy. Rick teared up a bit too as they continued their long embrace.

"Look, you lovebirds, we gotta get out of here," said Possum.

Jules laughed through her tears and jumped from Rick to hug Possum.

"Let's go!" she said.

Rick noticed a parts truck sitting between the buildings with the keys left inside. There was no time to worry about grand theft auto, so they all ran to the truck. Jules and her roommate jumped in the front seat with Rick, while Possum and Leo hopped into the bed of the truck. Rick peeled out and was off airport property in under a minute.

He took a side road, stopped, then pulled the magnetic sign from the driver's side door and threw it in a ditch culvert. Jules did the same for her side. They climbed back into the vehicle and sped toward Tabatinga.

"Rick, this is Mary, my roommate from Fonte Boa. She's also working with me on the research project."

"Nice to meet you, Mary. I wish it were under better circumstances."

"I'm just relieved you found us. I'm overwhelmed, actually."

"Can your dolphin project wait a few days, Jules? Unfortunately, I had to give up the jewel to get to you, and the lives of the Kayapó depend on it."

"Rick, I'm with you! The dolphins can wait."

"Where do you need to go, Mary?"

"I think I need to recharge my batteries after this," she said with a shaky laugh. "I can get a flight back home to Denver out of Tabatinga and stay with my family awhile."

Rick dropped off Possum and Leo at the Hotel Takana, while Jules and Mary stayed in the truck bound for the Tabatinga Airport.

"Possum, book us three rooms and decided who bunks with who," said Rick. "And let Gary know where we are. He'll probably be released from the hospital soon."

"You got it, amigo."

Rick sped toward the airport. His adrenaline was still flowing. Once they arrived, he parked the truck in long-term parking and put the key under the mat. The stolen truck was way too hot to be driving around anymore. They all walked to the main terminal, and Mary thanked Rick repeatedly for saving them. After she checked in, they all hugged and said their goodbyes before Mary disappeared into the security line.

"Let's see if we can get a ride back to the hotel and regroup," said Rick to Jules. "I don't wanna stay in this town any longer than we have to."

"Me neither."

Once on the curb, Rick flagged down a taxi and they climbed in.

"Hotel Takana," he said.

When they reached the hotel, Rick made his way to the front desk and was greeted by the hotel clerk.

"How may I help you?"

"Oh good, you speak English."

"Yessir. Are you checking in?"

"Yeah, I should have a room under the name Rick Waters."

The man typed on his computer keyboard, then handed Rick two keys and an envelope with the Wi-Fi passcode on it.

"You're in room 212 upstairs. Your room comes with a minibar refrigerator, shower, and a king bed. If you need anything, don't hesitate to call. My name is Francisco. Oh, and there's a free breakfast in the morning until ten."

"Well, thank you, Francisco. We'll probably be checking out tomorrow, but if we need to stay another night or so, will that be a problem?" asked Rick.

"No, it's very slow right now. I have plenty of rooms available. Just let me know before eleven and I can keep you and your friends all in the same rooms, just rescan the keys."

"Sounds good, my man. Have a great day."

"Thank you." The man nodded to Jules and said, "Obrigado," apparently assuming she was Brazilian. She just nodded back and smiled.

Rick opened the door of their room for Jules, and she set her backpack down on the edge of the bed, unzipped it, and pulled out a hairbrush with a heavy sigh.

"Boy, do I need a shower," said Jules. "And I've been wearing the same clothes for days. Rick, I need something fresh."

Rick unzipped his backpack and pulled out his MacBook. Once logged on, he did a Google search for nearby department stores. Los Americanos popped up; it was only a few miles away.

"Okay, Jules. Let's go shopping."

Jules brushed her hair and did a quick washdown in the bathroom sink, then put her hair in a ponytail. She walked back to the bed and put her brush back inside. Rick noticed the edge of a large book in her backpack.

"Whatcha reading, Jules?"

"Oh, I'm not really reading it. Evan and the guys were studying it before they locked us in the hangar. He accidentally left it sitting on the wheel of the Cessna, so I swiped it, hoping you could use it. It's a treasure book. Here, take a look."

Jules handed Rick the book titled, *Orinoco, The Jewel of God.*

"They had this book with them?"

"Yeah, I overheard Evan saying that the map used to be folded inside the book. I think he was talking about the map I got from the dying man. The same map you used to find the jewel."

Rick opened the book and shook it with the pages facing the floor. A small piece of paper slowly drifted to the floor. He bent over and picked it up. It was a receipt and badly faded, so he walked into the bathroom, the brightest place in the room, and pulled out a pair of readers and his LED flashlight. As he read the receipt, his knees got weak and he almost went down. Jules rushed over and grabbed Rick's arm to steady him.

"Are you okay? What's wrong?"

"I—I…"

Rick could barely speak and his face was white, as if he had just seen a ghost.

"I think you found a book that was stolen from Possum's wife a few years back. Look at this."

Rick handed her the receipt and she read it aloud.

"Thanks for your purchase on eBay. Please leave a good review for me. Don's Books."

At the bottom of the receipt were the last four numbers of a credit card, and a name.

"Jennifer Jackson?"

"Yes, that's the name of Possum's deceased wife. She told him she had ordered him a book on eBay but never got to show it to him. She was murdered, but the case went cold. The only thing taken from her was a book about a sacred jewel. I think this is the book...which means Evan, or someone working for him, murdered Possum's wife."

Jules covered her mouth with her hand in shock. "Ay, Dios mío! You have to tell Possum."

"I know, Jules, I know." He swallowed hard. "This may be the hardest thing I've ever done."

Rick walked over to the hotel house phone.

"Can you connect me to Mike Jackson's room, please?"

"Hold please."

The phone began to ring, and Rick sat down on the edge of the bed.

"Hello, Possum here."

"Hey, Possum. It's Rick. What's your room number?"

"I'm in 218. What's up?"

"Can you come over to my room? It's number 212. And bring a few whiskeys with you from the minibar."

"Okay, amigo. You drink all yours already?" asked Possum with a chuckle.

"No, they're for you."

The laughter faded from Possum's voice. "Sounds serious."

"It is, Possum. It is."

CHAPTER THIRTEEN

Possum's usual knock—two raps followed by three more—on the door announced his arrival. Jules opened the door for him. He had three small airplane-sized whiskey bottles in one hand and a glass of ice in the other.

"Sit down, buddy. I have to show you something."

Rick pulled up two chairs by the desk, and poured both himself and Jules whiskeys as Possum did the same. He clinked his glass with Possum's, but it wasn't a usual *ha-ha clink-clink* this time.

"Possum, we've been through a lot together over the years, and what I'm about to show you may be very painful."

Possum frowned and took a sip of his drink. Rick pulled open the drawer on the desk, revealing the book. Possum looked down at it. It didn't register at first. Rick pulled out the receipt he had stuck between a couple of pages and showed it to Possum. He passed Possum his readers and flashlight. Possum focused on the receipt and then dropped the flashlight in shock.

"Where did you get this?"

"Jules snatched it from the hangar when Evan and his crew must've left to track us to that cave. I think they tracked us for a couple of miles. They must've known the general area, because that's where they hid the jewel, but with all the clear cutting and rain, without the map that we had, they never would've found it. They just needed us to find it for them."

"Are you saying Evan owned this book?"

Jules interrupted. "Yes, Possum. I saw Evan pull this book out of his personal briefcase. He was in charge and it was his book. When they left, he accidentally left it behind sitting on the wheel of a Cessna in the hangar. I grabbed it and hid it in case they came back. When you saved us, I grabbed my backpack with the book in it I had hidden inside a couple of piled up tires. I had no idea it once belonged to your wife. I didn't even know her name was Jennifer until Rick told me what happened. I'm so sorry."

Jules reached over and cupped her hand over Possum's to comfort him.

Tears were welling up in Possum's eyes, and his look went from sadness to anger.

"I'm gonna kill that fucker myself, Rick. I'm going with you."

"Look, Possum, you're not a murderer. And I mean, we don't even know for sure if he did it or if he just bought this book on the black market from the perp who did do it."

"We need to find out. Let's get the jewel back to the Yanomami and save the Kayapó. Once we have it back, I'll deal with Evan personally. I have to know the truth." He clenched his hands into fists, setting his jaw hard. "I have to avenge Jen's death. She was my everything."

"I know, buddy," said Rick, barely able to get the words out. "I'll let you decide Evan's fate if he was indeed the killer. I won't stand in your way. That I promise."

They all sipped their whiskeys and reminisced about Jennifer. She and Possum had met in high school and were inseparable until her untimely death. It was a tragedy, and Rick was afraid at the time that he'd lose Possum too. He eventually recovered from the trauma and loss, and had put it behind him until today. Now his old feelings and fears had popped right back up. Rick could see the grief and anger in his friend's eyes. He would find out who had killed his wife, one way or another, and torture was not out of the question.

After a few more whiskeys, Possum went back to his room. Jules gave him the book to keep. It was meant to be his, after all.

"You okay, Rick?" asked Jules as she put her hand over his.

"Yep, that was tough, but he took it better than I thought." He sighed. "Let's go get you some clothes."

They strolled hand in hand out of the hotel. A couple of cabs were parked in the front, and Rick waved one over.

"Los Americanos, please."

The smiling cabby nodded and started the meter. It was a short ride to the department store. Jules picked out a few shorts and blouses, some sexy evening wear, and a few pairs of socks and undergarments. Rick paid with his credit card, and they headed back to the hotel.

Jules hopped in the shower first thing. She was in there for over an hour. It had been days since she was trapped inside that sweltering hangar. Rick went in after her and showered fairly quickly. It was late now, and Rick figured Jules would be hungry. He threw on a pair of shorts and walked out of the bathroom shirtless. Jules was in bed and gave Rick a sexy wink and waved him over with one finger. Rick was right; she was hungry—for him.

They made love in the cozy bed and held each other for a long time after.

"Rick, I'm so sorry I took the job down here. Not sorry about the job but sorry I had to leave you so fast when I took it. They really gave me no choice and I had been trying to get this grant for a long time. I hope I didn't upset you," said Jules.

"Jules, I'd never stand in the way of anyone following their dream. I knew I was gonna miss you, but I also knew from your letter how important it was to you. We had such a strong connection that I felt even after three years apart, we'd be back together. Besides, before I got your letter about your roommate being kidnapped, I was planning on making a trip down here and surprising you. Even though it didn't work out quite that way, at least we're together now. You wanna get some dinner?" he finally asked.

"Yes, what are you in the mood for?" asked Jules.

"Fish!"

Rick opened his laptop and did a search for restaurants. He didn't have a lot of luck, so he decided to call the front desk.

"Hey, my man. My girl and I are hungry and were thinking about fish. Can you suggest a restaurant?"

After a short pause, the man replied, "Yes, there is a place just over the Colombian border called Tierras Amazonicas. They specialize in local fresh fish. It's not a real long ride and crossing the border is very simple and quick. Just bring your passports. Shall I call you a taxi?"

"Sure, make it about thirty minutes from now. Get a large SUV if you can. My crew will probably be hungry as well."

"No problem. Hold, please. I have a note for you, Mr. Waters. Shall I bring it up?"

"Naw, just read it to me."

"Rick, I am back and I'm in room 216 with Leo. Come by the room when you get a second. Gary."

"Okay thanks, Francisco. I'll call you back shortly with the number of people going to the restaurant. Give me a couple minutes."

"No problem. I'll be waiting."

Rick hung up. "Jules, I need to pop over to Gary's room. Do you wanna come or stay here?"

"I'm gonna stay and put my face on, okay?"

He bent over and kissed her forehead. "Baby, you don't need any makeup, but go ahead. I'll just be a couple minutes."

He walked down the hall and knocked on Gary's door.

"Come on in. It's open."

When Rick walked inside, Gary said, "Hey, Rick. I'm back."

"I can see that. So, what's the verdict?"

Gary patted his leg. "They X-rayed it, wrapped it up, and gave me some sweet pain meds. The doctors said it's not broken. Surprise, surprise. You whacked it hard enough for it to look bad, but I ain't really hurt. It got us out of there, anyway. That little incident probably cost the military twenty K or more."

"Yikes," replied Rick.

"It's cool, I kinda see it as a real-life training mission for them boys. Hell, they probably spend more than that in a day just spotting coca fields over in Colombia. I mean, we're in cocaine heaven down here."

"Speaking of Colombia, Jules and I are going to a great fish restaurant over in Leticia. Do y'all wanna join us? I can ask Possum too."

"No, man. To be honest, I'm pretty whooped. I just spoke to Possum and we're gonna get together and order a pizza and play some cards. He told me about the book. He's pretty down and needs the company. I was just about to call you and see if you wanted pizza too."

"Okay, I think Jules is pretty excited to go to this place, so maybe I'll catch y'all when we get back and you can deal me in a few hands."

"Sounds good, buddy. Y'all be safe going over there. Leticia is a busy little place."

"No worries, man. I'll holler at ya when we get back."

Jules was slipping on a pair of sandals that perfectly matched the little black dress she had put on when Rick stepped back into the room. She looked stunning as usual.

"You ready, baby?"

"Yep, who's all going?"

"Just me and you, babe. A date night, sort of." He smiled. She smiled back. "I love it."

Rick made arrangements with Francisco, and soon a regular taxi was waiting for them outside. He opened the taxi door for Jules and she sat down, never letting go of his hand.

"You are eating at Tierras Amazonicas tonight, no?" asked the driver.

"Yes, that is correct."

"I can take you there and wait, so you come back in my car. Okay for you?"

"That will be fine. How much?"

"Thirty-five US dollars or 185 real."

"I tell you what, here's one hundred reals and I'll give you another one hundred when we return. A little tip for ya."

"Obrigado, senhor, I mean, tank you, mister."

"Call me Rick."

"Okay. I am Carlos."

"Nice to meet you, Carlos. This is Juliana."

"Olá, Miss Juliana."

"Olá."

Carlos put the car in drive and headed out to the potholed streets bound for Leticia, Colombia. It was only about a thirty-minute ride and immigration was a joke. They didn't even stamp their passports. The two cities were side by side, so commerce was constantly going back and forth. Once in front of the restaurant, Carlos quickly jumped out and opened the door for them.

Rick stepped out and helped Jules out.

"Coma," said Carlos.

"Obrigada," replied Jules.

As they approached the restaurant Rick asked, "What did he say?"

"He basically said, eat up, same as 'mangia, mangia' in Italian."

"I'm glad you speak a little Portuguese, Jules."

She shrugged. "You can't help but pick up words down here. I just know the basics, like obrigada for women and obrigado for men, which both mean thank you. Also, cerveja and banheiro," she said with a laugh.

"Let me guess, beer and bathroom?"

"Wow, you speak Portuguese, Rick?" She raised an eyebrow at him.

"Ha-ha, no, but those sounded similar to Spanish."

"Yes, some words are very similar but some are way, way different."

They were greeted by a nice older woman who sat them at a hand-carved wooden table under a fishing net adorned with many colorful fiberglass fish. The place was cute and welcoming.

"Qué les gustaría tomar?"

"Do you speak English?" asked Rick.

She shook her head.

"No, no habla ingles," she replied.

"It's okay, Rick," said Jules. "I'm Colombian, remember?"

"Oh yeah, duh! What was I thinking?" said Rick.

"My hometown, Ciénaga, is pretty much due north of here at the top of the country. Colombia is a fairly large country and Leticia is at the bottom. It's about a four-hour flight. Maybe when this is all over, we can visit there."

"That would be nice, Jules."

"What would you like to drink, Rick?"

"Um, I guess a local beer. And ask her what the best, freshest fish is tonight."

"Me gustaría una Costeña y un aguardiente. Cuál es el pescado fresco de hoy?"

"El pescado del dia es muy popular," the waitress replied.

"What did she say?"

"I ordered you a Costeña beer and an aguardiente on ice for me. She said the fish of the day is the most popular, but I didn't get the name. I'm sure it will be delicious."

"Sounds good, Jules. I'll trust your judgment."

They sipped their drinks, and about fifteen minutes later, the woman returned with two large plates. The look on Rick's face was priceless. Jules nearly spit out her drink laughing. She was holding her side from laughing so hard. Sitting atop pureed carrots and potatoes adorned with plantains was a deep-fried piranha, eyes, teeth, and all just staring at Rick, daring him to eat it.

Rick slumped back at his seat and rolled his eyes at Jules. "You've got to be kidding me."

"I kinda had an idea that's what it would be. Believe it or not, they are very tasty. Don't be a scaredy cat, Rick Waters!"

"Okay, okay, I'll try anything once. If I don't like it, I'm ordering something else. With my luck, I'll probably get some kind of steamed capybara or baked wooly monkey."

Jules continued to laugh and try to get her drink down. She raised her two fingers to the waitress for another round. Rick reluctantly dug his fork into the side of the staring fish. The meat looked white and moist. He slowly raised his fork to his mouth as Jules never took her eyes off of him, covering her mouth and trying not to laugh.

He slowly chewed, and a smiled crept across his face.

"Ha! Tastes like white perch! Some people call them crappy. I've caught and cooked them all my life. Who would've known? I approve, Jules. No capybara for me tonight."

They both enjoyed their fish, and Rick asked Jules to order dessert.

"Tienes Torta de Tres Leches?"

"Sí. Uno o dos?"

"Dos, por favor," she told the waitress.

"What did you order?" asked Rick.

"I ordered us two pieces of Triple Milk Cake. You're gonna love it. So moist and sweet."

"Just like you, Jules." He winked at her.

She blushed at Rick's comment.

The cakes were better than Rick could've imagined. They slowly finished dessert and sipped on a couple of coffees.

"You ready to head back, Jules?"

"Yeah, I'm feeling kinda sleepy now. I guess it all caught up with me."

Rick paid the bill, and they strolled back to the car. Their driver, Carlos, was leaning against the front fender smoking a cigarette and drinking an orange soda.

"How was dinner?" asked Carlos.

"It was perfect. That's a great little restaurant," replied Rick.

"Where to now? Back to the hotel?"

"Yeah, I think we're ready."

Jules nearly nodded off on the ride back to the hotel. She rested her head on Rick's shoulder. She had been through a lot in the past few days, and she needed to rest. Rick was still wired from the coffee when they arrived back. He gave Carlos the other hundred reals and threw in an extra twenty. Carlos pulled out a card with his number on it and handed it to Rick.

"Ju call me anytime. I be here for ju," said Carlos.

"Will do."

Rick almost had to carry Jules up to the room.

"Rick, I need to go to sleep," she moaned as she dragged her feet.

"No problem, Jules. Let me tuck you in. I need to check on the boys and see how Possum's doing. I may end up playing a hand or two of poker, if you don't mind."

"That's perfect, Rick. I'll be asleep waiting for you to come back and hold me."

Rick gave her a kiss and pulled a little money out of his go-bag. He walked over to Gary's room, ready to be dealt in and take their money. As he approached the room, he noticed that the door was slightly ajar. Stealthily, he got closer and peeked through.

He could see Possum sitting at the table. Gary's back was to Rick. Leo was with them, the visible side of his face looking rather pale. Possum noticed Rick and slowly moved his hand toward his chin as if he was gonna scratch his face. He held up two fingers and motioned with his eyes to his left, behind the door. Rick knew immediately what that meant. There were two men out of Rick's line of sight holding the crew at gunpoint. Rick quietly went back to his room and grabbed his .38 and returned. Jules was in the bathroom getting ready for bed, and didn't even hear him come in or out.

Crouching down, Rick slowly got his right foot to the edge of the door. He'd have the element of surprise but only one chance. With his revolver in hand, he used his right foot to kick open the door. The men spun around, but Rick had them dead to rights.

"Drop the weapons now! Okay, kick them over. Possum, get the guns."

The two dark-haired men did as they were told. One of them was visibly shaking, as he raised his arms high into the air. He couldn't be older than seventeen. The other one was even younger.

"No shoot, no shoot."

Possum grabbed the guns and unloaded them. They were both old ratty .45s. He could barely even get the slides open; they were so rusty. One of the boys had a wad of cash in his hand but dropped it as Rick waved his pistol toward him.

"Who are you and why are you trying to rob my friends?" shouted Rick.

"Meu amigo que entregou a pizza me disse que tinha muito dinheiro. Eu preciso de dinheiro."

"I got part of that. Leo, could you understand it? My Portuguese is crap."

"He said his friend who delivered the pizza told him we had lots of money and he needs it," said Leo.

"Okay, Possum, order another pizza. Gary, can you tie them up, please?"

Possum used the hotel phone to order a new pizza. Gary tied up the two boys on the couch out of view of the doorway.

About twenty-five minutes later, there was a knock on the door. Possum opened it and waved the kid inside. As soon as he was in, he kicked the door closed and Rick put the gun to the back of his head.

"You speak English?"

"Sim, um pouco. I mean, jes, a little."

Sweat was pouring off of the kid's forehead, and Rick placed the gun lower on his neck.

"You tipped these guys off about the money after you delivered the first pizzas?"

"Jes, I sorry."

"Why?"

He pointed to the younger kid sitting on the couch.

"He mama sick and can't work."

Rick looked over at the kid, whose eyes were wide with fear. "Mama sick?"

The kid nodded.

Rick cocked the .38. "Okay, I'm gonna teach you a lesson, all right?"

The pizza guy's knees were shaking, and he began to plead in Portuguese. "Por favor não me mate, eu nunca vou roubar de novo. Por favor, por favor."

Rick relaxed the hammer of the pistol. "How much money is in the pile, Possum?"

"About $300, I think."

Rick grabbed a paper sack sitting on the table that the beers were in and stuffed all the money into the bag. He handed it to the youngest boy.

"For your mama," said Rick. "Never do this again, compreendo?"

The boy nodded aggressively.

Rick noticed the older boy had peed his pants.

"Gary, go ahead and untie them."

"Are you sure?"

"Yeah, I think they learned their lesson."

"Obrigado, obrigado," repeated all three boys as they made prayer signs with their hands to their chests.

Rick opened the hotel door, and they scurried away into the darkness.

"So, what were you numbskulls thinking, playing cards with all that money on the table in a third-world country without weapons handy, anyway?"

"It's my fault," said Possum, shaking his head. "I guess I let down my guard with Jennifer on my mind."

"That's okay, buddy. Let's call it a night and meet here at eight a.m. to go over the plan for tomorrow."

Gary interrupted. "Rick, I figured we needed to get shaking, so I had the jet delivered to the Tabatinga Airport."

"You are the man! Let's rendezvous here at nine a.m. after breakfast and plan to depart at 10:30-ish?"

"Where are we headed? I'll have the jet fueled and the pilot on standby."

"Rio!"

CHAPTER FOURTEEN

Gina had already deposited one million dollars from the Museum of Natural History into the escrow account she had created after her meeting in Rio with the Yanomami leader. She sat anxiously in the office of the Smithsonian. A woman in a gray pantsuit wearing thick black cat eye frames approached the couch.

"Mr. McArthur will see you now."

Gina followed her to a large door of an office and was escorted to a table and chairs at the end of the room. She was well prepared and had everything she needed to persuade the curator to pay her two million dollars for the sacred gem.

"May I get you a coffee or tea? Mr. McArthur will be right in. He's just signing for some new displays."

"A green tea would be nice, if you have it."

The secretary soon returned with a hot green tea and some cream on a beautiful silver tray.

"Thank you."

"My pleasure."

The woman walked out of the room, closing the large, heavy door behind her. A couple of minutes went by, and a side door to the office opened. A tall man with gray temples and a pinstriped suit stepped into the room.

"I'm Barnaby McArthur. You must be Regina Russo."

"Please, call me Gina."

"Very well, Gina. Let's get down to brass tacks. The museum is incredibly interested in the Sacred Jewel of Orinoco. Did you bring some documentation with you?"

"Yes, of course."

Gina pulled out a blue folder and slid it across the table toward Barnaby. He pulled a pair of readers out of his coat pocket and began to flip through the pages. After a few minutes, he broke the silence again.

In a tone that told her he thought he was being shrewd, he said, "It has come to my attention from a trusted source that the Museum of Natural History has offered you one million dollars for the precious gem."

"Well, I hate to disappoint you, but your trusted source is mistaken. They offered me $1.75 million."

She pulled out her iPhone and slid it across the table. While she was at the hotel, she had made a mockup offer and transposed Jason Hillcrest's signature on the document. At the bottom it read: *$1.75 million, Final offer.*

"I see," replied Barnaby, looking pensive. "Can you wait here a few minutes? I need to make a call."

"No problem. My flight to New York is at three, so I'm good on time for now. I wanna get this wrapped up today."

Barnaby left the office through the side door and returned about ten minutes later.

"I have spoken with my people, and we are willing to pay you two million dollars if you will sign a contract that the jewel is ours. Where is it now?"

"It's in a safe in Rio. I can have it delivered by special envoy in ten to twelve days."

Barnaby leaned back in his chair in deep reflection, then slid the documents over for Gina to sign. He then pushed a button on an intercom in the middle of the table.

"Candace, come in here, please, and bring your notary stamp."

A few minutes later, the same woman who'd escorted Gina before stepped in.

"Whom shall we make the check out to?" asked Barnaby.

"Regina Russo, as it shows in the documents. I have power of attorney for Davi Kopenawa, the leader of the Yanomami. The trust account in Rio is in my name, and I will transfer the funds to the Yanomami as soon as the check clears."

Barnaby wrote her name on the check, stuck it in an envelope, and slid it to her. She gave him the documents as soon as Candace put her stamp on it.

They all stood up, and Gina shook both their hands and sauntered out of the office, trying not to show any emotions as she left the building. All she wanted to do was scream from the rooftops, but she maintained calm until she rounded the corner of the building. She clenched her fingers and did a huge fist pump. She had done it. The Yanomami would now have two million dollars to fight the building of the dam. She would have to return the one million to the New York museum, but that could wait a few days.

She headed for the airport, bound for Rio. It was time to call Gary.

Rick and Jules met the rest of the crew in the breakfast dining area. They all sat at a large rectangular table. Gary sipped coffee as he waited for his bagel to toast, and both Leo and Possum were chowing on a bowl of fresh fruit.

"Whatcha want for breakfast, babe?" Rick asked Jules.

"I think I'll have some oatmeal and a banana. You?"

"I'm gonna try one of those fruit bowls. It looks super fresh."

They didn't speak much as they ate breakfast, simply enjoying their food. Rick glanced down at his watch. It was 8:57.

"Shall we?"

They all put away their plates, grabbed to-go cups of coffee, and followed Rick upstairs to Gary's room. Once inside, they pulled the table closer to the couch so they'd all have a seat.

"Okay, the way I see it is, they have to fence the gem on the black market. It's far too hot to sell in the usual circles. Have you heard from Gina?" asked Rick.

Gary pulled out the sat phone.

"Crap, I forgot to charge it. It's dead."

He plugged it in and it pinged. New message.

Gary put it on speaker.

"Hi, Gary, it's Gina. I've managed to secure two million dollars from the Smithsonian. Please tell me you have the jewel. I'm boarding a flight to Rio. Can

*we rendezvous there? I have a room at the Emiliano
Rio. They have rooms available if you wanna book a
couple. I arrive at 8:15 p.m. Thursday. Call me back."*

"Where do you think they will sell it in Rio?" asked Rick.

"There are two main fences there. It's doubtful that they
will try and leave the country with it. I think we should split
up and case both buildings and wait for them to make their
move," replied Gary.

"That's a genius idea, Gary. Possum, myself, and Jules
will take one, and you, Leo, and Gina can canvass the other.
Sound good?"

"Yes, and I have two more sat phones on the plane. We
should get going."

They all went back to their rooms to pack as Gary called
the Emiliano Rio and booked three more rooms for four
nights to be safe.

The ride to the airport took no time, and the driver brought
them to the executive side of the airport, where all the
private jets sat on the tarmac. They had their own customs
and immigration, and it was quite plush for a third-world
country. As they walked toward the plane, the jetway stairs
slowly lowered to the ground, and out stepped Johnie with
Chief on his shoulder.

"Chief!" yelled Rick.

Chief flapped his wings and lifted off of Johnie's shoulders a bit, then back down softly.

Rick jogged up, shook Johnie's hand, and pulled Chief
to his chest.

"I've missed you, boy! We've gotta get you trimmed. You're almost fully flighted. I don't want you flying off."

Chief nuzzled Rick's whiskers as if he hadn't seen him in forever.

They all climbed into the Gulfstream, and the pilot did his usual spiel as they fastened their seatbelts and then taxied for takeoff. The takeoff was smooth as silk.

Rick and Jules were in the two seats at the table across from Possum; and Gary, Leo and Johnie all took the single solo window seats. Rick gave Jules the window on the two-seat side, but everyone had a nice view. Within minutes, the city disappeared and all they could see was vast rainforest as far as the horizon.

Rick thought about the forest and how important it was to the human race. The Amazon produced 54 percent of the earth's oxygen and held secrets to curing many diseases. If they could do their part to help the Yanomami and Kayapó stop the dam and deforestation—and prevent the Kayapó from being massacred—they at least had to try.

"Ladies and gentlemen, we are approaching Rio. Please look out the left side of the plane, and you will see the most famous statue in Brazil. Christ the Redeemer, a colossal statue of Jesus Christ at the summit of Mount Corcovado," said the pilot over the P.A. system.

Jules was glued to the window but moved over so Rick could see.

"Breathtaking," said Rick.

"Yes, it is. It seems surreal," she replied.

The plane touched down at a quarter to five with the time change. Gary had arranged for an airport transfer to the Emiliano Rio hotel. Gary tipped the immigration guy handsomely, and he let Chief come right through in his travel cage.

A huge black Sprinter van sat curbside, and they all climbed in for the thirty-minute trip to the resort. They were all pretty hungry and decided to try the hotel restaurant after they checked in. They pulled two tables together at the Restaurante Emiliano.

"Y'all get whatever you want; I'm charging it to the room. We all need a good meal," said Gary.

The menu was extensive. Gary started by ordering a couple of plates of ceviche for everyone to share and two bottles of champagne. Johnie talked the waiter into bringing Chief a small plate of fresh red grapes. The waiter didn't look too thrilled to have a bird in the restaurant, but once Johnie stuck a folded up hundred-dollar bill into his pocket, he suddenly didn't seem to mind at all. Rick grinned at Johnie, letting him know how proud he was of him being dad number two to Chief.

Possum ordered an appetizer of ostras frescas de Santa Catarina. Rick had no idea what that was until he saw it. It was fresh oysters with spicy peanut sauce. Possum put one on a plate for Rick to try, and he immediately ordered two more for the table. Rick decided to get the vieiras com farinha-d'agua, aka scallops, as his main course, while Jules was so full from all the appetizers that she just ordered a bowl of lobster bisque. Once they were all stuffed from the delicious meal, they headed up to their rooms.

"Gina should be here around nine," said Gary as they all got on the elevator. "How about we meet at 9:45 in my room? I booked the Cube Suite and canceled Gina's room. She's bunking with me, if you catch my drift. It has a 180-

degree view of the city and a heated pool in the living room. Sure beats the Motel 6 from years ago." He chuckled.

Gary gave everyone a sat phone, so they could keep in touch easier. Possum and Johnie were rooming together, and Leo had his own room.

It didn't take long for Rick and Jules to try out their bed. They put Chief on the balcony and let him soak up the remaining sun. A little while later, they joined him to watch the sunset as Rick opened a bottle of wine that came with the room. The accommodations were so beautiful and plush, and Jules looked so beautiful beside him, that he had a hard time remembering they were on a case.

At 9:15, Rick's sat phone pinged with a text message to meet at Gary's room in thirty minutes. Gina had arrived and would brief them all on her trip to the States. Rick put Chief in the travel cage so he wouldn't get into any mischief, and he and Jules headed to Gary's room on the top floor of the building.

"Welcome to my humble abode," said Gary as he opened the massive door to the suite.

Gina had changed into a t-shirt and shorts, and Gary was in quick-dry shorts. His hair was a little damp; it was obvious he had tried out the pool in the living room. They all gathered on the huge sectional couch as Gary poured everyone a glass of red wine.

"Welcome back, Gina," said Rick.

"It's good to be back." She smiled at everyone. "I'll get right to the point. As you all know from my message, I have secured two million dollars for the Yanomami tribe to fight the building of the dam. I only have nine days left to deliver the jewel to the Smithsonian. Please tell me you have it."

"Well, we did—" started Rick.

Possum interrupted. "But that fucking murderer Evan and his gang took it from us and left us to die in a cave."

Gina's eyes widened. Rick quickly filled her in about Possum's wife being possibly murdered by Evan or one of his associates. She put a hand over her mouth as she listened.

"I'm so sorry, Possum. How do we get it back?"

"We steal it back!" interjected Gary.

He passed a slip of paper with an address to Rick and one to Gina.

"These are the two largest fences in Rio. We need to get eyes on them ASAP. We'll have to work in shifts. Every team will have a sat phone. We each can do four-hour shifts, if that works for y'all. We have to watch these places twenty-four-seven starting tomorrow. There's no chatter on the dark web about the jewel being sold yet, so they've probably just made contact. I'll take the first shift in the morning at six. Rick, you and your team can decide what shifts to take."

"That's fine, but Jules and I will take the same shift. It's far too dangerous on the streets of Rio for a woman alone. Also, Evan's crew already knows what we look like, so we'll have to wear disguises," replied Rick.

"Way ahead of you," said Gary.

He pulled a huge box toward the table and opened it up. He tossed Rick a large sombrero and a bag full of oversized mustaches. Then he handed Jules a platinum-blonde wig and some oversized Dolce & Gabbana red clear lens glasses.

"Okay, y'all, dig in and pick out your characters." He winked at them.

"Where'd you get all this stuff?" asked Rick.

"Amazon. They now have same-day delivery in several large Brazilian cities. I ordered all these outfits while we were on the flight. It's too much fun to shop when you have nearly unlimited resources. I spent almost $5,000 on this order, but I don't even care. I made $300,000 yesterday on Dogecoin," said Gary with a laugh.

Rick raised an eyebrow. "That's that cryptocurrency, right? I've heard of it, but I don't know much about it."

Gary showed him a photo of the cute dog on the Dogecoin. "The best thing about cryptocurrency is that it's unregulated and untraceable. It's an incredible way, at least so far, to launder money. The government will eventually put a stop to it, I'm sure. They fuck up everything."

"So, who created Dogecoin? I'm still a little fuzzy on the whole thing. Where does it come from?" asked Rick.

"Doge was originally created as a joke by two software engineers named Billy Markus and Jackson Palmer. It gained huge popularity when Elon Musk started tweeting about it. It now has a market cap of eighty-five billion."

"So, those two guys were just goofing around and created a digital currency?"

"That's right, Rick. Anyone can create one."

Rick snorted. "We should create one called Chiefcoin."

"Why not? He's a cute bird; it might just take off. Get it—take off, as in fly?"

"That's crazy," said Rick.

Gary shrugged. "That's what they said about Dogecoin too, but now it's considered the people's coin. You never know."

Gina cleared her throat. "Can we get back to discussing the plan?" she asked.

"Right," said Rick. "How far away are these buildings where Evan might fence the gem?"

"We got lucky there. Only a couple blocks inland. The address of the one I gave you, Rick, is close to the Bank of Brazil on Rua Raul Pompéia, right next to Mama Rosa Pizza and Sapateiro Pompéia, a luggage shop. The only door leading up the stairs is directly in between them. The one I'll be casing is right beside Apetit Café, on Avenida Rainha Elisabeth. They are literally only three blocks apart and a couple of blocks from the hotel."

"Is there any chance Evan would go there tonight?" asked Rick.

Gary twisted his mouth. "I know for a fact they can't get into my building. It doesn't even open until nine. It's a shared tenement. Yours is possible but doubtful. They don't really keep normal hours, but even locals don't like to be on the streets at three a.m. The city has a bad criminal element. Drugs are everywhere."

Rick thought for a minute as he scratched his chin.

"I'm gonna case my building tonight. If there's even a tiny chance they will fence the gem tonight, I wanna be there. It's 10:15 now. I can be there by 10:45, I think."

He put on the ratty-looking pants and homeless man shirt and mustache.

"Are you sure you wanna do this tonight? Rio can be very dangerous at night," repeated Gary.

"I'm totally sure. Jules, I can't let you go, but you can join me at sun-up if you wish."

"Rick, it sounds dangerous," she said, frowning. "Maybe you should wait like Gary says."

"I can't, Jules. I'm too afraid we'll miss the swap. Besides, I'll have my revolver with me." He leaned closer to her and kissed her on the cheek. She didn't look any less worried, though.

"You'll also have me with you! I got your six, bro," said Possum, slapping Rick's shoulder.

"You don't have to, Possum."

"Yes, I do, and you know it!"

"Okay then, it's settled," said Rick. "Johnie can join Gary and Leo's team, since Possum is now on my crew. Y'all figure out the shifts."

Possum grabbed a pair of stained overalls, a ripped-up shirt, a faux leather top hat, and an '80s curly black rocker wig. He looked good as a homeless Slash. Inside his back waistband, he tucked a .45, and he slipped a bowie knife into his long sock under his left pants leg. He then tore off a large piece of the cardboard box, Googled the translation, and wrote something in Portuguese on it in permanent marker. *Sem-teto preciso trabalho*, which meant: *Homeless, need work*.

"Nice touch, Possum," said Rick.

Rick put his .38 in a shoulder holster and wrapped a camo shirt over his wifebeater undershirt. They looked like death warmed over.

Rick kissed Jules goodnight and walked her to their room.

"Be safe," she told him.

"I will."

Outside, he caught up to Possum on the street and stayed near him, but they didn't walk together. The phones Gary had given them were the latest technology. They were made by Iridium and had walkie-talkie push-to-talk features. Each came with Bluetooth earbuds, and Rick and Possum could communicate easily without being noticed. All they had to do was push one button on the phone in their pockets and speak. To anyone else, it would just look like they were homeless people with schizophrenia talking to themselves.

"You read me, Rick?"

"Yeah, Slash. I'm ten yards behind you. Look over your left shoulder."

Possum bent down and picked up an empty fountain drink cup, pretending to drink from it, and glanced back at Rick. Then he continued up the street until he came to the building. He found a cubby hole to sit down on. He unfolded the sign he'd made and set the empty cup in front of him.

Rick walked past him on the opposite side of the street, almost to the corner. He posted up under a streetlight and slowly did a 360-degree turn to take in the area. A few more homeless people were loitering around, and a couple of punks were dealing drugs in the park.

He settled in for what he expected would be a long night.

Several hours passed by, and Rick and Possum checked in with each other every fifteen minutes. It was almost 4:30 a.m. when Rick heard, "Rick, help!"

Rick bolted down the street on the opposite side of Possum. When he got closer, all he could see were three dark figures kicking at the cubby hole.

Possum!

Rick ran between two cars and was on them before they knew what hit them. He swept the legs of the biggest one out from under him, and he fell to the concrete with a loud *thud*. He dropped the bat he was holding, and Rick quickly snatched it and slammed it sideways into the man's ribs.

The shorter one pulled out a butterfly knife, but before he could even lock it, Rick swung the bat and shattered his hand, knocking the knife to the street. Holding the end of the bat, he slammed it directly into the man's nose. Blood exploded from his face.

The last guy standing was fumbling in his pocket for something. Before he could pull it out, Rick swung like Babe Ruth and caught the guy in the kidneys. He fell to the ground, holding his back and trying to get away. Rick moved toward him and kicked him several times in the side.

"You like beating up homeless people? You piece of shit."

Rick then remembered they couldn't understand him and yelled one of the only Portuguese words he knew. "Fujam! Fujam!" It basically meant *run away*.

The man rolled under a car to escape Rick's wrath, and then scurried down the street to catch up to the other two.

"Possum, are you okay?"

Holding his side and out of breath, Possum said, "Thank God you were here. They came out of nowhere." He let out a hard exhale, shook his head, and smiled up at Rick.

Possum was missing two teeth.

"Well, your homeless look just improved." Rick bent down and spotted the teeth, picked them up, and handed them to Possum.

"Shit! I guess I need a dentist."

Rick called Gary. "Gary, send a car to the Bank of Brazil. Some punks kicked Possum's ass, and he needs a dentist stat."

"Damn, okay, man. I'll have one there ASAP."

Rick walked with Possum across the street to the Bank of Brazil. He could still clearly see the building where Evan might try to fence the jewel. Within fifteen minutes, a black sedan rolled up. The man driving spoke perfect English.

"Are you Rick and Possum?"

"That's us."

"Hop in, Possum. I'm taking you to the best dentist in Rio."

"See ya soon, Rick. Be careful here alone."

"Okay, Slash. Good luck with your teeth."

Possum smiled, showing the gap again. They both laughed a little as the car sped off.

CHAPTER FIFTEEN

Rick paced the street as the sun began to rise. The same black sedan pulled up near the bank, and a man stepped out of the car and started walking toward Rick. He covered his mouth as if he was coughing. It was Johnie.

"Rick, I'm relieving you. Go back to your room. Possum and Jules are waiting for you. I'll be here until three. Get some rest."

Rick walked past Johnie as if he didn't know him. Johnie wasn't in costume, and just looked like a regular tourist. There was no need for him to be in disguise, as Evan had no idea what he looked like or who he even was.

Once back at the hotel, Jules met Rick in the lobby.

"Oh, baby, I'm glad you're back," she said, throwing her arms around his neck. "Possum really took a beating. He wants to talk to you."

Rick hugged Jules back and followed her to the elevator. She led him to Possum's room. He was sitting upright in bed with some ice bags and towels wrapped around his ribs.

"How you feeling, Possum?"

"I've been better. They couldn't save my teeth, but I got these for now until I get back to Houston." Possum smiled wide to show Rick. Both of his front teeth were gold.

Rick chuckled. "Man, with that grille, all you need is a couple of face tats and we can start calling you Lil Wayne."

"Oh, oh, don't make me laugh," said Possum, holding his side. "The dentist's office was in a medical building and he took me in to see a primary doctor after I got my gold implants. Luckily, there are no broken bones, just some bruised ribs. I'll live."

"Well, I'm glad you're okay," said Rick.

"Yeah, but I guess I'll be out of commission for a few days, until I can breathe again without wincing."

"Those punks sure kicked the shit out of you. Did they say anything?"

"One of them motioned for a cigarette and said something in Portuguese, and when I waved to tell them no, they just started wailing on me. I was backed into that cubby hole and sitting cross-legged. I didn't have a chance in hell to defend myself. I'm sure glad you came when you did. I really think they would've beat me to death if you hadn't."

"I bet they'll think twice about beating up a homeless guy again. Anyway, don't worry; between Gary, myself, and the rest of the crew, we'll cover your watch. We're gonna catch these mofos."

"I just wanna be there. I need to find out the truth about Jennifer."

"Once I get the jewel back, I will personally deliver Evan to you so you can interrogate him. You have my word. Now, just rest up and try to heal. I'll ask Gary if he knows any acupuncturists. They can really help speed things up."

"Thanks, Rick. I wish we had the shaman here who pulled your ass back from the dead after that centipede bite."

"Yeah, I don't think that's possible, unfortunately. I've gotta get a few hours' sleep and then get back to watch. They could show at any time."

"Okay, man. Go get some shut-eye."

Rick and Jules went back to their room, and Rick showered before collapsing onto the bed. He was sound asleep in minutes.

Jules sat by Rick's side and chewed on her lower lip as she watched him sleeping peacefully. She had slept most of the night while he was on watch, and wasn't tired anymore. Her heart beat fast as she made a decision.

The sat phone Gary gave Rick was sitting beside him on the nightstand. As quietly as a mouse, she picked it up and walked into the bathroom.

"Gary, come in. It's Jules. I want to relieve Johnie in three hours. Rick said it's okay."

"All right. Since it's daytime, it should be okay. But please use your disguise. If Evan's gonna recognize anyone, it'll be you."

"No problem, Gary. I'll bring Rick's sat phone and his .38 as well. He won't need it in the hotel."

She slowly tiptoed back to the bed, picked up Rick's iPhone, and turned off the alarm. She knew he'd be mad at her for going out on her own, but he had only set it for two hours and he needed much more sleep. He was stubborn, but so was she and she wanted to take care of him. She put the Bluetooth earbud in her left ear and listened to Gary and Johnie checking in with each other. It was slow and they hadn't yet seen any sign of Evan or his crew.

A few hours passed and she was ready to go. Rick was still in dreamland. She left a note for him in case he woke up. She didn't wanna freak him out and hated to lie to him, but she was doing this to help him. To help them all.

Rick,

I stepped out to grab some lunch downstairs. I'll be back shortly. I have your sat phone and iPhone. I'll wake you when the alarm goes off.

xoxo Jules

She put on her wig and outfit and headed outside toward the watch zone. Johnie walked past her and semi-nodded to her. He looked a little surprised Rick would let her be on the street alone like that. It was the middle of the day, though, and there was lots of traffic and business was bustling.

Jules took her spot and waited for the check-in with Gary. A few minutes later, she heard him.

"Jules, are you in position?"

"Yes, I'm here."

"Okay. Leo is relieving me. Check in with him every fifteen minutes. We're all monitoring communication, so if Evan shows we will all know and be there in no time."

"That's a big Texas 10-4."

Jules knew Gary would get a kick out of that, since Rick said it all the time. She watched cars come and go for several hours, and nothing caught her eye. She continued her check-ins with Leo. She just hoped she could get back to the hotel before Rick woke up. He'd be upset with her. They were supposed to be on this watch together, but he really needed his sleep. No doubt he would insist on doing the next overnight watch alone again.

A man approached her speaking Spanish. "Cómo te llamas?"

"Vete de aquí! Go away!"

"Oh, you speak English." He grinned at her. "You are one hot mama. What's your name?"

"I said go away," she snapped. "I'm waiting for my boyfriend. He's in the bank." She was used to getting hit on by strangers. She was tough and knew how to put someone in their place.

The man held up his hands. "Okay, Mama. Okay, I'll go."

She shooed him way with the flick of her wrist.

The man walked away and turned the corner. Jules kept her attention on the door to the stairwell.

A car pulled up. A man stepped out, with his back to her, and approached the door. Just as he was about to buzz himself in, he looked to the left and then to the right.

It was Evan. Her eyes widened.

He opened the door and stepped in. He had no briefcase or backpack with him. He couldn't have the jewel on his person.

"Gary, Leo, come in," Jules hissed into her earpiece. "Evan is here!"

Silence. She said it again and got no response. She pulled the earbud out, checking if it had lost the connection. She pressed the button on the sat phone and saw the screen was black. The phone had died. She'd plugged it in while Rick slept, but it must not have been a good outlet. Then she remembered the outlets against that wall only worked when the wall switch next to the main light switch was on. She had turned the lights off to help Rick sleep better.

Dammit! There's no time.

"What do I do?" she said aloud, thinking fast. If the jewel was in that car, she couldn't let it get away. This might be her only chance to get it back.

The driver of the car Evan had stepped out of was still sitting behind the wheel, next to another man. She dodged a few cars and crossed the street. As the driver looked to his left and the man next to him looked down at something, she quickly opened the back door of the passenger side and slid in, shoving Rick's .38 against the back of the driver's neck.

"Don't move, hijueputa!" she said, slipping into Colombian slang from all the adrenaline.

"I said don't move, you son of a bitch. I will blow your head off!"

The driver slowly raised his hands. She motioned to the other guy to do the same, and when he did, she saw his left hand was handcuffed to a metal briefcase with a long chain.

"Where's the jewel? Is it in the briefcase?" she asked. "You speak Spanish or Portuguese?"

"Portuguese."

She thought for a second, trying to translate Spanish into English into Portuguese. Her mind always thought in

Spanish, but she was quite comfortable with English and spoke it fluently. But not Portuguese.

"Onde está a jóia?"

"Que jóia?"

"The Sacred Jewel of Orinoco!"

The man's eyes widened as if he couldn't believe she'd said that, but he just made a gesture with his hands as if he didn't know. She kept looking back at the door Evan had gone through. He could appear at any time. She was freaking out and didn't know what to do. She could tell by the way the guy was dressed and the business cards on the dash that he was just a hired driver and didn't work for Evan directly. Probably just a family guy trying to make a living. She didn't wanna hurt him, but she had to intimidate him nonetheless.

She jabbed the gun into the neck of the man with the briefcase. The jewel had to be inside it.

"Where are the keys to the case? I mean, onde estão as chaves?"

The man pointed toward the door Evan had opened. Jules didn't know what to do and instinctively shoved the gun harder into the man's neck.

"Go! Guia! Drive! Vámonos, just drive! Ahora!" she yelled, mixing up all her languages.

The man threw the car into drive and peeled out. Jules looked back and saw the door fly open and Evan appear. He fired toward the car, but they were too far out of range for his pistol.

The driver whipped the car around the corner, almost losing control.

"Alto! Stop! Pare!"

She had to get the briefcase open. A super loud DJ was playing salsa music on the beach. They were right next to him. This was her chance. As the car came to a stop in traffic, she motioned to the driver to cover his ears. She pointed the gun at the flat part of the handcuffs attached to the briefcase and pulled the trigger. Her ears were ringing, but the handcuff slipped off of the metal handle of the brief-case.

They were only a block from the hotel. She told the driver to put the car in park, then shoved open her door and stumbled out, the suitcase in hand. She motioned for him to drive away, and went up an alley as they sped off. She ripped off the blonde wig and bright shirt and walked fast toward the hotel, keeping her head down and looking behind her every so often to see if Evan was closing in.

Once in the lobby, she bolted to the elevator and to her room.

CHAPTER SIXTEEN

"Rick, Rick, wake up."

A hand gently nudged Rick awake. His eyes slowly opened and he squinted, not knowing where he was for a second.

"Rick, I got it," said Jules. "I got it!"

"Got what?"

"The sacred jewel. I got it back."

"What? How?"

Rick was confused and thought maybe he was still dreaming. As his vision became clearer, he saw the briefcase.

"How did you..."

"Never mind, do you have a screwdriver?"

Clumsily, he dug through his backpack and pulled out his Leatherman. He was still trying to wake up and make sense of it all.

"Why are you dressed like that?"

"I'll explain. Don't be mad."

Trying to snap out of his grogginess, he pulled the briefcase closer and shoved the flat head into the slit where the two sides of the briefcase came together. With a hard twist, he popped it open. His eyes grew wide when he looked down at the leather pouch. It was starting to make sense. He loosened the drawstrings and pulled out the brilliant blue gem. It was even shinier than when they first saw it. It had been polished a little.

"Jules, how the hell did you get this? Call Gary."

"The sat phone's dead. Oh, let me plug it in."

She flipped the switch on the wall up and plugged in the phone. After about thirty seconds, it lit up.

"Jules, come in. Where are you?" Gary's frantic voice came through the phone's speaker. "I'm gonna walk over there if you don't respond."

"Gary, it's Jules. The sat phone died. I'm in the room with Rick. Please come down."

Minutes later, Gary knocked on the door and rushed in.

"What the hell is going on? Leo said you quit responding to his check-ins. Who's watching the building you were at?"

Rick held up the jewel for Gary to see. His mouth dropped open. Gary immediately got on his sat phone.

"Leo, come back to the hotel. Mission complete." To Jules, Gary said, "How did you get it? I don't know what to say."

"Can we all meet in Possum's room so I can tell the story once?" she said with a shaky laugh, wiping the sweat off her forehead. "I need a drink now. Is Gina here?"

Her hands were still trembling from the adrenaline.

Rick poured her a stiff drink and one for everyone else, and they walked over to Possum's room. Rick tucked the jewel into his front pants pocket, inside the leather pouch. Gina and Leo arrived at nearly the same time, and they all gathered around as Jules told her story, wide-eyed. You could've heard a pin drop in the room.

"I was standing across from the bank keeping my eye on the door," she started. "I had just checked in with Leo about ten minutes prior. A large black car pulled up to the curb next to the door. A man stepped out and I knew it was Evan. I tried to call Leo several times, but the sat phone had died. I knew it might be our only chance, so I snuck across the street and climbed into the back seat of the car. I stuck Rick's gun to the back of his neck."

"You had my gun?!"

"Baby, let me finish. I know you're gonna be mad, but just let me get this out." She told them the rest of the story, and when she finished, she gave Rick a nervous look. "Sorry I took your gun, and left while you were sleeping."

They all just stood there looking dumbfounded, and Possum started a slow clap. They all joined in and soon were cheering. Jules had saved the day. Her nervousness gave way to a beaming smile.

Rick wrapped his arms around her and squeezed her tight, letting her know he wasn't mad. "Just promise me one thing, Jules, and I will let this slide. Promise me you'll never do anything like that again without me!"

She smirked at him. "Okay, I promise to never again rescue a sacred jewel that could save an entire tribe from genocide without you again. Deal?"

"You little smart-ass, come here!"

Rick kissed her and raised his glass. "To Jules! The hero of the day! Hell—of the year!"

"To Jules!" they all said in unison as they clinked their glasses.

CHAPTER SEVENTEEN

Gary escorted Gina and Johnie to the airport for the flight aboard his Gulfstream to Washington, DC. Both checks from the competing museums were fully funded in the escrow account she had set up for the Yanomami. The flight would make a stop in Venezuela for refueling. Johnie had agreed to head back to the boat and resume charters. All that was left to do was present the Sacred Jewel of Orinoco to the Smithsonian and transfer the funds to the Yanomami. A truce had been called and peace was made with the Kayapó.

Jules, Rick, Chief, and Possum stayed back to spend some down time in Rio, and eventually head back to Fonte Boa so Jules could continue her research grant to help the pink dolphins. Gary planned to return with the Gulfstream in a few days and shuttle them to Tefé and then on to Fonte Boa. Rick and Jules just wanted to relax by the pool and catch their breath after all the excitement. At the moment, they were in Possum's room and Chief was on top of his cage flapping his wings like he was trying to put out a fire.

"Chief, you practicing flying?" said Rick. "I don't want you getting lost way down here in South America. You need your wings trimmed!"

Johnie usually took Chief to his favorite vet in Fort Walton for a nail trim and wing clip. He didn't really know how to fly, and he could easily get hurt or fly into a ceiling fan if they weren't careful.

"We're gonna go to the pool," said Rick. "Wanna join us, Possum?"

Possum was still intent on interrogating Evan about his wife's death when he could somehow make it happen. He was sure Evan would make an appearance trying to get the jewel back at some point.

"I'm still a little too sore, amigo," he told Rick. "Maybe I'll stroll down later and try the hot tub. Might do me some good."

"No worries, mate. We'll save a lounge chair for you."

Possum nodded and opened his laptop as Rick and Jules left the room. He had two things to research, and he needed some alone time. First, he was gonna try to order an acupuncturist to the room. He wasn't hurting as bad as he'd let on to Rick, but he was still quite sore.

Secondly, he was gonna try to set a trap for Evan. Possum searched the dark web for any info he could find on Evan Taylor. His plan was to find a quiet location nearby that was super soundproof and lure Evan to the building so he could do a proper investigation into his wife's murder.

"Strawberry, Jules?"

Rick dipped a fresh strawberry in whipped cream and gently put it in Jules's mouth. They had ordered room service to the pool. Two bottles of New Zealand sauvignon blanc and a bowl of strawberries and fresh whipped cream. They were living high on the hog, still celebrating Jules's amazing rescue of the Sacred Jewel of Orinoco. In one fell swoop, she had singlehandedly saved not just the jewel from the black market but also the genocide of an entire Amazonian tribe. Rick couldn't have been prouder of her.

"Wanna get wet, cowboy?" asked Jules, winking at him.

"Yeah, let's check out the water."

Rick stuck his big toe in the pool and the water was perfect. He turned around toward Jules as if he was gonna give her a big hug, and fell backward with his arms stretched outward into the warm clear water. Jules stepped in and swam over to him, wrapping her arms and legs around him.

She had a look of adoration in her eyes that made him grin. For a moment, she looked like she wanted to say something, but she didn't. He wondered if she was considering asking him to stay in Fonte Boa with her. But she must've known it wouldn't be feasible. His charter boat and life were in Destin. If they were meant to be together, time and distance wouldn't matter; somehow, they would make it work.

"Jules, I wish I could read your mind. I'm gonna try. Do you want me to stay in Fonte Boa with you until you finish your grant, or do you want to come to Destin with me?"

She was quiet for a few seconds then said, "After all I've been through here, I think I need a little break. I do still want to finish my work with dolphins, but I need time to equalize from the trauma. I also want to be with you. I guess I need some time to think about it. Let's just enjoy the moment for now."

Rick nodded in agreement, knowing she had a lot to process.

"More wine, Mr. Waters?" asked the pool attendant in perfect English.

"No, my man. Day drinking and the sun are giving me a headache. Can we get a couple bottles of water?"

"Still or sparkling?"

Rick grabbed his cowboy hat and threw it on his head. "Take a wild guess."

"Still it is, sir."

The attendant brought out two tall bottles of spring water in an ice bucket and set it beside the edge of the pool. The view was spectacular. Crystal-clear glass at the edge of the infinity pool overlooking the beautiful blue waters of the Atlantic made Rick feel like he was floating in heaven. He didn't ever wanna leave.

As Rick and Jules soaked up the sun, Possum devised a master plan to get Evan alone. If he could convince Evan that he had double-crossed Rick and Jules and would sell him the sapphire for a cool million, Evan would surely jump at the chance, knowing it was valued at well over $300 million. A small price to pay to get it back. Possum just had to somehow convince him that he still had it and that he was willing to sell out his friends.

He secured a room in a building nearby that musicians could rent for rehearsal. It was only forty dollars an hour, and he would only need a few hours once he set up the meeting. Always being prepared, he already had the necessary tools in his tool bag: a small electric screw driver and various screws and electrical tape. He ordered a few items from Amazon that he'd need once he got Evan to the location: two faux fur poms, a car battery charger, and an insulated stainless staff that he could turn into a picanha. It was basically two wooden-handled flat steak skewers that he could tie together, add the poms to the end covered in Vaseline, and connect each one to the positive and negative side of the charger. Once they were placed to the temple with a rheostat in between, he could raise and lower the amperage to adjust the amount of shock he would give Evan. It would be a painful yet persuasive tool to get the truth from him.

Now all he had to do was set the trap. Once he found Evan's company in England, he started to put the plan into action. He needed a burner phone, so he hobbled down to the lobby and then to the nearest convenience store and picked one up. It took six codeine for him to get numb enough to make the walk. He would be living off of those for a while.

Back at the room, he called the company. It was late in the afternoon in London and the voicemail came on.

"You have reached Armstrong Imports. At the tone, leave your name and number and one of our associates will return your call. If it is urgent, you can call +44 20 7946 0990."

He wrote down the number, hung up, and called it.

"You have reached Evan Taylor of Armstrong Imports. Leave your name and number and I will call you right back. I am probably in the field or on another call."

"Bingo!" said Possum aloud and quickly hung up before the beep.

He had to get his shit together before leaving the message or speaking directly to Evan. Evan was dangerous, after all. He'd already shot at Jules and might have killed Possum's wife, so Possum needed to be prepared.

The hotel phone rang and he picked up.

"You have a delivery from Amazon. Shall I bring it up?"

"Damn, that was fast. Did a drone deliver it?"

"Sorry, sir, what?"

"Never mind. Yes, bring it up please."

He tipped the bellman and locked the door. From his vantage point, he could clearly see the pool. Rick and Jules were all tangled up, kissing in the water. They'd be a while. He knew if Rick knew what he was planning, he would try to talk him out of it. He didn't care. It was his wife who was murdered, and he was gonna find out who did it at any cost.

He cut the clamps off of the charger, exposing bare wire. Then he cut the wire again and secured the pieces in line with the rheostat, and connected that to the positive and negative wires leading to the metal part of each of the skewers with a self-tapping screw. Then he taped them both together with electrical tape and fastened the poms to each end. He rubbed them down with Vaseline.

His makeshift cattle prod was complete. He just needed to test it. Turning it on, he set it to the lowest setting possible and placed it on his thigh. He winced when the shock came. It was equivalent to a cattle fence he'd touched once in Texas—painful but not jarring. He slowly turned the dial of the rheostat up, and his leg began to quiver. He cranked it up, and the shock jolted his leg outward, making him drop the wands with a cry. The sudden jerk hurt his ribs, and he knew his creation would work perfectly.

After covering the poms with a plastic bag, he crushed up ten codeine tablets and two muscle relaxers and put them inside the tea bag he'd picked up at breakfast. He knew Evan, being from England, would never say no to tea during a negotiation. It was the English way. With everything in a small backpack—including the book has wife had been killed for, *Orinoco, The Jewel of God*—he shoved it under the bed, and was ready to make the call. He practiced his best Italian accent a few times, then rang the number.

"You have reached Evan Taylor of Armstrong Imports. Leave your name and number and I will call you right back. I am probably in the field or on another call."

Beeeeep...

"Salve Evan, this is Michael and I have something you will be interested in. It's worth much more than I'm asking for it, and I am furious with the people who took it and I'm willing to make a deal. Call me back at +55 955 826 0633 so we can arrange to meet up in person. Just you and me, no one else. Ciao."

Possum hung up and waited. He paced the room and popped a few more codeine. His acupuncturist wouldn't arrive until 4:30, so he hoped to get a return call before dinner. He didn't want to explain the burner phone to Rick. He continued to look down at Rick and Jules through the window, hoping they'd stay in the pool long enough for him to complete the first part of his plan.

His phone buzzed in his pocket. He had written down a few Italian phrases to seem more genuine.

"Ciao, sono Michael."

"Michael, it's Evan, returning your call. You said you have something I am interested in? How do I know you?"

"You don't know me, but I know you. I have something blue that I know you once had and you want back. I know the value is above $300 million, but I have access to it, and I am willing to make a deal."

"How do I know you're not a cop?"

"You don't, but I know you shot at the woman who took it from you. I hate her and her boyfriend, and I know where they stashed the jewel. They trust me like a brother."

A short pause followed before Evan spoke again. Possum's heart was beating fast.

"Okay, where and when do you want to meet?" asked Evan.

"Let's say two days. I will text you the address in Rio."

"Okay, I'll be waiting."

"Ciao."

Possum hung up, already getting anxious about the plan. His hands were shaking a little. What he was attempting was dangerous, and he needed every detail to be perfect. He realized he needed a similar briefcase and a fake jewel. The briefcase would be easy. Amazon could have one to him by the end of the day, so he ordered it.

The jewel would be trickier. He got online and looked up art studios. He found one that specialized in glass forging. They made bowls, lamps, and huge paperweights.

Brinnnng, brinnnng...

"Olá, esta é a forja de Santiago."

"Do you speak English?"

"Yes, I speak English. How may I help you?"

"I'm looking for a fake sapphire for a funny wedding gift. Can you make something like that? It needs to be pretty large."

"How large?"

"I can text you the photos and sizes, if that will work?"

"Yes, use this number—955-757-7975."

Possum quickly jotted it down.

"How do you make them and how quickly can you have it ready? The wedding is tomorrow."

"First, we will make a 3D print of it, then create a glass mold based on the 3D model. We will forge it out of blue glass; our designers can duplicate anything. I'm afraid it is impossible to have something for you tomorrow, though."

Possum chewed on this inside of his mouth. "How much does something like that cost?"

"It depends on the size. Can you give me an estimate?"

"It's about twice as big as a grown man's fist."

"That would cost roughly a thousand and fifty reals or, hold on...about two hundred US dollars."

"I'll give you six hundred US dollars if you can have it ready by tomorrow afternoon."

There was a long pause. The man was cupping the phone and speaking to someone else in Portuguese.

"Okay, we will do it for seven hundred and fifty US dollars, and we can have it done by four p.m. tomorrow, if you get us the exact dimensions and weight with photos."

"You drive a hard bargain, but let's do it. Can I pay with a credit card?"

"Yes, text us the sizes of the jewel you desire and your credit card information and where you would like it delivered."

"Thank you, I will send them all as soon as we hang up."

Possum already had all the photos and sizes of the famous Jewel of Orinoco on his laptop. He pulled out his credit card, created an email fax, and sent it all to the number the guy gave him. Within a few minutes, his phone pinged. It was a thumbs-up emoji. He was good to go.

He took another muscle relaxer and headed down to the pool to visit with Rick and Jules. He still had time to do his acupuncture session.

"Hey, amigo, how's the water? Y'all are gonna turn into prunes," said Possum.

"Aw, Possum, it's like heaven," said Jules. "You should try it. Where are your swim trunks?"

"I just took a muscle relaxer for the ass whooping I got. I might drown if I get in the water. Besides, I have an acupuncturist coming in a little while."

"Oh, that's great, man," chimed in Rick. "I used one when I threw my back out once. They can work wonders. I'd order you a drink, but you probably shouldn't mix alcohol and pain meds."

"Always looking after me, huh?"

"Ha! You need looking after sometimes, you old codger," said Rick with a laugh.

"Well, I'll have you know this old codger has a date—not tomorrow, but the next day, with a very lovely lady I met in the lobby today."

"You serious?"

"Yep, she's a pharmaceutical rep who lives in town. I'm meeting her for dinner and drinks two nights from now around six at the famous Copacabana."

"You wanna double date?" asked Rick.

"I tell you what, let me get to know her a bit and text you, and maybe y'all can come meet us later. She may be a nut job; I wanna get a good feel for her first. Don't want Rick Waters cramping my style." Possum chuckled.

"Sounds like a plan. If she's not too crazy, we can meet up for some *ha-ha clink-clink.*"

"You read my mind, Rick. I'm so glad you looked into the international plan for the iPhones. I was sick of those damn huge sat phones."

"Me too. I added the plan to all our phones, even Jules's. I bought her an iPhone as a gift. She's still getting used to it."

"Cool, man. I'm gonna head up and take a quick nap before my acupuncture session."

"Sounds good. I hope it helps."

"Me too!"

"Bye, Possum," yipped Jules.

Possum headed back up to his room. His muscle relaxer was kicking in and he was getting sleepy, so he set his alarm for four and crashed in bed.

CHAPTER EIGHTEEN

Jules sat on the balcony playing with her iPhone and sipping a coffee. Rick crept up behind her and was gonna scare her, but decided to kiss her on the top of her head instead. Chief was sitting on the table munching on grapes as usual. Rick had walked down to the lobby and brought up a bunch of fresh fruit and danishes from the restaurant.

"Rick, I love this phone, but I'm so afraid I'm gonna lose it," said Jules. "I lose my glasses all the time."

"Here, let me show you something." He took her phone and pulled up the settings until he got to the Find My tab. "See where it says location?"

"Yes."

"Click on it."

A map popped up, and a blue dot appeared right at the hotel they were in.

"See, there's your phone," said Rick with a grin.

"Oh, okay. But if I lose my phone, how can I go to settings?"

"See the bottom of the Find My tab? What does it say?"

"Friends."

"Click on it."

"It says, Rick Waters and Michael Jackson and Johnie McDonald," she replied.

"Now look at my phone." Rick handed Jules his phone.

"It says, Michael Jackson, Johnie McDonald, and My Angel Jules."

"Exactly. In case we ever lose our phones, we can use any of our phones to find someone else's. As long as it's turned on and has signal."

"Why My Angel Jules?" she asked, smiling.

"That's how I have you programmed into my phone. That's the name I used, because you are my angel."

"You are so sweet! I'm changing your name now in my phone. Let me think." She bit her lip. "How about My Smart-ass Rick? Ha-ha-ha, I'm just kidding. I know... My Lover Boy Rick! That's it."

He chuckled. "You are something else, Jules."

"I know."

Rick dropped his phone on the glass table, startling Chief. The cockatoo flew up and hit the top of the ceiling and came crashing down on the table.

"That's it, we have to get your wings clipped ASAP, boy!" said Rick.

"Is he okay?" asked Jules.

"Yeah, look, he's blushing. I think he only hurt his ego. But seriously, as soon as we can, we need to clip his wings." He slapped his thighs. "You wanna go to the beach, Jules?"

"Yes! Let's do it!"

Rick picked up his iPhone and put it on speaker and began to play a song. It was "The Girl from Ipanema."

Rick took Jules's hand and pulled her close and began dancing. He started spinning around and did his best Captain Ron impression. Jules broke into laughter and hugged him tight.

"We can go to Ipanema Beach? I've heard that song a million times. It's here?!" exclaimed Jules.

Rick pulled Jules to the window of the balcony and pointed. "See that beach?"

"Yeah, that's it?"

"Nope. That's Copacabana Beach. Ipanema Beach is about a four-minute car ride to the right."

"What? Copacabana Beach is real too? I thought they were just songs. I thought Possum was being sarcastic when he said he had a date at the Copacabana."

"Well, there's the Copacabana Beach and the Copacabana Hotel, although the song is actually about the Copacabana night club in New York, which is named after the beach. Why don't we just see both?"

"Yes, yes, yes! I am so excited." She clapped her hands and grinned.

That was one of the things Rick loved the most about Jules: her childlike innocence. She was like a kid on Christmas day, and he grew fonder of her with each passing day.

"I'm gonna show you a new two-piece I got, Mr. Waters... I mean, my lover boy Rick!"

Jules skipped into the bathroom, and Rick finished his coffee while inspecting Chief's head. He would be fine. Not a mark at all.

Suddenly, Rick's phone whistled. It was a text from Johnie.

> Johnie: Hey boss, made it back to the boat. Thank God. I got tons of messages for charters. I'm gonna arrange a couple of captains to run the boat. Enjoy Rio and see ya soon.

> Rick: Thanks Johnie. I'm glad you're back safe. I'll keep you posted when I'll return. Thanks for doing what you do.

> Johnie: My pleasure boss!

"Tada!" exclaimed Jules.

Rick spun around and feigned a *Sanford and Son* heart attack.

"Oh, Lord. This is the big one. You hear that, Elizabeth? I'm coming to join ya, honey!"

Jules gave him a peculiar look. "Who is Elizabeth?"

He dropped his hand, frowning. "You've never seen *Sanford and Son*? Oh, I keep forgetting you grew up in Colombia. Never mind. I was pretending to have a heart attack because you look so fine!"

Jules was wearing what could only be described as a string bikini. The bright yellow colors against her tan skin looked neon. Rick walked over to her and kissed her.

"Can I pull this string?"

She giggled. "I thought you'd never ask."

Possum woke up not realizing he'd even fallen asleep. He was still in his shorts and tank top form the day before. His plan to get Evan to the location he'd picked out interwove in his dreams all night, and he didn't rest well. His heart wouldn't stop beating fast from anxiety. Partly because he desperately wanted to uncover the truth about his wife's death, and partly because he was keeping this whole plan from Rick.

After a bit, he couldn't take it anymore and decided to call Rick and spill the beans. It rang five times, but he never picked up.

Must have it on Do Not Disturb.

He hung up, knowing Rick would see his call and call him back soon enough anyway. About twenty minutes passed, and Possum's phone rang.

"Possum, que pasa, amigo?! Jules and I are heading to Ipanema Beach. Wanna join us? Please, I insist. How are you feeling anyway after the acupuncture?"

"Hang tight, I'll be right down. Let me throw on my swim trunks. See ya in five minutes."

Possum knocked on Rick's door a few minutes later. As soon as he opened it, Possum pulled up his shirt.

"Check this shit out!"

Rick leaned closer to get a better look. "What the hell? Where are your bruises?"

"They are gone, vanished, history!"

"But how?"

"The acupuncture worked like magic," said Possum as he stepped inside.

"What did he do exactly?" asked Jules.

"He used a bunch of tiny needles and it felt like they were hooked up to an electrical outlet. It felt like a tiny current running through my whole body. It was amazing. Then he took some type of suction cups and put them on various parts of my body. It was weird. All I know is I feel like a million bucks now and I'm a total believer in acupuncture."

They both sat there shaking their heads in disbelief, but the proof was in the pudding.

"Besides the bruises being gone, how do you feel mentally?"

"Honestly? It's like it never happened. I'm stunned."

"Damn, dude. Save that guy's contact info!"

"Damn straight!"

Jules was smiling and giddy to go to the beach, and so was Rick. Possum decided to keep his little secret to himself for now. He still had time to tell Rick before the plan went down, and he didn't wanna put a damper on the day.

Jules packed a little cooler with a few waters and some sandwiches she'd gotten from the restaurant, and they headed down to the lobby. The hotel had a free shuttle to the beach, so they took advantage of it.

Their first stop was Ipanema Beach. Rick paid for their beach chair rentals and they picked a spot close to the water. Rick wished he'd brought Chief along, but with his flight feathers grown in, it was just too risky.

Girls in thongs walked along the shore capturing the attention of Rick and Possum, as well as Jules. She didn't have a jealous bone in her body and could also appreciate the body of a beautiful woman. She was confident and knew she was going home with Rick. He could look all he wanted as long as he was with her. She trusted him and he trusted her. It was a beautiful thing.

A few vendors stopped by them, selling trinkets or snacks. They were all polite and not pushy at all.

Jules jumped up and pointed at one of the little carts. "Rick, look, caipirinhas! Let get one."

"Uh, okay, what is that?"

"It has rum in it. Well, actually cachaça. Same thing. I promise you'll like it."

"Count me in, baby! Possum?"

"Why not, amigo."

Rick gave Jules some cash, and she sprinted over to the cart like it was going out of business. She came back with three caipirinhas.

"Saúde! I learned that today. That means cheers in Portuguese."

"Saúde!" said Rick and Possum in unison.

They spent three hours lounging on the beach and finished off their sandwiches.

"Shall we go to *the Copa, Copacabana*? The beach, not the hotel," sang Rick.

Instead of calling the hotel shuttle, they opted to grab a cab. It cost nearly nothing anyway, as Copacabana Beach was only a mile away. The taxi dropped them off right at the lifeguard station, which was vacant. Right away, they noticed a difference in the two beaches and the people in general. It seemed a little lower rent. But Rick wasn't a snob, and as nice as Ipanema was, he was game to hang with some locals. The vendors were a bit pushier but could take a hint.

They spent two hours there, until they'd all had enough sun and decided to head back to the hotel.

"You look like a lobster!" exclaimed Jules when they were back in their room.

Rick looked in the mirror and saw she was right. She had been nagging at him all day to put on sunscreen, and he had, but apparently not enough. She went to the lobby and came back with some Aloe vera gel and rubbed it all over Rick.

"This feels like ice on a fire." said Rick.

"You never listen, lover boy."

Rick sat there on the edge of bed moaning.

"Shall we do room service?" asked Jules.

"Yeah, I'm too tired and burnt to go out. I'll call Possum and let him know."

"Possum, you cool if we get room service instead of meeting for dinner?"

"You read my mind, Rick. I'm kinda feeling the burn. You were looking redder than me, so I'm sure you're hurting. Plus, y'all got sun at the pool too yesterday."

"True dat. Okay, I'll holler at you tomorrow. Good luck with your date if I don't see you before you leave."

"Thanks, Rick. Y'all have a good night."

CHAPTER NINETEEN

Possum unboxed the delivery sitting in his room. The weight was perfect. The iridescent dark blue glass stone looked identical to the Sacred Jewel of Orinoco. He was beyond impressed. After putting it in the nearly identical leather pouch it was in when they found it, he placed it in the briefcase and slid it all back under the bed, where it would wait until tomorrow. He thought about telling Rick his plan, but decided against it. He knew the element of surprise would be to his advantage, and Rick would insist it was too dangerous.

Jules shook her head as Rick turned over in the bed and whined like a baby. His sunburn had turned sore and she could tell he was regretting those last two hours on the beach. Jules laughed then covered her mouth and gave him puppy dog eyes. She rubbed Aloe vera gel on him and told him she'd take care of breakfast. After kissing his burnt chest, she headed downstairs for some grub.

"Holá, amiga!" said Possum, who was toasting a bagel in the breakfast area.

"Good morning, Possum. How are you this morning?"

"Fit as a fiddle. How's lobster boy?"

"A little whiny bitch!" she said jokingly.

She made two waffles and filled a bowl of fruit as Possum munched on his bagel and sipped coffee.

"I don't know how much of a tourist Rick will be today. What are your plans?" asked Jules.

"I'm probably gonna check out a few local attractions and be back early. I have a big date tonight, remember?"

"That's right! Well, I hope it goes perfect, Possum. I'll tell Rick I saw you and you laughed at him, okay?"

"You are too much, Jules. Perfect for that numbskull."

Jules laughed and headed for the elevator.

Possum canvassed the room he'd rented for the interrogation to have the advantage and lay of the land, then returned to his room to get ready for what lay in store. Today was the day he'd find out who had killed his wife, Jennifer. He checked his burner phone, and there was a new message.

6:00 p.m. works. See you there.

He texted back: Confirmed.

Evan had taken the bait. The time was upon him.

Possum pulled the backpack out from under the bed and double-checked he had everything he needed. He had forgotten one thing—handcuffs—and had to come up with something fast. He planned to get there a half-hour early to set up the scene. His belt would make a great substitute, so he cut it into six-inch lengths, and pre-drilled one-and-a-half inch self-tapping screws with large washers into the ends of each strip. Having scoped out the room already, he knew that heavy wooden chairs and a table would be perfect to secure Evan during his interrogation. He could use his iPhone to record the entire event and would keep it out of sight in the oversized front pocket of one of his fishing shirts.

There was only one fear he had. If the mix of codeine and muscle relaxers didn't work fast enough, he might have to overpower Evan instead. He needed something more instant. Maybe if Evan drank the tea, it would slow him down enough for Possum to strap him down, but he really wanted a foolproof way. Chloroform.

Where the hell can I get chloroform? He went online and googled how to make chloroform. To his surprise, he needed only three ingredients: household bleach, acetone, and ice. It was a simple process, but pure chloroform would have to be distilled and he didn't have time for that. There had to be something else he could use. He searched again.

Drugs that can knock you out instantly.

The first page turned up GHB, Propofol, and Ketamine. The streets of Rio were littered with drug dealers, but they could also be selling saline solution and ripping people off. He was sure he could score as much of the date rape drug as he needed, but it was too risky in case he approached an undercover cop. Going to jail for soliciting drugs would throw a huge wrench in his plans.

Then he remembered an article he'd read in *The Houston Livestock Association* about Ketamine. It was a common animal tranquilizer available at your local tractor supply store. Street dealers had been buying it up and selling it on the black market as a new drug known as Special K. It had recently been removed from the shelves in Texas and could only be purchased through a licensed veterinarian. But not in Rio. Another search revealed a pet store only a few miles away that listed Ketamine on its website. He picked up the house phone.

"Front desk, Emiliano Rio. How may I help you?"

"Can you arrange a taxi for me?"

"Yes, Mr. Jackson. We have three in the queue of the hotel now. Come down when you're ready."

Possum went to the elevator and was in the taxi in minutes.

"Do you speak English?" he asked the driver.

"Yes, I do."

"Pet Market, please."

"Do you have the address?"

Possum handed his iPhone to the man, and he put the address into his GPS. It was only a 7.4-kilometer trip. He'd be back with plenty of time to spare. The driver pulled up to the Pet Market and parked.

"Can you wait for me and take me back to the hotel?"

"Yes, it's no problem."

As he walked down the equestrian aisle, there it was. Sitting on the shelf with three syringes in packaging—Ketamine HCl 500mg/10ml. He made his purchase and climbed back into the cab. Once back at the hotel, he filled all three syringes with Ketamine in case he had to grab one fast or Evan wrestled one away from him. He looked at his watch. It was 3:30 p.m. Time to touch base with Rick. He called him.

"Rick, what's up, amigo? How's that sunburn?"

"I hate it! Haven't left the room today. Jules has been rubbing Aloe on me though, and it's getting better. What're you up to?"

"Just checking in with you, amigo. I'm gonna hop in the shower and get ready for my date."

"That's right. Don't forget to text me how it's going and if you want us to join you. Jules has been reading all day about the Copacabana Palace and is stoked to check it out."

"No worries. You sure you're up to going out tonight?"

"I'll be fine. I'm sick of being cooped up in the room all day."

"Okay, I'll holler at you later."

"Cool. Later, man."

Possum pulled his .45 from out of the dresser drawer and tucked it into the back of his waistband. The last thing he wanted to do was get into a gun battle, but he had to be prepared.

It's go time.

Possum grabbed another taxi and gave the driver the address of the building. He'd be way early, but he had rented it for the day so it didn't matter. Once he got there, he put his iPhone on Do Not Disturb and started to set up the room.

His burner phone pinged at 5:30 p.m. It was Evan.

> *I've been detained. I*
> *can be there at 7:45 p.m.*
> *I apologize but it was*
> *unavoidable.*

"Shit!" said Possum.

He had to think before responding. He wanted to maintain control but not be too aggressive.

> *Be here by 7:45, not a*
> *minute later. I have three*
> *interested buyers besides*
> *you.*

> *I'll be there.*

Now he had to kill two hours and fifteen minutes. He started pacing the room. His anxiety was a mile high.

"Possum must be having a good time," said Rick, looking at his phone in the hotel room. "He hasn't returned any of my texts."

"It's okay. We can go visit the Copacabana Palace anytime. Let him have his fun."

"You're right. She must be something special. It's just rare that he doesn't text back ASAP. He's a serial texter."

He frowned for a moment, then set his phone down and shrugged. "I'll call him later. Maybe he's out of range."

There was a knock at the building door at 7:10 p.m. Possum hit record on his iPhone, shoved it down in his pocket, and looked through the peephole.

"Who's there?" he called.

"It's Evan."

"Are you strapping?"

"Are you?"

"Let's both remove our guns and hold them by the barrel, and I will slowly open the door."

"Deal."

Evan slowly pulled his Ruger from his shoulder holster and held it in front of himself by the end of the barrel with two fingers. Possum did the same with his .45, then opened the door.

"Let's set them on the ground," said Possum.

Evan agreed and set his weapon down in the doorway. Possum laid his .45 down and gently pushed them aside behind the inside wall.

"Arms out."

Evan put his arms out to the side, and Possum patted him down. Evan did the same to Possum and stepped inside.

"Let's get down to business."

The table was about twenty feet from the pistols, and now they were on an equal playing field. At least, Possum assumed that's what Evan thought. They both sat down in the heavy hand-carved chairs opposite each other at the table.

"Let's see it," said Evan.

Possum pulled the briefcase out from under the table. Inside it was the gem and one of the Ketamine syringes. He palmed the syringe with his right hand and spun the briefcase around to Evan in one move, keeping his palm flat on the table as Evan examined the precious stone.

"Tea?" asked Possum.

"I hate tea. Just because I'm English, everyone thinks I want tea. I drink coffee."

Possum was sure glad he'd brought the Ketamine, because the codeine-laced tea was out of the question now.

"I didn't know." He cleared his throat. "So, let's get down to brass tacks. I want $5 million cash for it. No negotiation. I want it in two days."

"Five million dollars?" Evan raised an eyebrow. "I don't think I can get that in two days. My partner is on a working vacation on his super cat on the Iguazu River, on the border of Brazil and Argentina. I can contact him and see what we can do."

"You want to call him now?"

"Okay."

"I need to make a call too."

Possum pulled out his burner and pretended to dial a number. The syringe was sitting on his knee out of view of Evan. Evan was speaking to his boss and took his eye off of Possum. As he hung up, Possum dropped his phone and it bounced off the table. Instinctively, Evan reached to try to catch the phone before it hit the ground. Possum grabbed the syringe and slammed it into Evan's forearm.

Evan's eyes widened in shock, and he slumped forward onto the table, unconscious.

He wouldn't be out too long, so Possum worked fast. With his electric screwdriver and leather straps, he secured Evan's wrists and legs to the wooden chair. The effect could last up to two hours, but he'd probably come to in about thirty minutes and be disoriented.

Like clockwork, Evan began to squirm about thirty minutes later. Possum had picked up his .45, which was now sitting on the table facing Evan, and plugged in the car battery charger. Evan shook his head, trying to figure out where he was. He tried to lift his hand to run his eyes and looked down at the leather straps.

"Where am I? Who are you?"

His eyes were coming into focus, and Possum slowly took off the glasses and removed his fake beard.

"I'm Possum, asshole. Remember me from the cave?"

"Possum?"

He was still drowsy and out of it, but seemed to be slowly regaining his mind.

"Wait, you were with Rick Waters, right?"

"Bingo, we have a winner. I only have one thing to say to you."

Possum reached into the backpack and slid the book, *Orinoco, The Jewel of God,* toward Evan.

"That's my book. Where did you get it?" asked Evan in a slurred voice.

"No, it's my book and you took it from my wife, Jennifer Jackson."

"Who?"

Possum leaned across the table and backhanded Evan as hard as he could.

"Don't you lie to me! You killed my wife for this book!"

"No, no, I swear. I bought the book from someone. I didn't kill anyone."

"You're lying."

Possum picked up the battery charger from under the table and turned it on.

Evan's eyes grew wide. "What are you doing?"

"I'm gonna get the truth out of you, one way or another."

Possum stuck the poms to Evan's forearm and slowly turned up the rheostat. Evan started convulsing. Clenching his fists, he screamed in pain.

"Stop! Stop! Please!"

"Who killed Jennifer? I know you did it."

"No, I swear!"

Possum walked behind the chair and put the poms to Evan's temple. His head shook violently and foam came from his mouth.

"Tell me, you son of a bitch."

The smell of burnt hair rose into the air. The side of Evan's head was red and looked scorched as well. His hands were trembling. Possum stepped around the table and picked up his .45 before walking back around and shoving it into the back of Evan's neck.

Rick texted Possum again. It was nine p.m. now.

"He's still not returning my texts. Must be one hell of a date. I'm gonna call him."

It rang several times and then went to voicemail.

Rick left a message. "Hey, buddy, it's Rick. Call me back. I'm getting worried. Either you're on the best date of your life or you've been kidnapped."

"Why don't we go to the Copacabana Palace anyway?" said Jules when he hung up. "It's a huge place. We won't cramp his style."

"I know you're chomping at the bit to see it, Jules. Let me throw a shirt on. Can you pull it up on your iPhone and get directions?"

"Sure, Rick."

Jules took her phone off the charger and unlocked it. After a moment, she said, "Rick, can you come here? Look at this. I can't make sense of it."

She was still learning how to use her new iPhone. Rick stepped over to help her.

"That's not the GPS, Jules." She had the Find My app open again.

"I know, but look. See where Possum is?"

Rick looked closer, and his body tensed. Possum was nowhere near the Copacabana Palace. It looked like he was in a commercial area of Rio.

Rick's eyes narrowed. "Something's wrong. Either someone stole his phone or he's not where he said he was gonna be. The phone is still on and he's not answering. That's strange. Let's go check it out."

He grabbed his .38, and they went downstairs and left the hotel through the lobby. He didn't have the exact address, but they just kept walking toward the beacon. They got to the building where the phone was and opened the door. The stair led to a sign that said *Ensaios de banda.*

"What does that mean, Jules?"

She squinted at the sign. "It says band rehearsals."

"Something's off," said Rick.

Rick ran up the stairs with Jules right behind him. He could hear the muffled sound of a band practicing behind the left door in the hallway. He stuck his ear to the door on the right and covered his left ear to hear better.

"Tell me now, or I'm gonna blow your fucking head off!" came a muffled, familiar voice. Possum.

"It was my partner, Nate. Nate Armstrong. It wasn't supposed to happen." That was a second voice, also familiar.

"Time to die!"

Click-clack

"Don't kill me!" yelled Evan.

Rick turned the handle of the door. It was locked. He stepped back and ran toward the door and kicked it with all his weight. The wood of the door jamb splintered, and the door flew open.

"Possum, stop!" he yelled, entering the room. He took in the sight of his friend holding a gun to Evan's head. "What are you doing? Put down the gun!"

Possum barely noticed Rick kicking the door down, but he recognized his friend's voice behind him.

"Step away, Rick. This guy has to die," said Possum through gritted teeth.

"No, Possum, don't," pleaded Rick. "You can't do that."

"He and his partner killed Jennifer."

"You are not a cold-blooded killer, Possum. Please put down the gun."

The gun shook in Possum's grip. He couldn't keep it steady. "Step away, Rick. This is my problem to deal with."

"Listen, take a deep breath. Put down the gun and let's talk. It's me, Rick. You trust me, don't you?"

Possum's shoulders slumped a little, and at last, he lowered the gun with trembling hands. Tears welled up in his eyes. Rick was right; he wasn't a killer. He was so torn. He had to avenge the death of his wife, but he knew he couldn't pull the trigger.

He dropped the gun.

Evan let out a huge sigh as Rick picked up the .45 from the floor. Jules ran over to Possum and wrapped her arms around him, and they both wept.

CHAPTER TWENTY

Rick looked at his watch. It was almost midnight. The interrogation of Evan was almost complete. They'd learned that Evan's partner had shot Possum's wife because he was afraid she would identify them. It wasn't supposed to go down that way. It was supposed to be a simple snatch and grab, but Nate Armstrong never left any loose ends. Ever.

"We can use Evan to our advantage," whispered Rick in Possum's ear. "He knows you won't kill him, but he has no idea about me. Good cop, bad cop. Follow my lead."

Rick grabbed Evan by the hair and pulled his head back. "Live or die?"

"Live, please."

"I'm not talking to you. I'm talking to Possum. He's no killer, but I couldn't care less if I splatter your brains all over that wall."

"Tell us exactly where we can find Nate Armstrong," said Possum. "You need to set up a meeting with us and take us to him."

"Are you crazy? He'll kill me and then kill all of you."

"Okay, Rick, shoot him. I'm going to the hotel."

Possum grabbed the briefcase and backpack, and headed for the door and kept walking.

"Tough break, man." Rick cocked his .38 and placed it on the back of Evan's head. "Any last words?"

"Wait, wait. I'll do whatever you want!" cried Evan, panicking. Sweat glistened on his face.

Rick picked up Evan's phone and waved it at him.

"What's the number?"

"Speed dial one."

Rick pressed the button, held the phone up to Evan's ear, and kept the gun tight to the back of his head.

"Nate, it's Evan. Change of plans. Don't wire the money in the morning. They want cash and he wants to do the exchange in person on *Sabbatine*."

Rick leaned in and could hear the other voice.

"On my boat? Why?"

"I don't know; he just said that was the only way. I'll get back to you with a time we can fly into Cataratas Airport and shuttle over to the dock. I'll keep you posted."

"Okay, Evan. Don't fuck this up again. I need to have that jewel." Nate hung up.

Rick pulled the gun back and slowly released the hammer.

"Okay, listen and listen good. You're coming with us. You're gonna be a guest of my hotel room. Or, should I say my hotel room's closet, until we figure out what to do with you. You so much as hiccup on the walk back to the hotel, and I will shoot you in the back. People get shot every day in Rio. You got it?"

Evan bobbed his head. "Okay, I got it."

Rick pulled his Leatherman from his pocket and cut the leather straps holding Evan to the chair. He rubbed his red, swollen wrists.

"Jules, check the hallway."

Jules peeked out of the door. A band was still jamming in another part of the building. "It's clear, Rick."

Rick helped Evan up and turned him toward the door, shoving his .38 against his ribs.

He walked out the door with Rick close behind him and Jules taking up the rear.

The streets were dark and not many people milled around. When they got to the lobby, Jules ran up to the front desk guy to distract him, and Rick and Evan made it to the elevator. They got into the room and Rick secured him to a chair, shoved a handkerchief in his mouth, and put him in the walk-in closet.

Jules came in a few minutes later. "Where is he?"

Rick raised his index finger to his mouth to indicate she should hush, then pointed to the closet. Jules shook her head and winked in agreement.

They quietly opened the door and knocked on Possum's door. He opened it. His eyes were red, and he was clearly still emotional from everything that had gone down.

"You gonna be okay?" asked Rick.

"Yeah, man." Possum wiped his eyes. "The whole reality of Jennifer's death kind of hit me all at once, and I almost killed a man point blank. It was all a little too much. Where is he now?"

"He's in the closet."

Possum half laughed. "Where he deserves to be. What's the plan?"

"I think a little double cross might be in order. That faux gem you have is a perfect match for the Sacred Jewel of Orinoco. We can use it to get to Armstrong. We all need to get some sleep, though. Let's check in with Gary in the morning. I'll come back to your room. We don't wanna be talking around Evan."

"Here, pour this in a Coke or something and give it to Evan." Possum handed him a bunch of pills. "He'll sleep for twelve or more hours."

"What is it?"

"Ten codeine and two muscle relaxers."

Rick raised an eyebrow. "You trying to kill him still?"

"It won't kill him. But he won't be able to bother us for quite a while."

"Okay, we'll be back here at 7:30 a.m. to go over everything with Gary. Have a good night."

"Y'all too."

Rick knocked on Possum's door at 7:31 a.m.

"Good morning, amigo. How'd you sleep? Better yet, how'd our guest sleep?" asked Possum.

"I checked on him this morning and he was still breathing but out cold. That's a good sign. Jules will be here shortly with breakfast. I texted Gary and told him to call us at eight a.m. on the dot. He's in the jet headed back with Gina."

"Sounds good, man. I guess now we just wait."

Jules returned with a carafe of fresh coffee, some bagels, and fresh fruit. Shortly after they finished the bagels, Rick's phone rang.

"Hey, Rick. Can you hear me okay? We're at 30,000 feet. We already fueled up in Caracas. See ya soon. I'm gonna put you on speaker. Gina's with me and wants to listen."

"Okay, Gary. I'll put you on speaker too. We're all here."

Rick told Gary how the entire night went down and how he planned to use Evan to get to Armstrong.

"How long is that runway in Cataratas Airport?" asked Gary.

"Hang on, let me check," interjected Possum. After a minute, he said, "You're good, dude. It's an international airport."

"Okay, great. Let's set it up for tomorrow. We can refuel in Rio and fly out in the a.m."

"Hey, everyone, Gina here. Gary dropped me at the Smithsonian and I gave the Sacred Jewel of Orinoco to the curator. All I have to do now is transfer the funds to the Yanomami. It's Friday and by the time we get settled, the banks will be closed, but I can do it on Monday. We are way ahead of schedule and I've already filled in the Yanomami about the transfer. That two million dollars will go a long way to help their fight against the dam."

"Great job negotiating, Gina," said Rick.

"Thanks, Rick. Yeah, I should've asked for four million and kept two for myself," she said with a chuckle.

"Right!"

"Okay, y'all, we'll be at the hotel around six p.m. Once we land and refuel, wanna grab dinner at the Copa? My treat?" said Gary.

Jules's eyes lit up. "Yes, please!"

"Anything else we need to go over?" asked Gary.

"Naw, we can rendezvous tonight and go over the finer details after dinner," said Rick. "I'm gonna take Jules to see Christ the Redeemer up close right now. Any of y'all wanna go?"

"I'll tag along," said Possum.

Rick and Jules returned to their own room to get ready to go out. Evan was groggy but awake, so Jules hand fed him and gave him some water, and Rick watched him as he used the bathroom. They zip-tied him back to the chair, and Rick gave him one more drink of water, this one with codeine mixed in it again. A few moments later, Evan was out like a light.

Rick closed the closet, put the Do Not Disturb sign on the front door of the room, and they headed for the lobby to meet back up with Possum.

There was a long line to get to the base of the statue, but it was well worth the wait. The view of Rio down below was only surpassed by the glory of the ninety-eight-foot Art Deco statue with his arms spread wide overlooking the city. It was glorious. Only a poet could put into words the feeling it gave them all.

"Rick, it's so beautiful," said Jules.

"It truly is breathtaking. Possum? Any words?"

"I'm speechless, amigo."

They all took lots of photos and decided to be real tourists and eat at the restaurant at the base of the statue. It was called Corcovado, and they weren't expecting much but were pleasantly surprised. The food was quite good and not overpriced, and the drinks were exceptional. They all had a couple of caipirinhas, and Rick and Jules got the steak salad, while Possum opted for the freshwater prawns. It was all fresh and filling and they left happy and full.

"Pool time?" asked Rick.

"How's your burn?" asked Possum.

"I'm good thanks to Jules."

"Let's go, boys. I wanna swim!" Jules took their hands and began to skip, pulling them along like two puppies.

They spent the afternoon lounging by the pool. Even Chief joined the excitement. Rick tethered a small cord to the ring on his foot so he couldn't fly off. He didn't like it at first, but eventually lost interest and destroyed a tray of red grapes.

Jules checked on Evan once they got back to the room and he was still sound asleep in the closet.

"What are we gonna do with him, Rick? He can't stay in there forever."

"We're taking him with us in the morning. We need him. Remember, Armstrong still thinks we're trading him the sacred gem for five million dollars and Evan is the broker. Once we get to the boat, we'll sort it out. Until then, he sleeps. As much as possible."

Gary texted Rick that he had already left for the Copa. He had arranged a large table in the restaurant. Rick called Possum and they all met in the lobby once again. Poor Chief had to stay behind. No pets allowed at the Copa. Rick would make it up to him, though; he always did.

"Ay Dios mío, Rick. This place is incredible," said Jules, looking around the Copa.

Rick and Possum were also both impressed. The hotel and restaurant brought the song to mind. Rick started to sing the words and do the cha-cha.

"You are silly, Rick Waters!" said Jules as she stood on her tippy toes and kissed him.

"Are you gonna dance with me later?" he asked, still humming the song and taking her hands into his.

"What do I get if I do?"

"You get coffee, tea, and me, sweetie."

"I guess I will, then."

"Rick, over here."

Rick looked over and saw Gary waving at them.

"Hey, y'all, what do you think? Beautiful, huh?" Gary said as the group joined him.

"It's stunning, Gary," replied Jules. "Where's Gina?"

"She's at the restaurant ordering a martini. Let's go. I have a great table for us. We are dining at Restaurante Mee. It's a Pan Asian restaurant specializing in fresh seafood. Who wants sushi?"

"Raw fish?!" said Rick.

"Raw everything. Wait until you see the size of the prawns. Don't worry, Rick, you can also order fresh seafood cooked on a lava stone. That's right up your alley." Gary patted Rick on the back, laughing. "Let's go, cowboy."

Gina took the liberty of ordering a round of dirty martinis.

"Gina, I knew I liked you for some reason," said Rick as he lifted his martini to his lips.

They all sat down and did the *ha-ha clink-clink* and shared sushi. Only Jules passed on having some.

"What the hell is that?" exclaimed Rick as a waiter passed the table carrying a huge, colorful dish.

"Those are the prawns I was talking about," replied Gary. "I'm getting those!"

Possum, Gary, and Gina ordered the Seleção Atum Bluefin do Chef, which was a specially prepared fresh bluefin tuna. Jules ordered an Asian salad and a bowl of Kara Miso Ramen. It was way more than she could eat.

"Oh my God!" exclaimed Rick when his entrée arrived.

Sitting atop some jasmine rice and sautéed mango slices were two of the biggest freshwater prawns he'd ever seen. He'd have to cut them like a steak. The rest of the gang's meals arrived, and they all chowed down.

A couple of hours passed as they devoured their food and a few more rounds of drinks. At one point, Rick noticed Jules had barely touched her meal.

"You okay, Jules?" he asked.

"I'm fine," she said, though she didn't look it. Her forehead had a sheen of sweat. "That was a pretty big lunch we had, and I'm still kinda full and don't feel great. I have a little headache and I'm a little nauseated."

"You probably need some water. Here, have some of mine."

She took a big swig and got Gina's attention to follow her to the ladies' room. The girls grabbed their purses and headed out. Rick ordered another martini and a dessert Jules would surely love. It was on fire.

The dessert arrived and the girls still weren't back yet. Rick looked at his watch. "They've been gone a long time," he said.

"You know girls, Rick. They probably got distracted by the décor of the hotel," said Gary.

"That's true."

Rick was about to get up and go look for them when they walked in.

"Did you fall in?" he asked.

"Sorry, Rick," said Jules.

"It's okay, baby. I'm just messing with you. Check out the dessert."

Jules glanced at the fire atop the dessert as she sat back down, but she seemed to be somewhere else. Kind of distant.

"Did your cat die or something?" Rick joked with a smile.

She just looked up at Rick with a blank stare. Trying to pull her out of whatever was going on with her, Rick stood up.

"A toast. To friendship."

They all raised their glasses.

"Here's to you and here's to me,
Friends may we always be!
But, if by chance we disagree,
Up yours! Here's to me!"

They all laughed. Jules leaned over and whispered in Rick's ear, then handed him something under the table. Rick looked down at it and then back at Jules. He was stunned and couldn't speak. She leaned over and whispered in his ear again, and he nodded.

"Another toast. To Rick," said Jules, standing up and raising her glass of water.

"Here's to Rick, he's quite a laddie
He's in great shape and not a fatty
And what I told him knocked him flatty
Here's to Rick, he's gonna be a daddy"

Silence fell over the table, followed by joyful claps and whistles of jubilation. The girls had gone to the gift shop inside the hotel and gotten a pregnancy test. Rick still held the plastic bag in his hands.

He looked down at it again, even closer, still in shock. Jules was pregnant.

CHAPTER TWENTY-ONE

"Don't pick up that bag. Let me get that!"

"I'm pregnant, Rick, not handicapped."

"I know, I know. I just don't want you lifting anything heavy."

"Rick Waters, you listen to me. I love you and I am fine. But I'm perfectly capable of lifting my own carry-on bag. I appreciate the concern, but I'm a strong girl. I got this."

Rick relented, although he didn't want to. He'd tried to talk her out of coming with them to the meetup with Armstrong. In the end, he'd agreed to let her come on the jet to Argentina—but that was it. The airport was just across the border from Brazil. He made her promise to stay behind at the Airbnb Gary had arranged for them to rent in Iguazu during the trade. It was far too dangerous, and she'd finally conceded he was right.

Once Jules had left to take her bag down to the van, Rick called Possum. "How the hell are we gonna get Evan out of this hotel? It's busy as hell down there in the lobby."

"Is he awake?"

"Yeah, but he's pissed and with all those people down there, he's likely to cause a scene. He already tried to yell once when Jules fed him. I shoved my handkerchief back in his mouth. We can't take a chance of him going ballistic in the lobby. Kidnapping is a big no-no, even in Rio."

"I have an idea. Give me fifteen minutes."

Soon there was a knock on the door. Rick opened it. Possum stepped in, pulling a Dakine double rolling bicycle case.

"You've got to be shitting me. Where'd you get that?"

"I saw it in the luggage storage when I went to get some coffee this morning. There's a big bicycling road race in town this week. There are tons of these around. That's what all the bustling is about downstairs. We'll fit right in."

Possum walked over to Evan, grabbed him by his hair, and turned his face toward his own.

"Goodnight, asshole!"

He stuck the needle into Evan's arm, and the Ketamine's effects were instant. His head dropped and he slumped over. Possum and Rick heaved him up and zipped him inside the bike case. Rick left the top cracked open to let a little air in. He wouldn't be in there long anyway. Their van was already waiting downstairs and Gary was driving. All they had to do was get him into the van without arousing suspicion.

"Let's do this," said Rick.

He grabbed one side of the bike case, and Possum grabbed the other. It was a comedy of errors. Evan's limp body kept flopping back and forth in the canvas case. Every time his body would bulge onto Rick's side, Rick would nudge him with his knee toward Possum's side. The cycle would continue. They made it through the lobby, and all Rick could think about was *Weekend at Bernie's*. He almost burst into laughter in the middle of the lobby, but bit his lip to stop himself.

They made it to the van and opened the double doors in the back. Jules had pushed the back seat forward, making more room.

Haaa-haaa-haaa! Chief was mimicking the laughing gulls on the beach.

"You silly bird," said Jules. "You're not a seagull."

"One, two, three," said Rick.

They lifted the entire bike case into the van and shut the door. Gary would pay someone at the rental car company to return the case to the hotel after they got Evan on the plane.

"Let's go!" said Gary, as Rick and Possum climbed into the van.

Gina was sitting in the front passenger seat, and Rick and Jules sat in the second row, along with Chief in his travel cage. Possum had the back row all to himself just in front of the bike case.

Gary slowly pulled into the traffic bound for the airport. Jules had grabbed sandwiches for everyone from the hotel, not realizing Gary had already catered the flight, but Rick thanked her for them nonetheless. He couldn't help but rub Jules's belly every few minutes. Her stomach was still flat as a board and every time he did it, she just looked at him with loving eyes and smiled. They made small talk on the way to the airport. Not being on a super tight schedule, they stopped every once in a while to take in the scenery. Gary took the beach route, which took longer but had a lot more interesting things to see along the way. Rick hoped it would help distract Jules from her morning sickness.

"Rick, I've thought a lot about it and I want to come to Destin with you. The dolphins can wait."

"Are you certain, Jules? That would sure make me happy."

"I'm totally sure, Rick," she said with a reassuring smile.

Rick gave her an even tighter hug.

"Jules, look out the right side of the window. That's the Museu do Amanhã. It's one of the top-rated museums in Brazil," said Gary, playing tour guide.

As they approached the Rio-Niterói Bridge, Jules yelled, "Stop! Stop!"

"Are you gonna be sick?" asked Rick.

"Yes, but look at those coconuts!"

She pointed at a man with a large cooler at the foot of the bridge selling ice-cold coconuts.

"Who wants one?" she asked.

Gina, Possum, and Jules got coconuts, and Rick took a sip of Jules's. Back on the road again, Gary pointed out several beach bars that he had always wanted to try out but never had the chance. They vowed to come back under different circumstances.

As they approached the last turn to the airport, the traffic came to a dead stop. There was construction up ahead and it wasn't moving.

"We only have a mile to go," said Gary.

There was a large delivery truck behind the van, inching closer than Gary was comfortable with. He rolled down the window and shot the finger at the driver and shouted obscenities at him that he wouldn't be able to understand anyway, as they were in English.

Without warning, the back doors of the van flew open. Rick and Possum spun around to see who had opened them, and saw Evan roll out onto the street and take off running. What they didn't know was that Ketamine only had a half-life of eight hours. So, every eight hours it got half as strong. It still worked the same for the first few minutes but was metabolized quicker in the liver, so Evan had been slowly unzipping the bike case every time someone was talking. When the van stopped, he made his move.

"I got him! Just go, I'll catch up!"

Before anyone could open the doors, Possum had climbed over the back seat and out the back doors. He slammed them shut, and Gary peeled out, running over a small curb to get to the feeder road of the highway. They all watched as Evan ran toward a tin fence covered in graffiti, with Possum hot on his trail. They had to keep going.

Just beyond the bridge, Rick saw blue lights. Someone had obviously seen Evan fall out of the van and called the police.

"We've gotta ditch this van and get to the jet," said Gary, and Rick agreed.

The punishment for kidnapping in Brazil was twelve to twenty-four years, but it would be better to get the death penalty, as bad as Brazilian prisons were. Gary sped to the airport on surface streets, avoiding the construction, and pulled into the executive side of the airport. They all jumped out, and a dark-skinned guy helped put the bags onto the plane.

"You speak English?" Gary asked the guy.

"Yes, I speak English."

"You wanna make five hundred bucks fast? Take this van across the bridge to Fonseca. Have it detailed and return it to Rio Car Rental. Here are the keys. Take the side streets. Don't get on the highway. You understand?"

"Yes."

"Well, what are you waiting for?"

Gary handed him a wad of hundred-dollar bills and the van keys.

When the guy was gone, Gary said, "We have to get out of here. Possum's on his own. We're gonna fly to São Paulo and fuel up again. I'll have the pilot call in that we need a maintenance check. If Possum can get Evan before Evan gets to the cops, I'll send a chopper and fly them both to São Paulo. I know a guy there who's a chopper pilot. I can trust him."

Rick nodded. He hated leaving Possum behind like this, but he knew they had no other choice.

The plane touched down in São Paolo with still no word from Possum. Rick tried his number a few times, but it went straight to voicemail.

"All we can do is wait," he said with a sigh. "I pray he's not in jail."

"We can hold here for three hours," replied Gary. "If we haven't heard from him by then, we'll have to head to Argentina and go with plan B."

"What's plan B?"

"I don't know, but we'll have to think of one to get to Armstrong and hope Evan hasn't made contact with him."

CHAPTER TWENTY-TWO

Possum chased Evan over the rusty tin fence into a field beside the Hospital do Fundão, but lost him in the high brush. He cursed under his breath. He was out of breath from running for so long. Evan had a head start on him and probably had gone straight for the hospital. Evan didn't speak Portuguese, so if he made it inside, the language barrier might help Possum catch up to him, unless he got an English-speaking doctor or nurse.

Even though Evan hadn't shot the gun that killed Possum's wife, he was just as guilty as Armstrong in the eyes of Possum, and they both were gonna pay.

"Where is that son of a bitch? Evan! Where are you? I'm gonna get you," yelled Possum.

He looked toward the hospital just as Evan ran toward the front door and fell face first. Even from that distance, he could see Evan had busted up his face really bad. He probably had a lack of coordination from the Ketamine. He just lay there not moving, right in front of the entrance doors.

Possum started jogging toward him through the high grass when two men in green scrubs stepped out with a gurney. Possum hit the deck, hiding in the grass. He watched them lift Evan's body onto the gurney and roll him inside.

When he fell, he must've knocked his own damn self out.

On the side of the building, out of view of the entrance doors, was a cop car. It was empty. Possum needed to get into the hospital but wasn't sure if Evan would be conscious or not. He waited near the cop car, hoping the guy would come back and leave. He had no idea if he was there looking for a person who fell out of a van or not. He could just be there moonlighting as a security guard. There was no way to tell.

A few minutes later, a slob of a cop waddled out of the hospital eating a pastry. He was a fat cop and way out of shape. It gave Possum an idea.

He walked perpendicular to the cop car, trying to look as nonchalant as possible. When he got to the rear of the car, he ducked down behind it. An old pack of cigarettes and a Coke can were sitting next to the curb beside the car. He picked up the pack of smokes and threw it over the head of the cop, who was leaning against the hood of his car, finishing his pastry. The pack landed a few feet in front of him. He looked down at it, then looked up at the hospital and then behind him, trying to figure out where it had come from.

Possum picked up the empty can of Coke, reared back, and threw it as hard as he could at the cop. It grazed his shoulder and bounced away from him. He spun around just as Possum ducked out of sight. The cop began to walk toward the back of the car. Possum could see his feet as he crouched down. He only had one chance. As soon as the cop got to the end of the car, Possum lunged as hard as he could and drove his head into the overweight cop's gut, sending him backward to the ground.

"Uggghhh!" yelled the cop as he hit the concrete hard.

Possum was on him like a cat, and pulled out his nightstick and whacked him across the side of the head. Blood trickled down the cop's temple. Possum dragged him to the car, took his pistol and car keys, and threw him in the back seat. He was hurt and unconscious but would be fine. Possum climbed into the cop car and spun it around, heading for the parking garage. He drove all the way to the top. The first two floors were almost full, and as he drove higher there were fewer and fewer cars. Only two vacant cars were on the top level. No one liked to drive this far.

He backed into a spot and climbed out. He dragged the cop to the rear of car, and it took all his strength to get him into the trunk. His body still was limp. Possum check his pulse; he was breathing and had a heartbeat.

"Sorry, hombre, this isn't your lucky day," said Possum to the unconscious man.

He pulled off the cop's clothes and put them on over his own, glad he had only worn shorts and a tank top today. After slamming the trunk closed, he threw the car keys on the front seat. He knew the underwear-clad cop would eventually wake up and kick in the back seat to escape. It was only a matter of time. He might be so embarrassed he wouldn't even call it in, though.

Once inside the hospital and on the elevator, Possum did his best to make the fat man's clothes look normal on him. It would have to do. He walked down the hall, looking for the drug distribution cart. If he could find it, he could get something to knock out Evan again.

"Poor guy, he's lost a lot of brain cells in the past few days," said Possum to himself, laughing inside.

Then he saw it. A nurse was doing an inventory of the cart, which they did every day several times a day. This was his chance. He tried to think of what to say in Portuguese; all he could think of was código azul or code blue. He had been watching reruns of *Grey's Anatomy* in his room, a show he and his wife Jennifer used to watch all the time when she was alive. He knew the show by heart.

He ran up to the nurse. "Código azul!"

He pointed to the front of the hospital, then pointed at both his eyes with his two fingers and then at the cart, letting her know he'd watch the cart while she was gone. She took off running toward the entrance. As soon as she rounded the corner, he started looking. There it was—Propofol. He grabbed a vial of it and a syringe and began to look for Evan.

It took him twenty minutes to find his room. He peeked in, and Evan's face was bandaged and he was lying down with his eyes closed. Hanging above the bed was an IV bag, attached to his arm. Possum had no idea if he was unconscious or resting. He grabbed a wheelchair and placed it beside his room door. Evan still hadn't moved. Possum needed to get out of this cop uniform and find some scrubs. He ran into a nurse on rounds and nodded to her; she barely even looked up at him. He opened a few doors until he found laundry. A stack of scrubs lay on a shelf. He ripped off the police uniform and buried it deep in the bottom of a towel bin, pulled on the scrubs, and headed back to Evan's room.

He had to be stealthy. If he wasn't unconscious, he'd have to give him the Propofol. It would take fifteen minutes for the drug to take effect.

God, help me be quiet!

He slowly opened Evan's door. He was snoring. As quiet and as slow as he could be, he tiptoed toward his bed. After filling the syringe with what he thought was the appropriate amount of Propofol, he injected it into the IV and slowly backed away into the bathroom. He looked at his watch and waited.

Suddenly, the door opened and a nurse came in. Possum stiffened, holding his breath. She checked Evan's vitals as Possum peeped through a crack in the bathroom doorway. He kept waiting for her to notice something wrong and call for a doctor, but she didn't. After a few minutes, she left the room, humming to herself.

Sweat was running down Possum's forehead and his heart was beating a thousand miles an hour. Fifteen minutes seemed like an eternity.

When enough time had passed, he stepped out. It was now or never. He reached over to Evan and shook him.

"Wake up!"

He didn't budge. Possum opened the door and pushed the wheelchair into the room. He slid Evan off of the bed and propped him up in the chair.

Now what?

He had smashed his iPhone to pieces while chasing Evan, and his burner phone was in his backpack on the jet. He began to stroll toward the exit doors when he saw a wall phone hanging in the hall. He knew Rick's number by heart and called it.

"Rick, it's me, Possum," he said in a low voice, glancing around to make sure no one was nearby. "I got him."

"Where are you?"

"I'm at the hospital."

"Can you get to the airport? Gary can send a chopper for you."

Possum tried to think of how he could get a car and make it all the way to the airport without getting caught. Then he saw the shirtless cop drive right past the exit doors onto the feeder road, bound for the highway.

"Fuck that! Tell him to land on the roof of the parking garage of the Hospital do Fundão. I'll be waiting."

CHAPTER TWENTY-THREE

Possum pushed the wheelchair out of the elevator and planted it in the far corner of the parking lot in the shade of a satellite dish. He kept looking at his watch, pacing. Minutes seemed like hours. He occasionally reached down and checked Evan's wrist for a pulse. He had no way to call the jet and see what the ETA would be, so he had to wait. He prayed no one wanted to park on the top floor. The two floors below him only had a smattering of cars, so he figured he was okay.

Where is that chopper?

The faint *chuf-chuf-chuf* sound of helicopter blades came into earshot. The chopper landed dead center in the parking lot, and Possum pushed the wheelchair with the slumped-over Evan, not moving.

"Grab his arm!" yelled the man who climbed out of the helicopter.

Together, they pulled Evan into the helicopter, and laid him on the floor of the aircraft.

"Hey, I'm Nathan. Mr. Haas sent me. Who is this guy?"

"Just a guy. Where are we headed?" replied Possum.

"I was hired by Mr. Haas to fly you to São Paulo. Is he okay? He looks a little blue."

"Oh, shit!"

Possum stuck his index and middle finger under Evan's neck. No pulse. He bent over to try to see if he was breathing. No dice. Quickly, he ripped open his gown and began CPR. He must've given Evan too much Propofol. It was ironic, considering Possum's real name was Michael Jackson and Propofol was what killed the singer with the same name.

"Come on, Evan! Breathe, dammit!"

He compressed his chest over and over and counted, as he blew air into his lungs. He was unresponsive.

"Move over!" yelled Nathan. He was agitated and angry now. "Gary never told me I was transporting a dying man. Why the hell are we leaving the hospital? We should turn back."

He opened a large first-aid kit and pushed Possum aside.

"Did he overdose? What's he on?"

"I think he was administered too much Propofol," replied Possum.

"Propofol. Why?"

Possum had to think fast. "I'm with the D.E.A., and this man is in protective custody and is testifying against the leader of a large cartel. Someone on the inside of the hospital tried to kill him and make it look like he died in his sleep. We can't return to that hospital. It's been compromised."

"Are you sure it's Propofol?" asked Nathan.

"I administered it. I'm not a doctor, but I guesstimated based on his size and weight."

Nathan hissed through his teeth. "Man, this stuff is nothing to play with. You could have killed him. You may have killed him."

"Well, someone was coming for him from the cartel, and I had to get him out of there somehow undetected. He's a hostile witness," lied Possum.

Nathan pulled out a syringe and stuck it in a vial, then raised it up to get the exact measurement. He wrapped a tube around his arm and started tapping for a vein.

"Keep doing compressions on him! I have to find a vein."

He found one and squeezed the syringe into the dying Evan. His body jolted and he started convulsing.

"That's a normal reaction." Nathan felt for a pulse and put his ear against Evan's nose. "He's alive. He may have brain damage, though. How long was he flat-lined?"

"Couldn't have been long. I checked his pulse as soon as I heard the chopper approaching," replied Possum.

Evan stopped convulsing, and Nathan wiped the spittle from his mouth. One eye slightly opened, and Nathan shined a light into it and then forced open the other one, and did the same.

"I'm getting pupil constriction. That's a good sign. You're lucky your buddy hired this chopper. We run it as a medevac contractor for all the hospitals in Rio and the surrounding area. I'm an EMT on assignment here from Miami, where the company is based. Being able to speak English saved valuable time for your unconscious friend."

"He ain't my friend. Just a federal witness," said Possum again to keep his story straight.

Nathan and Possum lifted Evan onto a flat gurney and strapped him in. Nathan shook his head and gave Possum a look of distrust, then got back in his seat and fastened himself in. Possum strapped in too.

"The flight will be a little over an hour," said Nathan. "When we land, just help me get him over to the plane. I don't wanna know any more than you've already told me."

"Understood."

Gary's Gulfstream was easy to spot; it had a toucan painted on the tail. That was one thing Gary and Rick had in common. They really dug exotic birds.

Once Evan was on the jet, the helicopter lifted off and spun around, bound for Rio. Possum climbed into the Gulfstream and collapsed into the seat like a bag of potatoes. Rick and Gary moved Evan into a seat and handcuffed his feet and wrists to the chair. He was groggy but conscious.

"What the hell happened to him, Possum?" asked Rick.

"Let's just say I gave him the Michael Jackson treatment."

CHAPTER TWENTY-FOUR

The Gulfstream lifted off and climbed to 20,000 feet. The flight time to Cataratas International Airport was a little over an hour and a half. Once they had leveled off, Rick unbuckled his seatbelt, poured a bourbon over ice, and handed it to Possum. He grabbed one for himself as well. Gina and Gary followed suit, and they all moved closer to Possum.

"Spill it. What the hell happened back there, Possum?"

"Man, it was insane. I'm still a little shaken, I think. Okay, here's what happened in a nutshell. I ran after Evan, but he got to the hospital before I could catch him. So, I knocked out a cop and threw him in the trunk of his car, stole his clothes, stole some Propofol, and nearly killed our guest, swapped the cop uniform for scrubs—obviously." He was still wearing the scrubs. "And then I got him into the chopper. That pretty much sums it up."

"Damn, dude. That's extraordinary," said Gary.

"I'm exhausted just thinking about it. Rick, when this is all over, can I fly to Destin and go fishing on your boat? I need some serious R & R, amigo."

"You know it, Possum. You're all invited. Jules already said she's gonna take a leave from her dolphin assignment. It's no place to have a baby," said Rick as he rubbed her belly.

Suddenly, Chief, who had been sitting on top of his travel cage, flew from the far back of the plane and landed on Rick's shoulder.

"Holy crap, Chief. You're flying! We have to keep an eye on him, y'all. He can't be out of the cage outdoors until we get his wings trimmed."

Chief flapped his wings hard as if he was showing off. It was the first time since Rick got him that all his feathers were fully grown in, maybe ever.

"I'll watch him, Rick," Jules piped up.

"Gary, is it okay if I go sit in the cockpit?" asked Gina. "I wanna see the falls as we go over them."

"No problem. I'm gonna tell the boys the plan, but I can fill you in later. You and Jules won't really be involved in the heavy lifting anyway," said Gary.

Gina walked to the cockpit and sat next to the pilot and shut the door.

"So, what's the plan, y'all?" said Possum. "We have Evan. How are we gonna get him to double cross Armstrong? He'll never go along with it."

"I've got it all figured out."

Gary reached into one of the overhead compartments and pulled out a brown leather bag. He carefully set it on the seat next to Possum and opened it up. Inside the bag was a black vest taped up with red wires and enough C4 to blow up the Astrodome.

"Holy shit!" yelped Rick. "Be careful with that. Where'd you get that?"

"I made it. See this?"

Gary unzipped a side pocket of the bag and pulled out a small black remote. It had a clear hinged cover that protected a red switch with an LED flashing above it.

"Jesus Christ, you're freaking me out," replied Rick, his eyes widening.

Without warning, Gary flipped open the cover and flicked the switch up with his thumb. They all instinctively covered their faces, some of them scrambling to hide behind the seats, knowing it was all over.

Gary almost fell over laughing.

"It's fake. The C4 jacket is a prop I made out of clay and electrical wires I got from my tool kit. The detonator is real, but it would require real C4 and blasting caps."

"You son of a bitch! You damn near gave me a heart attack," exclaimed Rick, putting a hand to his chest.

Possum was hyperventilating, and Jules had curled up on the floor in the fetal position. Even Chief was flustered from all the excitement and had flown back to his travel cage and crawled inside, shivering.

"I'm sorry, guys," said Gary, still laughing. "I had to test y'all to see if it would look realistic. Mission accomplished. The only one who doesn't know it's fake now is Evan."

Evan's head was still plopped over. Rick slapped him gently to make sure he wasn't listening. He had passed out again from the aftereffects of the Propofol.

"So, here's the plan. Gina and Jules will stay in the rental house, with Chief of course. Rick, me, you, and Possum and will accompany Evan to Armstrong's yacht to make the switch. Evan will have to go along with the plan. He'll think he has five pounds of C4 attached to him. I'll strap it to him and cover him in an oversized denim shirt. Once we get to the boat, I'll open the briefcase. As soon as Armstrong examines the fake jewel, you can rip open Evan's shirt, exposing the C4. I'll hold the detonator. We should be able to walk right off the boat with the money. I'll give Possum time to do whatever he wants to do with Armstrong. I know it's personal, Possum."

Possum nodded, his jaw hard.

"That's a great plan, Gary!" said Rick.

"I thought so."

Rick and Gary slipped Evan's arms through the vest and fastened the leather straps holding it tightly to his chest. About ten minutes before they arrived at the airport, Evan began to come to and move a little. Gary sat down across from him. Once Evan's eyes adjusted to his surroundings, he focused on Gary with squinty eyes.

"Well, good morning, Sleeping Beauty."

"Where am I?"

Gary waved the detonator in front of Evan's face and said, "You're in my jet approaching the airfield. Look down at your new outfit."

Evan looked down at his chest, covered in wires. His eyes went wide and his mouth fell open.

"What the fuck?!"

"Just a little insurance, Evan. When we meet with Armstrong tomorrow, I'm taking no chances of you tipping him off."

Evan huffed with frustration. "You're making a big mistake. He is ruthless. He'll get you one way or another. I work for him and even I don't trust him."

"Look, all you have to do is get us on the yacht and we'll do the rest. If you cooperate, you'll live. If you don't...well, *boom!*"

Evan winced, obviously shaken.

The plane touched down softly at the airport, and a black Hummer pulled up to the jet on the tarmac. They all grabbed their luggage and climbed into the SUV. The driver took their passports and checked them into the country. Gary handed him a roll of hundreds. He returned shortly.

"Bienvenidos a Argentina. I be your driver. My name es Alberto. You stay on Brazil side near Iguazu Falls?"

"Yes, here is the address." Rick handed him a small piece of paper with the Airbnb address on it. "Can we cross over to Brazil without going through customs?"

"Si!" replied Alberto as he switched the Hummer into four-wheel drive mode and squealed all four tires.

He drove down the main road toward the checkpoint into Brazil, but veered off the main road to a dirt road before the border came into view. The road was bumpy and every time they hit a pothole, Evan gasped. Rick gave Gary a look, sensing he was struggling to not burst out laughing. Chief was in the very back, squawking away at the bumpy ride.

After close to an hour on the dirt road, the driver pulled up to a gate. He jumped out, unlocked it, and dragged it open. Once he drove through it, he stopped and closed the gate again and locked it. He drove down a curvy path and stopped at the river's edge. At the bottom of the path sat a flat barge with two outboards on it. Two men wearing straw gaucho hats approached the Hummer.

They peered inside through the driver's side window and one of them said, "Treinta mil."

"Thirty thousand dollars?" yelped Gary.

"No, silly. Thirty thousand pesos is about three hundred dollars," replied Jules.

Gary peeled off three hundred-dollar bills and handed them to the man. The other man guided the Hummer onto the ferry. They were quite a ways downstream from the massive Iguazu Falls, and the water was slow-moving and glassy. They crossed the river, and the driver got off the ferry and turned east, then joined a main road. They drove past the falls on their right. The view was breathtaking. The side closest to them was known as Devil's Throat, a sheer drop of over 279 feet. The far side of the falls had drops anywhere from 100 to 150 feet. It made Niagara Falls look like a small river flume.

"Llegamos!" said the driver as he pulled up to the Airbnb and stopped the Hummer.

They helped Evan, whose legs were still a little wobbly, into the house. The driver paid little to no attention. He was being paid well to be discreet. They handcuffed Evan to a sofa and gave him enough room to stretch out and sleep later. Gary and Gina took the room closest to the living room, where they could keep an eye on Evan. Possum gave Gary the briefcase with the faux gem in it, since Gary planned to plant a bug in a compartment beneath the jewel.

It had been a long day and they were all hungry. Gary had paid extra to have some groceries delivered to the house before they got there, knowing the nearest store could be miles away. Fruit trees abounded in the yard, so Jules picked a few ripe papayas and mangoes and prepared dinner. She made pan-fried fish over wild rice, with a chutney from the fresh fruit. They all enjoyed it. She even gave some to the indignant Evan, who scarfed it down regardless.

Tomorrow was a big day and they knew anything could go wrong, so they wanted to be fresh and get a good night's sleep. They all went to bed before ten o'clock.

"What's that sound?" asked Jules as she lay next to Rick in their bedroom.

Rick listened intently, trying to discern the sound Jules was talking about. A low rumbling could be heard off in the distance. It almost sounded like the beach waves in Destin when a storm kicked up the Gulf.

"That's the falls," he said, "I didn't notice it before because we were all talking, but now that it's quiet, I hear it. Can you imagine the power of that water?"

"It's kind of peaceful," replied Jules.

"Yeah, as long as you don't go over it in a barrel like those idiots in Niagara Falls did."

"People intentionally went over the falls?" she asked in amazement.

"Yeah. A few of them lived. It ain't nothing compared to the drops at Iguazu, though. That's insanity. Don't fall in, Jules," said Rick as he rubbed her gently.

She laughed and gave him a huge hug, as Chief awoke and squawked gibberish a few times. Rick got up and covered Chief's cage so he could sleep. He climbed back into bed and started rubbing Jules behind her neck softly and seductively.

"Rick, I want to, but I'm shy and these walls are thin," she said, pulling away from him.

"You're right, Jules. We can wait 'til this whole mess is over and we are out of here. I can't wait to show you the boat!"

One by one, everyone in the house fell asleep. Wind rustled the leaves as frogs and crickets chirped in the darkness, creating a peaceful ambiance that kept everyone in dreamland. Everyone, that is, except for Possum. He was too wired to sleep. He kept tossing and turning, reliving his insane kidnapping of Evan.

After a while, he gave up trying and opened his laptop and connected to the house Wi-Fi. It was slow but he was able to get online. He did a search for the flora and fauna near Iguazu Falls. Always the inquisitive type, he read about all the animals that were in the area. Cougars, jaguars, capuchin monkeys, and red brocket deer, among others. He read about the spectacled bears that used to live in the area but now only resided in the mountains due to agriculture and deforestation. That made him sad. He hated to see the earth's natural resources destroyed for the almighty dollar. It actually sickened him.

He came upon an article about the ancient tribes nearby and was fascinated by the story. It gave the background of the Iguazu Falls and surrounding area. As he read, his eyes began to get heavy. He closed his laptop and drifted off to sleep.

A little after midnight, a scream came from the living room. Rick popped up in bed, instantly grabbed his pistol, and ran into the living room, where Possum and Gary joined him. In the door stood a shadow on four legs. Rick squinted to see the big cat clearly.

"Shoot it, shoot it!" yelled Evan.

Rick reached over and flicked on the lights. They all started laughing. A giant anteater stood there frozen in its tracks.

"Shoo! Shoo!" said Rick as he moved toward the animal. It spun around and slid though a rip in the screen door.

"Ooh, a big scary panther almost got you, Evan. Ha-ha-ha-ha," said Rick.

"Kiss my arse, wanker!" replied Evan.

"I think that's enough excitement for one night." Rick closed the wooden door and locked it.

"Yeah, we don't want any anteaters coming in and licking us to death," added Gary.

Evan shot Gary a *go to hell* look as Rick turned off the lights.

CHAPTER TWENTY-FIVE

Rick arose earlier than almost anyone but Possum, who always seemed to be the first to rise.

"Good morning, amigo."

"Morning, Possum," said Rick.

The smell of sausage and eggs filled his nose.

"Java?" asked Possum.

"Does an anteater shit in the woods?"

Possum poured Rick a cup and looked over at Evan, who was scowling at them, not the least bit amused. Within a few minutes, everyone was up and they all sat down at the great table. Rick was well aware Evan was listening to them talk, no doubt hoping to overhear a kink in their plan. But the detonator was always in Gary's front pocket, and he made sure Evan knew it. He didn't have any choice but to go along with them, as long as he thought he was booby-trapped.

The meetup was set to take place at ten a.m., and the driver showed up promptly at nine. The drive to the dock of Armstrong's yacht was only twenty minutes from the house. At 9:30, Gary, Rick, and Possum put Evan into the Hummer. Rick kissed Jules goodbye and gave Gina a hug.

"Chief, you take care of these two. I'm counting on you, boy."

Chief hopped up and down and raised his crown while flapping his wings, lifting a little off the perch each time.

"We'll be fine, Rick," said Gina. "Y'all be careful. Jules and I will watch the fort. Godspeed."

The boys climbed into the Hummer and took off. Rick tried to keep his breathing even. He couldn't help feeling a bit nervous, hoping everything would go according to plan. Now, he had a baby to worry about getting back to, along with Jules.

They arrived at the dock and were greeted by two thick-necked dudes, who patted them down.

"Hands off Evan. He's ours until the switch," said Gary.

The guys glanced over at Evan, obviously recognizing him, and jerked their heads for the group to follow. Gary had handcuffed his left arm to Evan's right wrist to sell it even more. They climbed into the inflatable and rowed halfway across the massive river to where the yacht, *Sabbatine*, was at anchor. The giant catamaran was opulent, brimming with Jet Skis and rows of paddle kayaks with carbon fiber paddles fastened to their sides. There was no shortage of toys on the boat. Even a twenty-three-foot fishing boat was floating behind the yacht on a mooring line. They all climbed up the stern swim ladder and were greeted by a man who could only be Armstrong.

"Welcome aboard *Sabbatine*. I'm Nate Armstrong."

"This is Gary, Possum, and I'm Rick. You already know Evan."

"What happened to you, Evan?" said Nate. "You look like you were beat with an ugly stick."

"Never mind him. Let's get down to business," replied Rick.

"Okay, follow me."

They walked into the main salon of the mighty cat and sat at a large round table.

"So, you have the Sacred Jewel of Orinoco?" asked Nate, clasping his hands on the table.

Rick slowly spun around the metal briefcase and opened it, exposing the leather pouch containing the jewel. Nate's eyes widened.

"You want five million dollars for it, right?"

Rick just nodded.

Nate snapped his fingers, and one of the thick-necked goons brought over an aluminum briefcase and opened it. Stacks of hundreds in wrappers appeared. He quickly closed it.

"Listen, I'm a civil man," said Nate. "Before we do the swap, let's have a drink."

"Look, we're not here to socialize. Let's just get this over with," replied Rick.

"Rick, Rick, Rick, you seem like a man of the world." Nate smiled at him. "I just wanna have a smooth business transaction and celebrate our deal with some of the world's finest cognac."

Rick hesitated but agreed. After all, if he planned to get five million dollars and let Possum get his revenge on Nate anyway, he might as well indulge in the guy's expensive cognac.

"Okay, but I pour. I ain't taking a chance of getting poisoned."

"Pour away!" Nate slid the bottle and snifters toward Rick and laughed. "So untrusting, Rick Waters."

Rick poured the brown nectar into all the glasses and passed them around.

"Shall I make a toast?" asked Nate.

"It's your boat. Go for it," replied Rick.

"Here's to sun, here's to fun. Okay, boys, whip out your guns."

The two thick necks pulled automatics from their waistbands as two more men came into the salon from behind with shotguns and surrounded the crew.

Rick calmly took a swig of his cognac. "That's delicious," he said.

"You didn't really think I was gonna give you five million for the jewel on my boat, did you? What were you thinking? I mean, you're not even armed. What a numbskull plan," said Nate, laughing. "Now, slide over the briefcase."

Rick slid it over to him, and Nate pulled back the money.

"Well, boys, time to die," said Nate.

"Not so fast."

Gary ripped open the snaps of the denim shirt, exposing the C4 vest Evan was wearing. He raised his arm, showing Nate the detonator.

"One move and we'll all become little pieces of meat for the crocs in the river."

Gary waved Possum over.

"You'll kill us all, including yourself," said Nate, shaking his head. "You'll never flick that switch."

"You're right, but he will," replied Gary. "This is Possum. That's the name his friends use. His real name is Michael Jackson. Does that ring a bell?"

"The singer? Michael Jackson is dead," replied Nate.

"Well, how about Jennifer Jackson? Does that ring a bell?" asked Possum.

Nate just frowned, looking confused.

From his front pocket, Possum pulled a photo of the book Armstrong stole when he killed Possum's wife Jennifer. He slid the photo over to Nate.

Nate studied it for a moment. Then his confusion turned to fear. "It was an accident. I swear."

"Well, you are about to have a similar accident."

"Stop!" said a familiar voice from behind the crew.

Rick spun his head around. It was Gina. She stood in the opening of the sliding glass doors, pressing Rick's pistol against Jules's temple. Her mouth was bleeding and her face was swollen. She had Chief in her arms and he was shivering with fear.

"What the fuck?!" said Rick.

"There's been a change of plans, Rick." Gina smirked. "Remember when I said, 'I should've asked for four million and kept two for myself?' The more I thought about it, the more it made sense. I'm sick of this third-world country and all the damn bugs. With this kind of money, I can live the rest of my life in a high-rise in Miami Beach. I made separate deals with both the Smithsonian and the American Museum of Natural History in New York, but I also kept the jewel to sell on the black market. Sorry about Jules. When I paid the guys to take us here, they took advantage of her a bit. There wasn't much I could do."

Rick's heart was pounding fast. He couldn't believe she'd let those men hurt Jules.

"You double-crossing little bitch!" said Gary.

Gina shrugged. "You got me there, Gare Bear. I guess I'm just a material girl after all. Now, hand Nate the detonator."

Gary clenched his teeth in anger, but slowly handed the detonator to Nate.

"Well, that's quite the turn of events," said Nate, grinning. "Double crossing a double cross. I adore it! Give me the key to the handcuffs."

Gary pulled out the chain from under his shirt, revealing handcuff keys. Nate waved one of his goons over, who released Evan from Gary's wrist.

"Get this thing off me and throw it in the river!" said Evan, still sweating from fear. "Hurry!"

"I have a better idea," replied Nate.

They slowing unbuckled the leather straps from the vest, and Evan slid one arm at a time out of it. He winced once it was off. Nate motioned to his goons.

"Put it on him," he said, pointing at Possum.

They put the vest tightly on Possum and made sure it was snug.

"Now, Mr. Jackson, before you go boom, I'm gonna tell you how I killed your wife. It wasn't an accident. It was pleasurable. I tried to rip the book from her, but she fought back. She scratched my face while trying to hold on to the book, so I pulled my trusty Sheffield Dagger from my pocket and jabbed its entire six-inch blade into her side. For good measure, I twisted it a few times. No slag is gonna scratch my face and get away with it."

Possum moved toward Nate, snarling in anger.

"Uh, uh, uh, don't want that to go off prematurely," said Nate, and Possum froze again, remembering. "Gina, please show me the real jewel."

Gina had already contacted Nate and given him the heads up that she had the authentic jewel. She walked over and began to unwrap the gem as one of the goons grabbed Jules's arms and held his own gun on her.

She placed it on the table next to the faux jewel Possum had made in Rio. Nate picked them both up, examining them. He whistled. "This is quite extraordinary. I'm not a jeweler, and I honestly can't tell which one is the real one. I think I'll put the real one in the briefcase. Don't wanna mix these up! Here, Possum, you can keep the fake one."

Nate tossed the glass gem to Possum, who caught it.

"So, here's what's gonna happen. We'll tie Rick to one of the kayaks and let him go. The falls will do the rest. You seem like a rugged guy, and I've always wanted to send someone over those falls. The rest of you can get in the fishing boat. We'll have a fireworks show. Yippee!"

He clapped his hands together like an excited little child. It startled Chief, who flew out of Jules's arms toward Rick. The ceiling fan clipped him, and he flew right into the face of Nate, who waved his arms violently, trying to get the bird away from him.

In the brief moment of distraction, Possum tossed the glass gem to Rick, who switched it with the real gem and shut the case.

"Whose fucking bird is this? Is this yours?" shouted Nate as he pointed at Jules.

Chief hopped across the floor toward Rick and climbed up his leg.

"He's my bird," said Rick proudly.

"Well, la-di-fucking-da! Now that feathered menace can join you on your little river trip. Enough bullshit. Let's do this."

The goons tied Rick's hands behind his back, and shoved Chief in between his legs in the kayak. They secured him to Rick's beltloop with a piece of nylon string around the identification ring on Chief's leg.

"I'm gonna enjoy this. Let's all gather on the stern for Rick's grand send-off."

"No, no, please," begged Jules, tears streaming down her face. "Don't do this!"

The thick-necked guy holding a gun to Jules's temple hit her as hard as he could in the stomach, making her fold over in pain. She gasped for air.

"You fucking piece of shit," yelled Rick. "Come do that to me."

"Now, now, everyone, relax," said Nate. "You'll all be together soon. In Heaven? Hell? Purgatory? Whatever you believe."

Nate reached down and untied the line holding the kayak to the stern of the yacht. It began to drift backward toward Iguazu Falls. Rick's chest heaved in anger, but he couldn't do a thing to stop it.

"Bon voyage, Rick Waters!" shouted Nate, laughing like an insane man.

CHAPTER TWENTY-SIX

Two of Nate's men pulled the fishing boat closer to the stern of the yacht and put the others in it at gunpoint. Everyone but Gina. She looked on, avoiding Gary's angry glare, as Nate had his goons zip tie them all to the rail of the fishing boat. Jules was still crying silently, murmuring Rick's name.

Nate put his hands up above his brow, blocking the sun to try to see Rick's kayak, which had drifted far downstream toward the falls. "He's gone! Ha-ha, I should've strapped a GoPro to him. I'd love to see his face as he makes the big drop."

He directed his men to start letting out the line. The boat drifted slowly behind the yacht in the current.

"Let out as much as we have. I don't wanna get any brain matter on my yacht."

They added a few lines to the existing painter, until the boat was at least a hundred feet behind the super cat.

"Let's let them sit there for a while in fear of what's to come. I'm famished. Gina, are you hungry?"

She hesitated. "You know, you don't have to kill them."

"Gina, thanks for bringing me the real jewel. I was offering you your last meal. But since you are being so boring, goodbye."

Nate pulled out his pistol and shot her in the eye point blank. Her head was thrown back and she fell backward. Her body bounced off of the swim platform into the water.

"Tsk-tsk. So naïve. Clean up the mess," said Nate as he waved his hands backward in a dismissive way toward the swim platform.

Nate stepped back into the salon and poured himself another cognac. One of his crew set his lunch down in front of him. He nibbled on his foie gras and water crackers as he admired the Sacred Jewel of Orinoco.

"That was tasty. Who wants to see some fireworks?" he said to the crew.

They all just laughed and followed him to the stern. He picked up his handheld and began to speak. Another handheld was affixed to the bottom of the T-top of the fishing boat.

"I know you can't respond right now because you're tied up at the moment. Ha-ha. Get it? Tied up? Anyway, the famous Rick Waters and his ridiculous bird are probably only a few hundred yards from the falls. I wanted him to know you all went boom before he makes his plunge. Well, anyway, it's been fun! Ciao."

He waved goodbye and held the detonator high in the air.

Gary and Possum looked at each other and grinned.

Nate flipped open the cover of the detonator without a care in the world. With the flick of a finger, he flipped the switch. The red LED turned green.

Kabooooooom!

A massive explosion rattled the trees of the rainforest. A mushroom cloud rose into the sky, and pieces of fiberglass, metal, and human remains began splashing all over the river. Flocks of birds sprang from the trees from the massive sound.

Gary and Possum were stoic, as they'd known what was gonna happen, but Jules looked on in bewilderment.

"Qué mierda? What the fuck?!" she yelled. "I thought you said it was fake!"

"Oh, it is fake—the one in the vest, and the detonator I showed you on the plane was fake too. But the C4 I put under a hidden compartment of the briefcase?" Gary laughed. "That was real. Genuine grade A."

"How are we gonna save Rick?" cried Jules.

"Oh, shit. We have to get to him before he goes over the falls," replied Possum.

The zip ties on their wrists were police issued. There was no busting out of them.

"I have an idea," said Gary. "We need to work as a team. Jules, can you reach the key in the ignition with your mouth and turn it?"

"I can try."

Jules leaned over and stretched with all her might. She tilted her head sideways and got the float of the keys in her mouth. Spinning it with her tongue, she got it tight and with a hard right turn of her head, the engines started.

"Possum, you steer with your right knee and I'll steer with my left. Jules, you push the throttle forward with your chin."

They all worked as a team and began moving closer to the falls. The rumble of the mighty falls grew louder as they approached. They scanned the horizon, looking for the red kayak. They got within a hundred yards of it and still no Rick. They turned left and went across the far side of the river, eyeing the falls and trees, praying he got stuck somewhere.

As they reached the farthest northern falls of the river, they spotted him. He had untied himself and was frantically paddling toward the far bank.

"Rick, we're coming!" shouted Jules.

The current was strong as they moved closer to Rick.

"Rick, Rick!"

With her nose, she pushed the button on the glovebox and spotted an air horn. She got the horn out with her teeth and wedged it against the glass. Using her chin, she pressed it and the horn blasted.

Rick looked back toward the sound as his kayak shot forward over the edge of the falls. Jules began crying uncontrollably. Gary and Possum managed to steer the boat to the shore, and ran it up onto the bank. Two fishermen saw them and ran over.

"Você está bem?" they yelled.

"Sueltanos!" screamed Jules in Spanish. "Cut us loose!"

The men came closer and saw the zip ties on them. One pulled out an old rusty knife and began to saw at Jules's zip tie. She was hysterical and crying. As soon as she was free, she leaped from the boat and began to run. The men were still finishing cutting Gary and Possum free.

"Jules, wait, wait!" yelled Possum.

She was out of sight before he could step off of the boat. He and Gary ran to catch up to her. She disappeared into the rainforest, trying to get to the bottom of the falls.

CHAPTER TWENTY-SEVEN

Rick heard the explosion and tried to look back. The large plume of smoke in the sky reached a hundred feet. There was no time to worry. He could only hope their plan would be successful.

He pulled at the nylon lines tightly bound around his wrist. He could see the falls up ahead, some five hundred feet. His only chance was to free himself and fight the current to try to reach the shore. Slowly and carefully, so he wouldn't flip the kayak, he arched his knees and sat up on his hands. The kayak rocked and he almost went over, but managed to catch his balance just in time.

"Chief, come here. Get on my chest."

He pulled at Chief's tether with his teeth, coaxing the cockatoo closer. Chief climbed up and cuddled under Rick's chin. Slowly, he slid his hands forward under his butt. Once he got them under his knees, he pulled back his feet and stretched with all his might until he got his legs over his arms. He was still tied up, but at least his arms were no longer behind his back. There was only one way out of these cords and that was to chew through them. He pulled his wrists to his mouth and began to rip at the cords. A small piece loosened and was hanging. Chief grabbed at it with his beak, thinking Rick was playing a game.

"That's it, boy. Tear it up. Tear it up. Good dog!"

They had played a similar game many times with strong yarn. Chief would shred things to pieces. Rick moved his wrists by Chief's beak and began jerking back and forth, getting him into the game. Chief grabbed hold of the biggest pieces, and Rick wrestled with him. The bird bit down hard and shook his head violently like a pit bull. Suddenly, one of the cords snapped in two, and it all came unraveled.

"Yes, you did it, Chief!"

Rip ripped the paddle from its lock and started paddling as hard as he could against the current. That didn't get him anywhere, so instead he started paddling toward the bank at an angle. He was making progress, but the current was too strong. He spotted a huge submerged tree about a hundred yards away. It was his only chance.

He got within two feet of it and reached out to grab it, only to be swept farther downstream. His arms were Jell-o. There was no way he could beat the current.

"Chief, you are a good bird," he said, fighting back tears. "I need you to listen. You have to fly! That's the only way you'll survive. I doubt I'll make it, boy. I love you."

He kissed Chief on the beak and began to untie the cord attached to his identification ring. The falls were ten yards away. He finally got it undone.

A boat horn sounded somewhere behind him. He looked back as the end of the kayak tipped down over the falls.

With all his might, he flung Chief out in front of him. He leaned back in the kayak as Chief disappeared in the mist.

Down he fell.

Down, down, down.

"Our Father, Who art in heaven, hallowed be Thy…"

All Rick could think about as he descended was the statue of Christ he and Jules had visited in Rio: Christ the Redeemer.

Jules rolled down the steep terrain, cutting herself on the branches, desperately trying to get to the bottom of the falls. She pushed through the rainforest, racing like a wildcat through the thick overgrowth.

"Rick, Rick!" she screamed. "Please don't leave me. I love you!"

Possum and Gary tried to follow her trail, but got lost themselves. They trekked to the edge of the incline, trying to spot the kayak or Jules. It was hard to see, as the water from the massive falls filled the air with mist and fog.

"Jules! Where are you?!" shouted Possum.

The sound of the falls was deafening. It was no use. They continued on downhill as fast as they could. The hill was steep and the drop-off dangerous. They raced down, trying to get to the bottom, and praying for a miracle.

"We gotta find Jules. The chances of Rick surviving this are almost impossible," Rick said to Gary.

"I know, man. Let's try not to lose her too."

Jules made it to the bottom. The water was filled with rocks and boulders, lots of deep holes and pockets. She didn't care. She had to find her Rick. She called for him over and over, then waded into the cold water and made her way closer to the pounding falls. She swam and climbed onto rocks, yelling Rick's name. Her tears dried and her fear turned to anger. She was determined to find her man.

Then she spotted something. She tried to see what it was through the mist. She dove in and swam with all her might. There it was—the kayak. The bow of it. It had broken in half. She wrapped her arms around it and began to cry uncontrollably.

"Oh, my Rick. Why, God? Why did you take him from me?"

She pulled herself up on top of the broken kayak and kept on searching. All she could see was white water.

Out of the corner of her eye, she noticed something black bobbing in the water. She wiped her eyes and looked harder. It was just a log. No—there was something shiny on it. She ditched the kayak and swam over to it. As she got closer, the object flashed again. She swam harder. The reflection of the sun made the object look like a bobbing light.

It was Rick. His necklace had spun around, and the gold fishhook he had molded from Fletcher's treasure was now upon his back. She swam as fast as she could to reach him. He was face down in the water and lifeless. She flipped him over. Blood was in the water around him. His collarbone was busting out from his skin.

"Rick, wake up! Please, Rick!"

She kissed him and felt for a pulse. He wasn't breathing. She began to breathe for him and pounded his chest the best she could while keeping them both afloat. She wrapped her arms under his and began to kick, pulling him toward the shore, stopping every few seconds to give him CPR. She had to get to a hard surface. They reached a smooth rock with tufts of grass growing from it. She knew there was no way she could pull him up on that rock by herself. Swimming around the front of him, she pushed him with all her might up against the boulder. She continued CPR and stopped every few minutes to yell for help.

She checked his pulse again. Nothing.

"Rick, please come back to me. God, take me instead. Please bring Rick back."

She was running out of strength.

"Now, you listen to me, Rick Waters! I love you and we are having a baby. You come back to me. I can't raise him on my own."

In frustration, she clenched both of her hands together, reached behind her head, and swung as hard as she could, slamming the center of his chest. The air rushed out of his lungs, and he spit up water and began to cough.

"Rick! Rick!" she yelled.

Rick cracked open his eyes, smiled, and fell unconscious again. She took his pulse and checked his breathing. He was alive! She cried and screamed for help, spinning around looking for anyone. Slowly, she dragged Rick the rest of the way to the shore, checking him every few feet. His breathing was shallow.

"Help! Help us!" she yelled.

"Jules! Over here!" shouted Gary.

Jules looked over her shoulder and began waving frantically. Gary leaped into the water, splashing his way over the rocks. He got to them and saw the blood in the water.

"Is he breathing?" he asked.

"Yes, but he needs help."

Gary and Jules continued to drag him toward the shore. Once they got him to dry ground, they could see his injuries better. He had a broken leg and a broken clavicle. Blood was coming from the tear in his shoulder where the bone had poked through, and he had a huge gash on his right leg.

"We have to stop the bleeding. He's gotta be airlifted out of here," said Gary.

He ripped off his shirt and tied it around Rick's bleeding leg. He grabbed two branches and placed them along each side of his broken leg, and tied them into place with the rest of his shirt.

"Jules, you stay with him and comfort him. I'm gonna go get help. I remember seeing some tourist lookout points when we drove over in the Hummer."

"Please hurry."

Gary ran downriver and soon disappeared. Jules wondered where Possum was, and hoped he was okay. But at the moment, all she could focus on was Rick.

"You hang in there, Rick. I need you. We need you."

She held his hand and prayed.

Two hours went by and Jules never left his side. Then she heard it. *Chuf-chuf-chuf.* She looked up and saw a helicopter approaching. She waved her arms to make sure they spotted her.

A man with a stretcher was eased down on a long stainless-steel line. The man assessed Rick's condition, and he and Jules slowly got Rick onto the stretcher. The man waved his hands in a circle and it began to rise back up. Once inside the helicopter, the line came down again, along with two harnesses. The man assisted Jules and then donned his own. The chopper slowly lifted them both into the air and inside.

The copter spun around, bound for Hospital e Maternidade Cataratas. The flight took only twenty-five minutes. Jules never let go of Rick's hand.

Doctors rushed Rick into the ER when they arrived. Jules ran behind them, but they stopped her at a certain point. She pleaded with them to let her in. A nurse showed her to the waiting area. She paced back and forth, waiting for news for hours.

"Jules, I'm here."

Jules looked up and saw Gary jogging toward her.

"How is he?"

"I don't know. He's been in there for over three hours. I'm scared, Gary."

Gary wrapped his arms around and her and hugged her tight.

"Rick is a fighter. If anyone can make it, he can."

She nodded and walked toward the seats to sit down. Suddenly, she fell to the ground. Gary ran to her. She had fainted.

"Nurse, nurse!"

A nurse came running. Gary helped get her into a wheelchair, and the nurse pushed her down the hall, until they disappeared behind closed double doors.

Gary was a mess now. Both Rick and Jules were inside, and Possum was nowhere to be found. Several hours passed and then a doctor came into the waiting room.

"Are you Gary Haas?"

Gary stood up right away. "Yes, how are they? How is Rick? Jules?"

"Rick lost a lot of blood and has serious trauma. Luckily, he has no internal bleeding. But we are unsure about a head injury. We have put him into an induced coma for now, and he has been moved to the ICU. Juliana will be fine. She told me you are family. I have to be honest with you, Rick is touch and go. We will do everything we can. Jules is asking for you. She also mentioned a guy named Possum?"

"Yeah, we are all family."

"Okay, I will add his name to the visitation list up front. You may go visit Juliana now. She's in room 145."

Gary found the room and went straight inside. Jules looked up at him from the bed, her eyes tired.

"How is he, Gary?"

He went to her bedside, took her hand, and squeezed it. "He's in the ICU. They have him in an induced coma. That's usually to avoid swelling on the brain. All we can do is wait now."

She nodded, sighing. "Is Possum here?"

"I have no idea where he is. As soon I know, you will know."

Jules was released from her room, and Rick was moved from the ICU to a regular room to begin recovery. Over the next few days, he had several surgeries to repair his shattered leg and collarbone. He also had four broken ribs and more cuts and contusions than a frog in a blender.

"Can I see him?" asked Jules on the fourth day.

"Yes, you both can. He's awake and alert. That is one lucky guy. He's in room 167."

Jules pulled Gary down the hall like a little kid. She slowly opened the door to his room and peeked in, trying not to cry.

"Rick?"

"Oh my God, Jules, come here," said Rick with a quivering voice.

Tears were welling up in his eyes. She ran to him. Touching his arm, being careful not to hurt him, she said, "I thought I lost you, Rick Waters! I was so scared."

"It takes a lot more than falling down a waterfall to kill the old Rickster."

Gary stepped into view.

"Gary, you're here too. Where's Possum?"

"I'm not sure. It's been four days since we were separated. I'm sure he's okay. I have the local authorities looking for him. He probably has no idea you're here and is still looking for you. He is one dedicated friend. I can say that for sure."

"Jules, the doctor told me what you did," said Rick. "He said the EMT told him you saved my life. Well, both you and Gary. I don't know what to say."

"You don't have to say anything. Just get well soon. Very soon. I'm ready to visit that boat of yours in Destin."

"Sounds like a plan."

"Gary, can you give Rick and me a moment alone? Just a couple of minutes, then you can come back in."

"No problem."

Once he was gone, Jules reached down and took Rick's hand.

"I love you so much, Rick. There's no easy way to say it, so I'm just gonna say it. Rick, I lost the baby."

Rick looked up at Jules, who had tears in her eyes. "I'm so sorry, Jules."

"Thank you, Rick. It just wasn't time. We can try again sometime. Or at least we can practice." She cracked a smile, trying to lighten the mood.

"Ha-ha-oh-oh, don't make me laugh."

She leaned over and kissed Rick's forehead. The door creaked open, and Gary poked his head inside.

"Is it safe to come in?"

"Come on in, Gary," replied Jules.

"Look what the cat dragged in," said Gary as Possum appeared behind him.

"Possum!" both Rick and Jules said at the same time.

"Hello, amigo and amigorette? Is that how you say it?" he said with a chuckle. "You look like warmed-up cat shit, Rick."

"You always know what to say, Possum. Chief? Did he make it?" asked Rick nervously, as if he really didn't wanna know.

"I got good news and bad news, Rick. I spent four days looking for Chief. I called the hospital and they have been updating me on your progress. I didn't have Gary's number. I left a message with the nurses' station. The language barrier is tough. I guess y'all didn't get it."

"Did you find him?"

"Well, that's the thing. I looked for four days. Man, I looked under every rock, crevice, and tree near the falls. I even looked at the visitor center and asked around for him. I found a few things washed up on the shore. One, I think will really interest you. It was an aluminum briefcase, but I'll get to that later."

"Get to the point!" demanded Rick.

"Take a look at this."

Possum reached into the pocket of his windbreaker and pulled out the Sacred Jewel of Orinoco.

"Shiny, huh?"

"What about Chief?!!!"

Possum unzipped his windbreaker, and out popped Chief's head. Rick let out a relieved laugh.

Ruff, ruff, ruff

"I couldn't find your cockatoo, but this dog followed me home."

The End

ABOUT THE AUTHOR

Eric Chance Stone was born and raised on the gulf coast of Southeast Texas. An avid surfer, sailor, scuba diver, fisherman and treasure hunter, Eric met many bigger than life characters on his adventures across the globe. Wanting to travel after college, he got a job with Northwest Airlines and moved to Florida. Shortly thereafter transferred to Hawaii, then Nashville. After years of being a staff songwriter in Nashville, he released his first album, Songs For Sail in 1999, a tropically inspired collection of songs. He continued to write songs and tour and eventually landed a gig with Sail America and Show Management to perform at all international boat shows where his list of characters continued to grow.

He moved to the Virgin Islands in 2007 and became the official entertainer for Pusser's Marina Cay in the BVI. After several years in the Caribbean, his fate for telling stories was sealed.

Upon release of his 15th CD, All The Rest, he was inspired to become a novelist after a chance meeting with Wayne Stinnett. Wayne along with Cap Daniels, Chip Bell and a few others, became his mentors and they are all good friends now. Eric currently resides in Destin, Florida with his fiancé Kim-Cara and their three exotic birds, Harley, Marley and Ozzy.

Inspired by the likes of Clive Cussler's Dirk Pitt, Wayne Stinnett's Jesse McDermitt, Cap Daniels Chase Fulton, Chip Bell's Jake Sullivan and many more, Eric's tales are sprinkled with Voodoo, Hoodoo and kinds of weird stuff. From the bayous of Texas to the Voodoo dens of Haiti, his twist of reality will take you for a ride. His main character Rick Waters is a down to earth good ol' boy, adventurist turned private eye, who uses his treasure hunting skills and street smarts to solve mysteries.

FOLLOW ERIC CHANCE STONE:

Website:

www.EricChanceStone.com

Facebook:

www.facebook.com/RickWatersSeries

Made in United States
North Haven, CT
17 May 2023

36699638R00154